PRODUCT
GHETTO

Loyalty And Respect

By Sputnic

Table Of Contents

DEDICATION

To the flesh of my flesh, the blood of my blood: Diadra D. Williams, Kaneesha L. Brown, George M.Brown, and Jasmine Brown. Whatever profit comes from this book is for the four of you. Daddy loves you four to no end.

To my homeboy from the Ville, Willie 'Big Will' Nabritt II. Thank you bruh for looking out when times got rough and for sharing a lot of the things with me that kept my drive to write alive. I seriously doubt that this book would've gotten this far without you. You are amongst the few real brothers that I know and I count you as a blessing in my life.

To my lil homie Antonio 'Luke' Lucas out of North Cack, you are what a real friend means. When most raise up out of the tombs, they leave everything and everyone from the inside on the inside. You have ridden this thing out with your boy and I am proud to call you my friend

ACKNOWLEDGEMENT

First and foremost, I give thanks to the Almighty Father for holding me together here behind these prison walls. When things seemed to be about to overwhelm me, you would step in and humble the storm that raged within. I thank you Father for giving me this creative mind as an outlet and a way to relieve the daily stress of being alone and so far from home. I thank you Father for loving and constantly blessing me, despite my many shortcomings.

In loving memory of the three greatest, most influential women to ever bless my life with their love and presence. My three queens: Carolyn A. Grant (mother: 1944 - 2005), Georgie L. Merchant (grandmother: 1927 - 2001), and Sarah E. Williams (great grandmother: 1910 1992). May the three of you be reunited forever inside the pearly gates of Heaven. I love and miss y'all dearly. You may be gone, but never, ever forgotten.

I'd like to shout out all of my brothers that I left behind the wall: Anthony 'MWATA' Cade, Clayton 'C.C' Covington, Anthony 'Jake' Jacobs, Daryl 'Big Pun' Johnson, Christopher 'P-Nut' Jones, Oran 'Root man' Kennedy, Robert 'Leather Cal' Boyd, Clarence 'Bug' Grice, Hasain 'Jamaica' McKnight, Calvin 'Mac' McKnight, Herbert Slater, and Matthew 'Mosi' Williams, I'll always be a phone call away.

CHAPTER: 1

Born Ja'Marius Brown, the third of three children, my mother's only man-child. The result of a fatherless home. Until I was 13 years old; my sister's alcoholic grandparents were the only parents that I'd ever known. Basically, raised and destroyed by my two older siblings Jesikah and Juleyka, because their grandparents were always passed out drunk. They often abused me mentally, physically, and sexually. I was too afraid to say no or stop whenever they had the desire to use me because I knew that if I resisted or told anyone and they were questioned, they'd only deny it or no one would believe me.

Then I'd have to fight a losing battle against those two bitches. Both of them at the same time more than likely. So instead of trying to get some help, I suppressed it and endured but not without a price. A fury had grown within me. A fury that was so strong, that it could be seen in my eyes.

I was 10 years old when my best friend White Boy started calling me Fury. Not only because he could see it in me but also because he knew of my situation that caused the anger that dwelled within. And the nickname stuck with me.

Many days after school, I wouldn't go home until well after dark, because it was always a put-out or get beat-up situation with one of the horny broads that I shared a bedroom with and

I was tired of it. The beast that was growing inside of me became rage and hatred, which started me to rebel at home. Not only because of the abuse that I was suffering at the hands of my sisters but also because of the neglect from the only two people that I looked to for love and protection. They gave less than a fuck about me. Juleyka was their first-born grandchild, the princess. She could do no wrong. Jesikah was their second, the angel. I was the bastard, the product of an extramarital affair, something that I heard quite often from my sisters in the face of adversity.

I did everything that I could think of to gain the approval and love of those that I knew as my grandparents; from making straight A's in school to mowing lawns to buying my own school clothes and supplies but it all went unseen. All that they ever cared about was their deceased son's girls, the welfare check and food stamps on the first of the month, and how much money they would have after bills to buy their next bottle or six pack.

White Boy and I were like brothers because he too was going through some abuse at home with his crazy mother. She was very abusive towards him as a result of the abuse that she suffered from her husband. Abusing him was her outlet because he was the center of her husband's anger for he too was the result of an extramarital affair, but of the interracial nature. He and I had plotted to escape the misery a million and one time, but neither one of us knew how to do so.

One Friday afternoon, White Boy and I were walking home from school when out of the blue, he stopped and turned to me.

"Fury, one day I'm gonna leave home, and when I do. I won't ever come back," he said. "I hate the way I live, and I hate the people I live with. No one really cares for me but you. And If you ever need me, I'll be there for you if I can. You're my only true friend, so I'ma show you my hideout just in case you're ever in need of one."

"You ain't got no hideout nigga," I ribbed. "So stop the madness. Besides, you know that if you stay out after dark, your ol' girl is gonna beat your ass down."

"Whatever Fury, just meet me at the elementary school at first dark and don't be late. Or I'ma go on without you."

I should have realized that something was wrong before we parted ways because he never spoke about being out after dark before now but I didn't before I got home. So, first dark found me standing next to the Middleton - Burney Elementary School's fence waiting for him which only took about two or three minutes before he came up running. Silent tears were running down his cheeks and blood was on the front of his shirt. When he finally stopped close to me, I could see a nasty

bruise on his left cheek and that his top lip was busted and swollen as he had just been punched.

"Damn dawg. What happened to you?" I asked.

Instead of answering, he just stepped by me and kept it moving. So I fell in behind him as he went down the side of the fence and across a field behind the school. We came to a church on Cherry Street called The Pillar Ground In Truth. He stopped momentarily and looked both ways to make sure that no one was coming or saw us, then broke into an all-out sprint across the street towards the church.

I was right on his heels as he went down the left side of the church and around to the back which was facing a wooded area. We climbed into an unlocked kitchen window that was on the ground floor of the upstairs apartment that was connected to the church. Inside, the one-bedroom apartment was fully furnished, with working utilities. I could tell that White Boy had been coming here for quite some time, as he gave me a silent tour of his sanctuary because he had clean clothes and personal hygiene products here already for whenever he had to make a break from home like tonight.

"Don't ever come here before dark. If you don't want anyone to know where you are,' he said as we sat on the sofa watching the Matrix on the television in the small living room after the tour.

"What happened to you when you went home after school, dawg?" I asked, ignoring his warning.

"I don't wanna talk about it, Fury," he replied.

"Did your ol' girl jump on you again Martellus?" I asked, using his government name.

"No, now let it drop."

"Then who?" I asked, being persistent. "Was it that nigga that she's married to?"

"Don't stress over it, Fury, I'll handle it," he said, never taking his eyes off of the television the entire time that he was talking.

Falling silent, even though I was watching him, I started wondering what could he do to handle his situation, he was only thirteen. He must have been reading my thoughts because he got up off the sofa and went and got a backpack out of a chair across the room. He unzipped it and pulled out a loaded .38 Special.

"Fury, I'ma stop'em from punching on me," he said with fresh tears running down his cheeks.

"Where the fuck did you get that gat from White Boy?" I asked, gaping at it in wide-eyed astonishment.

"Your ass is gonna go to jail if you get caught with that thing."

"I don't care," he replied. "Can't be no worse than that hellhole that I live in now. I'm tired of getting beat on every time that nigga raises his voice at my ol' girl or when that spoiled little bitch Takiyah can't have her way and decides to tell a lie on me. And I'm gonna put a stop to it."

"You're one bad muthafucka dawg. Lemme hold it?"

"Nah Fury, you ain't big enough yet."

"The hell you say! Your ass is only two years older than I am. Shidd nigga! I take care of myself just like you do. So lemme hold that gat."

"No Ja'Marius, and I mean it!" He said, a little more forceful than he intended, putting it back in the backpack.

"Fuck that shit then nigga, since you wanna act like that. I'm outta here."

"My nigga White Boy is a real goon. That nigga's got a gat and he ain't taking no shit off of nobody," is all that I could think about on my way home. Lost in my own thoughts as I was cutting across Booker Park on 9th street. I walked on my sister Juleyka bent over a picnic table with a guy behind her. When I got closer, I could see what they were doing. He had her

miniskirt up over her ass and her panties down around her ankles. He was all up in her from the back. I turned my head and tried to sneak past them but the guy saw me.

"Hey lil nigga," he called out. I froze in my tracks. "Ya wont some of dis good, hot pussy?"

Juleyka looked up to see who he was talking to and saw me looking. When we made eye contact, my heart sank and I took off running.

Big Mama and Papa were in their room passed out drunk as usual when I got home. So I took a long, hot shower and

stretched out on the living room sofa to watch Monday Night Raw before I went to bed. Juleyka having come home while I was in the shower, came into the living room and sat straddling my back.

"Listen you little bastard," she growled. "If you open your fucking mouth about what you saw tonight, I'm gonna get Tough Luck to fuck your punk ass up. Do you hear me?"

"Yeah Jule, damn," I replied. "I don't care who you're fucking. As long as somebody is playing in your nasty ass, you ain't bothering me. I mind my business and don't see or say shit. Now get the fuck off of me and go wash your funky ass, I don't want that nigga's cum dripping outta your ass on me."

She slapped me hard on the back of the head and pointed her finger at me. "If I hear one word lil nigga, it's on!"

*   *   *   *

The next year and a half went by pretty much the same, except my body seemed to grow abnormally fast on its own. White Boy and I would still end up in the apartment behind the church at least twice a month. His mother or step-father were still beating the shit out of him for nothing, and I'd get fed up with the bullshit that my sisters were putting me through when they couldn't find anyone to fulfill their desires.

12

By Sputnic

On my 13th birthday, my whole life changed. I was getting off of the school bus after school when a police car passed the bus with the siren blaring and an ambulance in tow. I stood on the

sidewalk and watched as they turned on the street that went towards White Boy's crib. The first thought to enter my mind was that something had happened to my best friend. I took off running for his house as fast as my legs would carry me. I really hadn't noticed that he hadn't been in school all week until now, and that gave me even more strength to run faster.

I got to his house just in time to see the fire department cutting him down from the Oak tree in his front yard that he was hanging from. I was momentarily paralyzed in my tracks as silent tears fell from my eyes like a waterfall. Never in my life had I been hurt so deeply or felt as much hatred towards a person as I felt towards White Boy's mother at that moment. The only thought that I had beyond wanting to kill her, was how could a woman that carried a child in her womb for nine months and gave birth to it, have so much dislike for it?

I forced myself to move closer to the house. There was so much chaos going on that I was practically invisible and no one even noticed me when I walked into the house. There, in the living room, I learned the truth of what really happened. White Boy had handled it, just like he'd said he would a year and a half back in the church apartment. He had shot and killed his mother and stepfather while forcing his sister to watch. The empty .38 Special was laying on the floor where he'd dropped it before going out the door to hang himself. All of his pain and suffering was over. I walked out of the house numb and in a daze.

I can't tell exactly what time it was when I walked into my apartment and went into the bedroom to change clothes

before starting on my homework but I do remember that Jesikah was in the room when I walked in, sitting in front of the mirror, primping her hair.

"Fury, you need to find somewhere to go for a while," she said, looking at me through the mirror. "I'm having some company come over before Big Mama and Poppa get home."

I was in no mood for the usual bullshit that I'd been living through over the past 13 years. I had just seen my only real friend hanging from a tree with a rope around his neck.

"Not today, Jesi," I replied. "I'm not in the mood for your foolishness. If you can't wait for me to change my clothes and do my homework, take your company in the living room or in Big Mama's room to handle your business. Whoever you've got coming over is only coming for a booty call anyway."

"You think that you're beyond an ass whoopin' don'cha lil nigga? Now that you're 13 and got a couple of hairs around your little nuts," she said, turning from the mirror to mean-mug me. "Ain't nothing changed, Fury. I'll still kick your ass like you stole something from me. Now do what the fuck I told you to do and get light."

"Jesi, find yourself someone else to bully. Like I said, I ain't in the mood for your foolishness today,"

"Don't have your black ass up out of this muthafuckin' house by the time Jule and the fellaz get here. And I'm gonna show you what kinda mood I'm in."

Ignoring her, I walked out of the room and went to the kitchen. I opened the refrigerator and took out some sliced turkey and Kraft

singles to make a sandwich before I started on my homework. When I closed the refrigerator door, Jesikah was standing there with her hands on her hips, and a frown on her face.

"I guess you think that this is a game huh black ass nigga?" She asked.

I turned and walked over to the kitchen counter without saying a word. Hoping that by me continuing to ignore her, she would go away. But my hopes were short-lived because she was right on my heels continuing to threaten me. I knew then that the only options I had were to concede or fight because she was going to continue to push until I did one or the other.

"Jesi please, you don't wanna do this today," I begged, without looking back at her. "It's gonna get ugly up in here if you keep pushing. So please leave me alone, or give me enough time to do my homework and then I'll get light. I don't wanna hurt you, so please stop fuckin with me."

"You might as well give me what you've got then. Because your ass is getting the fuck up out of here this minute."

Putting the turkey and cheese on the counter, I turned and punched her in the eye all in one motion. All of the pent-up anger from the abuse that I'd suffered at her hands over the years and the hurt from losing my best and only friend rose to the surface and boiled over. My intentions were to punish her for all that she had ever done to me but the fight was short as

my second punch landed flush on her chin, crossing her eyes and putting her to sleep on her feet.

Juleyka walked into the kitchen with two guys in tow, just as Jesi's knees buckled and she went down hard to the floor. Seeing her face down and unconscious, she fled into a blind rage.

"OH HELL NO MUTHAFUCKA!" She yelled. "YOU DON'T PUT'CHO MUTHAFUCKIN DICKBEATERS ON MY SISTER!" She then attacked.

I met her half way, and we fought like lifelong enemies. I punished her for the old and the new. I mean that I beat her like she was a man.

When the two guys that were with her finally pulled me off of her, I snatched away and turned on them. Ready to rumble with the both of them, if it came down to it.

"Chill lil homie," said the taller of the two. "You've handled yo business. We ain't got no beef witju. Jus tell Jesi and Jule dat we'll catch up wit em on the rebound."

I left Jesikah and Juleyka both laying on the kitchen floor and bounced myself. I headed across town to a park across the street from the Gunby Courts Projects over on Franklin and Jesse which I had heard some of the guys in school talking about.

I was still in combat mode when I reached my destination and I wasn't to take no bullshit or slick rap from any of these clowns today either. Even if I was out of bounds.

The park was jam-packed when I got there. Niggas were out there stunting big time. There were so many candy-painted wet rides, sitting on shooz ranging from 20 to 32 inches, gutted out in all colors and with so much get down in them that any one of them could have been used to provide the music for a block party. Not only that, but there were so many fine ass females of every flavor. When I say every flavor, I mean every flavor. Black, white, Mexican, Puerto Rican, you name it,

they were there. Parading around in boy shorts and halter tops or daisy dukes and bikini tops. Ass cheeks were hanging out everywhere.

I was truly mesmerized by what I was seeing, and I knew that it showed on my face but I didn't care. This was the kind of thing that I'd only seen in music videos on BET's 106 and Park and that didn't even come close to what I was witnessing with my own eyes, up close and personally.

"Damn lil nigga, have you been wallowing in the dirt or something?" A female voice asked, from behind me.

I turned around to see a tall, thick redbone with a grill full of lucky charms on gold teeth leaning against a convertible, candy apple red BMW 650i. I was so caught up looking at all of the tight whips and fine females that I never heard her drive up behind me, nor get out of her car. I looked down at my clothes and the fight that I'd had at home instantly invaded my thoughts. But instead of entertaining her with an answer, I just moved on. I took my time and walked the long way back home. I wasn't in a hurry to get there because I knew that when I got there, Big Momma and Poppa would be in their usual state and I'd have to go another round with Jesikah and Juleyka. Both of them at once more than likely. I crossed 7th Street and stopped to the Handy Way on the corner of 7th and Monroe to buy a soda and a bag of chips. I dropped fifty cents in the Ms Pacman machine and played it for a while. Anything to delay what was to come when I got home.

After about thirty minutes, I headed for home. Expecting the usual or maybe a little worse after the fight that had taken place earlier. My

first thought was to go to the apartment behind the church then the comment that Red had made back at the park crossed my mind, and I realized that I didn't have any clean clothes there and White Boy's were too big for me. So, I went home instead.

To my surprise, Big Momma nor Poppa was drunk when I got there. In fact, they both were sitting on the front porch in their rocking chairs. Big Momma looked mad as hell for some unknown reason.

When I walked up to the porch, I stopped in front of them.

"Fury, what the fuck were you doing with somebody in my house when I wasn't home?" Big Momma asked.

If she could have read my facial expression. She would have known that I didn't know what she was talking about. "I haven't had anyone here Big Momma," I replied. "When I came ...." "Stop!" She snapped, putting her hand up to cut me off. "Both of your goddamn sisters ain't gonna tell me the same damn lie. And who in the fuck made you the king of this castle that you can be putting your damn hands-on people like they're your damn children?"

I knew that there was no need for me to try and plead my case. Jesikah and Juleyka had plotted and flipped the script and that was all that she was going to believe. So I kept my mouth shut.

"Now get your black ass in that house and take off them clothes. I'ma teach you about having them little hot-in-the-ass wenches in my house with your mannish ass. You won't be putting your hands on nobody else when they're trying to get your hard-headed ass to do what's right. Not as long as your ass lives in my house."

I don't know if it was survival instincts from the years of abuse that I had suffered or the stubborn Jamaican blood that flowed through my veins that caused me to take a step backward, but I did.

"Oh! You wanna be a tough guy huh?" asked Poppa as he got up out of his rocking chair. "What did Big Momma just tell you to do boy? This ain't that bastard that fathered you's house and it damn sure ain't that whore of a mammie of yours own. Now, get your black ass in that damn house like she told you to do before I put my hands on you right now."

From that accusation, I realized that Jesikah and Juleyka had been right all along about Big Momma and Poppa not being my biological grandparents and that I was a bastard. Dropping my head, I did as I was told and went inside.

Jesi and Jule were standing just inside the screen door listening. Despite the fact that I had beat the shit out of them both and Jesikah's right eye was swollen shut, they still had that 'we got the last laugh' smirk on their faces as I passed them going to our room.

Sitting on my bed waiting for what was to come, I was at a crossroads and my thoughts were all over at once. I could either sit there and wait for Big Momma or Poppa to come in here and beat the hell out of me for nothing or I could make a break for it and take my chances of taking care of myself as I've done practically my whole life anyway. These people were not

related to me, and the two that were, hated me more than the two that weren't.

By having to share the small bedroom with my sisters, my clothes were practically always packed in my sports bags. All I had to do was put my shoes in my bags, get my backpack with my school books in it, and go out the window. I could be long gone before they knew I had left. 'I refuse to be beaten for something that I haven't done or for defending myself,' I said, thinking out loud as my thoughts drifted to White Boy and what he had gone through.

Making up my mind, I got off the bed and went to the door. I looked out into the hallway to make sure that no one was coming. When I didn't see anyone, I silently closed the door and hurriedly packed my things. I flipped over my mattress and got the money that I'd saved from mowing lawns out of my stash spot. Easing over to the window, I slowly raised it, took the screen out, and dropped my bags outside on the ground. I went back to the door and put my ear to it. When I didn't hear anything and was sure that the coast was clear, I hurriedly walked back to the window. Looking back at the door one last time, I jumped out of the window and into the night. Picking up my bags, I got light. Running through the back of the projects to cut across Laurel Avenue. This way, I wouldn't be seen and when I would have to cross back over Magnolia, I'd be only a few blocks from the Middleton-Burney Elementary School.

It took me less than fifteen minutes to make it to Cherry Street despite taking the long route because I was running for my life. The only stop that I made other than for traffic was when I was across the street from the church. There, I looked both ways, the same way that I'd seen White Boy do the first time that he'd brought me here. Once I was sure

that the coast was clear, I broke into a sprint for the apartment in the back of the church. I was finally safe.

CHAPTER: 2

For the next couple of days, I laid low and stayed out of school out of fear that Big Mama would be looking for me there to take me back to her house. I'd get up early every morning and clean the apartment. An invaluable lesson that I'd learned during those horrible, abusive years that I lived on Magnolia Avenue, I can cook, clean, and do laundry better than a maid, thanks to Jesikah and Juleyka.

I had perfected the ins and outs of getting to and from the apartment without being seen while White Boy was still alive. I could pretty much come and go as I pleased but I never deviated from his warning about going to the apartment before dark. Once I was satisfied that no one was looking for me, I forged a sick note and went back to school. With White Boy gone, I always had more than enough time to kill before I went in at night. So every day after school, I'd hide my backpack and go across town.

Whenever I got over to the park across the street from the Gunby Courts projects, there was always a crowd hanging around the entrance of the projects and up on the corner of Jesse Street, two of which were running up to cars, then going back to the curb counting money. I often wondered why on this side of town would a person be giving these guys their money for simply coming up to their cars or for a few seconds of conversation. There was no way that they could be selling anything because I never saw anything in their hands whenever they went to a car. The Gunby Courts were so much

different from Magnolia Arms because over on my side of town, them stingy ass niggas ain't giving you shit.

For two weeks, I had sat across from the projects and watched the daily activities. All while wondering what was really going on. That was just how little I knew about that type of street life. This was totally different from the bootleg or gambling houses that were over in Magnolia Arms. There wasn't half as much traffic going in and out, and there sure wasn't as much money exchanging hands as I'd seen over here.

On several occasions, I saw that same thick redbone from my first time coming on this side of town, only she wasn't always in the red Beemer. She would holla at a heavyset guy on the block that I'd seen running cars. He would hop in her ride for a few seconds, then she would drive off.

For some reason, slipping was becoming a bad habit of mine on this alien turf. One Friday evening, I was in my usual spot, but I was so preoccupied with watching the activities going on across the street. Trying to figure out what they could possibly be selling to be getting the kind of money that I've seen exchange hands over the past couple of weeks, that I never noticed that someone had walked up behind me.

"Hey punk, whatja doin' on my playground wit'out my permission?" I heard coming from behind me. I turned around

to see a bighead, fat dude with two other guys standing there with their arms folded across their chests.

"You ain't from round here nigga," He went on menacingly. "Meanin' you ain't got no business on dis side of town. So once again what tha fuck yu doin' on my playground?"

"Look dawg," I replied, getting up off of the bench. "I ain't looking for no trouble. I'm just chilling here, minding my own business."

"Yu ain't got no business ova here nigga. So yo punk ass betta kick rocks befo trouble start lookin' fa yu."

The people across the street must have anticipated that a fight was about to go down because almost everyone off the corner and in the projects entryway started coming over to the park hoping to see some action.

"Look, my man," I said, not wanting the extra attention and trying to avoid the confrontation if at all possible. "I'ma get on through. Not because you told me to but because I ain't looking for no trouble."

"Fuck dat shit Klint, kick his bitch ass," says the skinny, brown-skinned guy in his crew to appease the crowd that had gathered and made a circle around us. "He's scared anyway, and once ya spank dat ass good. He won't come back round here no mo."

That little bit of boosting from slim was all the Gunby Courts bully needed for him to try me. He threw a wild right hook at my face. I ducked and stepped inside to his left, and went to work on his ass. I

had his nose bleeding, his left eye swollen shut, and a cut over his right eye before his boys decided to come to his rescue.

I was holding my own considering they were trying to triple-team me. Then out of nowhere, a short, stocky guy jumped into the fight, and to my surprise, he was helping me. It was only a matter of seconds after that, that the fight was over.

After everyone had dispersed and gone back over to the project's entrance or back up on the corner where they had been before the fight, I sat back down on the bench contemplating my next move, considering that I still had a couple of hours of daylight to burn before it was safe for me to go in.

The same guy that had just fought on my side, walked up in front of me. Not knowing his intentions, I stood up, just in case he wanted to start some more shit about me being in the park. "Hey my man," he said, offering a pound. "My name is LaVale, but everybody calls me Juice. Yu're one fightin' son of a bitch. I ain't neva seen a nigga throw hands like dat."

"Thanks for the help, Juice," I replied, without giving him a pound. "I doubt I could've lasted much longer fighting the three of them by myself."

"It ain't nuttin' my nigga, but..." A horn blew interrupting him, and we both looked towards the street. Red in the Beemer had stopped and rolled down the window.

"Juice, come your ass on before I leave you," she said. "You know that I got things to do."

I accepted the pound from him this time, and he ran up to the street to get in the car. Seeing me once Juice was in the car, Red pulled down in the park where I had sat back down, rather than pulling off.

"Haven't I seen you sitting out here every day for the past couple of weeks?" She asked.

"Yes, is there a problem with it?" I answered with a question of my own. "You're the second   person today to mention me being in this park."

"No, don't get offended or take what I said the wrong way. I was only asking. You aren't from around here, are you?"

"No."

"Where are you from, if you don't mind me asking?"

"Does where I'm from make a difference on whether or not I'm allowed in this park?"

"No," she replied a second time. "Not to me anyway, I'm just curious."

"I'm off of Magnolia. Out of the Arms."

"Vik, dat nigga dere gotta set of hands on him," Juice interjected. "He jus beat tha shit outta Klint and his boys, when they tried ta put down on'em."

"What's your name?" She asked, ignoring her brother.

"Fury."

"Fury," she repeated as if testing the name for substance. "Can I give you a ride somewhere, Fury?"

"Nah, I'm good."

She stared as if she was appraising some prize bull before putting the car in gear.

"Be safe my nigga," Juice said, as she drove off. "I'll be seein' ya sound."

"No doubt, Juice. You be safe too."

The following week went by without me going across town. Whenever I wasn't making my lawn mowing rounds, I was studying for midterm exams. Although I spent the majority of my time alone, I felt free, and I took advantage of the situation. I was proud to be on my own. I didn't have to worry about the abuse that I'd once suffered anymore and I had my own space. Nobody told me what I could and couldn't do. Yet

nothing that this new freedom allowed me to do interfered with my going to school or my grades.

Some nights though, Big Mama and Papa would cross my mind and I'd wonder if they were alright. Even Jesi and Jule would

evade my thoughts from time to time. But sad as it may sound, beyond wondering if they were alright. I didn't really miss any of them

CHAPTER: 3

Friday after school, I was back in the park, sitting in my usual spot when Juice came across the street and sat down beside me.

"Whutz up nigga?" He spoke, giving me a pound. "Where yo ass been all week? Dere's been mad talk bout tha way datju beat Klint's ass up. Yu got mad props in tha Courts fa dat shit my nigga. Cuz he wuz straight terrorizin dem fools ova dere as well."

"I've been working and studying, dawg," I replied. Ignoring what he had said about the fight because that kind of talk don't make me.

"Workin?" He said, repeating what I'd said in a questioning manner.

"Yeah nigga, I said working. Ain't nothing wrong with having a job. Besides, ain't nobody going to give me nothing."

While Juice and I were talking, Vik walked up. "What's up Fury?" She said. "Where have you been all week?"

"Dis nigga gotta job, Vik," Juice answered for me.

"A job," she repeated with a frown.

"Yeah sis, a job."

"What's wrong with having a job?" I asked defensively. "I like having nice things and money in my pocket just like the next nigga. Besides, ain't nobody gon gimme shit."

"How old are you, Fury?" She asked.

"Why? I hold my own."

"Yeah, I've heard a thousand times over from the buzz in the Courts and from this nigga," she said, pointing at her baby brother. "What kind of money do you make on that job of yours?"

I stared at her for a long minute, trying to figure out where all of the questions were leading to. "It depends on how much work I get," I finally replied. "If I get it all like I did this past week, I'll make about a yard fifty."

"How would you like to make that right now?"

"I'm always down for greasing my pockets, but how?"

"Come with me," she replied, and walked off before I could say anything.

I looked over at Juice who was still standing there. He nodded his head before walking off himself so, I got up off the bench and caught up with him. First, we went over to where the guy that I had seen get in and out of her car, was standing at the entrance of the projects with another guy.

"Whut up Vik?," He said, acknowledging only her. "I see datju gotcha bad ass lil brutha witja today. Who is dis otha cat?" He went on, trying to be sarcastic and make small talk at the same time.

I was tall for thirteen, standing at about five-eight so those who didn't know me always assumed that I was older than I actually was.

"Yu ain't still trippin bout it takin me a coupla days to turn in my trap money. When I had ta go and see   bout my ol' gurl are ya? Yu ain't boutta cut a nigga off or put a nigga on extended probation, are ya?"

"No fool, and stop whining like a little bitch," she replied. "We came over here so I could introduce my man here to you."

"This is Fury," she said, "and Fury this is Thin."

"Fury, Fury," he said, closing his eyes and tapping his temple with his right index finger as if trying to draw the name back to the surface of his memory. "Damn, I've heard dat name, but I can't rememba where or why."

The guy standing there with him sniggered at his sarcasm.

"Stop frontin nigga," Juice said indignantly. "Y'know damn well y'know where and why ya heard his name. Tha whole fukkkin projects is on fie bout how he kicked Klint's ass ova in tha park last week. Sumthin yo fat, soft ass ain't neva been able ta do. As many times as he's jumped on yu, and yu're a grown ass

man. If ya didn't keep dat raggedy ass gat witja, Klint would prolly still have his foot knee deep in yo punk ass right now."

"Shut up, Juice," Vik said, cutting him off. "Thin, I introduced y'all because I want Fury to know that it's okay for him to come over here anytime that he wants to come across the street."

"No doubt Vik, yu're da boss. Whateva yu say, is whut it's gon be."

"You good with that Fury?" She asked.

I didn't say a word. I just nodded my head in agreement, keeping my eyes on this nigga Thin and his henchman the entire time because even though she didn't introduce the other cat, my instincts were telling me that something wasn't right with these two.

We left Thin and his boy and walked over to her car that was parked in the projects. This was the fliest non-tricked out whip that I'd ever been close to. Not to mention about to ride in.

"Juice, get in the backseat and let Fury ride up front with me. I want to holla at him about something."

Once we were in the car. She reached into a purse that was in between the front seats, and pulled out a fat knot of money. She counted out seven twenties and a ten, and handed it to me.

"Here you go Fury, just like I said."

"I want that money Vik, I ain't going to front but I haven't put in no work to earn it. And I don't accept charity."

"Oh yeah, you have earned every penny of this money. First, by making the decision to come along and hear me out. Secondly, you have passed several tests over the past few weeks, without even knowing that I was watching you or that you were being tested."

Not sure of what she was talking about but deciding not going to debate with her either when it came to making money, I took it and put it in my pocket. No other words were exchanged between us until we pulled into the Ice Cream Station's parking lot on Atlantic Boulevard.

"Damn Vik!" Juice exclaimed as we got out of the car to go inside. "Yu ain't neva brought me here befo. Whutz tha special occasion?"

"Shut up boy, and go enjoy yourself," she replied.

I followed her inside and to a table. I took a seat across from her and waited patiently and quietly for her to tell me what she wanted to talk to me about.

"Why didn't you go and shoot some pool or play some video games with Juice?" She asked.

"You said that you wanted to talk to me about something. And I'm sure that it couldn't have been about me enjoying myself. Besides, you have given me a hundred and fifty dollars for

nothing while saying that I've earned it. Keeping it real, I'm waiting on you to get at me about what you really want."

"You're right," she said after having gauged my maturity level for several seconds. "Actually, I have a proposition for you and I'll explain to you the test that earned you that yard fifty." Without saying another word, I sat back in my seat to hear her out.

"I can remember the first time that I saw you in the park across from the Gunby Courts," She went on. "You were so out of place, and everyone that saw you knew that you weren't from around our way. Yet, you showed no fear. You minded your business, took in the sights, and then moved on. The next time I saw you, you were in the park again. Only this time, you were sitting on the bench

watching the daily activities that go on from the corner of Franklin and Jesse Street to the entrance of the projects."

"I could tell by how attentive you were that you were curious about the activities that you saw but you never moved a muscle to interfere or to ask questions about things that weren't any of your business. Even after Juice befriended you, you never asked a single question about what was going on when the average Joe would have tried to get all up in the mix."

"When Klint and his crew rolled up on you and tried to punk you like they've done so many others in the Courts successfully. You made a statement by not backing down and holding your own. Despite being outnumbered and on his turf so to speak, and with everyone else glorifying the ass whipping that you put on Klint. You haven't said a word about the fight. If none of the ones who'd been boasting about your hands hadn't been in the park to see it for themselves and it was left up to you to tell the story, no one would ever know anything".

"The day that I decided that it was time to holla at you. The little bit of conversation that I did get out of you was cut and dry, that in itself says a lot about you as a man. The same with when I introduced you to Thin earlier, and he got sarcastic. He already knew who you were. Shid! Everybody in those projects knows who you are. But you didn't even sweat his sarcasm".

"Fury, I like your cool, calm, and collective, nonchalant demeanor. The tests that you have passed are; you're not a coward, nor do you run off at the mouth. You prefer to stay low-key and fly under the radar.

You are good under pressure and you'll only give up enough to keep whoever is asking questions guessing."

"I could use you on my team Fury. I know that you are green to certain aspects of the streets but anything that you don't know or understand, I will make sure that it is taught to you properly. I will pay you three hundred dollars a week while you are being schooled. Then we will go from there. What do you say?"

I sat there for a long minute and thought about everything that she'd said. I could use the three hundred a week. It was twice as much as I make mowing lawns whenever the work was available. Not only was it more money but it would eliminate pushing that lawnmower altogether. And from what I've seen, I won't ever have to worry about missing out on a week's pay.

"You're right about me being curious about the activities that I've seen going on," I finally said. "If I decide to take you up on this, do I answer only to you?"

"Yes and no. Yes, because I'm the head of this organization. No, because I have a lieutenant who's in charge whenever I'm not around, whom you will meet in due time."

"I want you to know up-front before we go any further that I go to school from seven-thirty till two and nothing is going to stop or interfere with that. So whatever I am supposed to do or learn, it will have to be after school and on weekends."

"That will be fine."

"Okay then, Vik. I've already accepted half of my first week's pay. So, I'm in."

She smiled, showing her gold grill. "The money that you got earlier is yours. You've already earned it.

"You won't be put on the payroll until Monday when your training starts."

She then reached into her purse once again, pulled out some gold links with a gold DMB for a medallion, and set it on the table.

"This will let everyone on our turf know that you're a part of the Dirty Money Brothers family until they're familiar with who you are."

She closed the meeting explaining that the medallion was the big boss's insignia and the history behind it.

Over the next six to eight weeks, every day after school, Vik would pick me up at Jack's liquor store on the corner of Main and 16th Street at two thirty. Daily, she would ride me around and school me on the ins and outs of certain parts of street hustling. She would explain things and then ask me questions to see if I grasped what she was telling me. She would even take me on rounds with her to do business or to pick up money. To me, that had a double meaning to it but I'd never comment on or ask questions about it.

I'd never seen so much money in my life. Vik showed and told me things that I didn't even think Juice knew about. She even taught me how to drive and made sure that I got my license as well.

I picked up street knowledge like it was second nature and absorbed it like a dry sponge in a glass of water, routinely passing her little tests with ease. But on the same note, unless I was in school or at the apartment, she hardly ever let me out of her eyesight during work hours. Nor had she allowed me to get close to the actual product that was being sold on the tracks.

Vik got so much respect that just being a part of her team and being seen with her so often got me the same respect and saved me from a lot of unnecessary conflict with the guys off of this side of town, being that I am off of Magnolia. In all actuality, I never imagined things being like this. Because for once in my life, things were actually going good for me. Not only was I seen for who I am and got some respect, I could actually afford to eat out whenever and wherever I wanted. I had more name-brand clothes and shoes than I'd ever be able to wear and more money than I'd ever imagined that I'd be able to call my own.

CHAPTER: 4

One Thursday afternoon about three months after I'd joined Vik's team, I called her from school and told her that I needed to go home right after school, that I'd be in the Courts by four-thirty. When I got over to Cherry Street, I saw some guys outside of the church looking around. It looked like a pastor and his sons, but I couldn't be for sure. All that I was sure of at the moment, was that all of the money that I'd saved and everything that I owned was in the apartment. And other than here, I had no place else to go.

I walked back up to Magnolia Avenue, took out my cell, and called Vik.

"What's up Fury?" She answers on the second ring. "It's not four thirty yet."

"Yeah, I know," I replied. "I need for you to come and scoop me up over on Magnolia by the Middleton-Burney Elementary School."

"If you're ready right now, I'm only a couple of blocks away on Randolph getting my hair and nails done at Shai's."

"I can walk over there
if it's all good with
you."

"I'll be right here," she
said and hung up.

I took my time walking the four blocks to Randolph Street, the whole time contemplating how to tell Vik that I was soon to be homeless if the guys that I saw at the church were about to take it over.

I was caught up in my thoughts that I'd gotten to Randolph a lot faster than I'd anticipated and still hadn't got my thoughts completely together. When I saw Vik's car parked in Shai's yard, I headed to the back of the house to the salon.

A little bell rang announcing my entrance as I pushed the door open and only one person looked in my direction. To my surprise, that person was my sister Juleyka whose eyes nearly jumped out of their sockets when we made eye contact.

She elbowed Jesikah who was sitting next to her reading an Ebony magazine then nodded her head in my direction when she looked at her.

"Look Jesi," she said, talking loud enough for everyone in the salon to hear. "If it ain't the runaway himself. We ain't seen his punk ass in almost six months."

"I know, right," Jesikah chided in, following Juleyka's lead. "Not to mention nicely dressed and from the looks of it, still going to school."

I didn't say a word to defend myself or in response to what they were saying. Not because I couldn't have but because I was too

embarrassed by them airing out my dirty laundry in front of all of the ladies in the salon who had also turned their attention to me. None

40

of whom I knew beyond the two of them except for Vik who I knew was also listening to their every word as well.

Ignoring them and their taunts as if they weren't talking about me. I went to where Vik was sitting, sat my backpack down, and had a seat next to her. I had bigger problems than them to deal with. Besides, whatever damage they'd intended to do by what they were saying was already done whether I said anything in retaliation or not.

"What's poppin, ma?" I asked as I sat down next to Vik. She nodded her head. "When we leave, I need to talk to you about something important."

"Alright," she replied. "And what are those two skanky bitches talking about?"

"I'll explain it all to you when we talk."

Jesikah and Juleyka were all eyes the entire time that Vik and I were talking. Straining their ears trying to catch a word of what we were talking about. My cell rang just as Vik was being put under the hair dryer. I looked over at them and shook my head

as I got up to answer the call. They both were staring at me with animosity and jealousy in their eyes after all of the time that had passed since we'd last seen each other. My only guess was that my life had improved for the better since I'd left and they were still living the same miserable hoodrat lives.

Vik having peeped the looks, decided to do some taunting of her own. "Lil Daddy, can your girl get a cold soda?" She asked.

"No doubt," I replied, hanging up the phone and walking back over to where my backpack was sitting on the floor. I unzipped the pocket on the front and pulled out the money that was inside. "Shai, do you have change for a hundred?"

Jesikah was looking so hard that she grunted when she saw the fat knot in my hand. I looked up at her and laughed out loud when I saw how wide her mouth was hanging open in astonishment.

About an hour later, Vik was finished. Jesikah and Juleyka who had been finished for some time, had been sitting around making meaningless conversation with the other ladies to stall for time. I guess in hopes of seeing what time it was with Vik and me when it was time to leave.

I think that Vik saw through their phony meaningless conversation as well as caught their casual glances in her direction to see how close to finish she was.

"Fury," she said, getting to her feet to pay Shai. "I had your whip detailed while I was out making my rounds today. Thank

you for letting me use it." She dug into her purse and handed me her keys, winking at me as she did.

"That wasn't necessary," I replied, catching her cue. "You know that what's mine is yours."

Jesikah and Juleyka rushed out the door as Vik was paying for her service. If they were still like they were when I was there, they wanted to see this car of mine that Vik had mentioned. They were just reaching the corner of Randolph Street and Magnolia Avenue when I pulled up to the stop sign with the top down on the vert. I blew the horn at them, just before making the left onto Magnolia.

The entire time that I was driving, Vik was sitting with her back against the door staring at me.

"Are you ready to talk yet?" She asked.

"Yes," I replied, taking the next right and pulling into Babylon Park. Once I parked, I turned in the seat to face her.

"I have a question before you get started," she said. "Who were those two bitches that were taunting you back there at Shai's?"

"They were my half-sisters, Jesikah and Juleyka," I answered.

Then I ran down my life living in the two-bedroom project apartment in Magnolia Arms with them. Leaving out nothing. By the time I got to my current situation surrounding the

church apartment and what I feared was about to happen. Vik was just sitting there staring at me as if she was in a trance.

"I have no place to go if I'm right, Vik. Do you think that you could get someone to rent me an apartment in the Courts?" I said after she'd sat there in silence for a minute longer than I thought she should have. "I can pay my own bills."

She still just sat there staring at me without saying a word.

"What's up, Vik? I refuse to go back to Magnolia Arms, and I can't afford to chance losing everything I have by trying to stay in the church apartment much longer."

"You surprise me more and more with each passing day," she finally said. "All this time, I thought that you were going home to a family at night when you have been living on your own. You're as rare as you are real. So, this is what I'm gonna do for you. We're going to go and get your stuff, and then you're going home with me until I can find someone to rent you a place of your own. What do you say to that?"

"I'll accept but only if you will allow me to pay my own way while I am there. Oh wait! How am I gonna get to and from the bus stop?"

"I'll handle that," she replied. "Now, let's go check out the scene to see if we can get your stuff now,"

CHAPTER: 5

I was out in the Courts leaning against Vik's car rapping with Juice. When five guys were approaching the car. By the way that they were sporting the identical yellow-gold links and charm, I could tell that they were a crew. Once they got close enough for me to recognize Thin and his boy, my thoughts instantly went to the links and charm around my own neck and I knew that this was the rest of Vik's team, with the exception of the tall light-skinned brother who was dressed totally different from the others and sporting platinum Gucci links with a diamond-encrusted, platinum Jesus piece draped around his neck.

"Whut up, Juice?" Thin said, once they were right in front of us, and as if I wasn't standing there.

"Where's Vik?"

"I dunno. She's round here somewhere," he replied.

"Why da fukkk would she tell us ta meet her here and she ain't no fukkkin where ta be found?" He complained. "I got otha shit dat I need ta do."

"Stop alla dat fukkkin cryin nigga, and leave sumthin' fa da baby ta do," Juice said. "Besides, yo punk ass ain't gon tella dat shit ta her face."

"Look lil nigga," Thin says, steeping up on him. "Da only reason dat I ain't spanked yo young ass already is cuz of Vik. Don't make me shake loose on yo ass right da fukkk now."

I raised up off of Vik's car and stepped in between them to face Thin. "It ain't gonna be none of that, my nigga," I said to him. "Not unless you plan on shaking loose on me too. Besides, Juice be clowning you because he knows that you wear your feelings and emotions on your sleeves and he can easily get under your skin. You're the fool for always entertaining him with the madness."

About that time, Vik walked up with two fine ass females and sees Thin and I standing face to face.

"Hey, what's going on here?" She asked.

"Nuttin Vik," Thin answered.

"Don't bitch up now nigga," Juice taunted. "Talk dat slick shit now fukkk boi."

"What's going on then, Juice?" She asked her brother.

"Thin came outta his mouth all aggressive and shit, and Fury wuz bout ta serve his bitch made ass."

"Is that true?" She asked firmly, but no one said anything. "Is there a beef between you and Thin, Fury?"

"No Vik, I don't know him like that. I have no reason to be beefing with him." I replied.

"Good, because you're going to be working with him and his boys."

Turning to face Thin and the others, she introduced me to the three that I hadn't seen before as well as to the one that was standing with Thin on the day that I'd become a member of the Dirty Money family. Immediately, I realized that the light-skinned brother named Cee Lo was the lieutenant that she'd told me about at the Ice Cream Station on day one.

"I called y'all here because I'm ready to put Fury to work. He's going to start as a lookout. So, I need for J.R and Po Boy to alternate days training him and getting him familiar with the different posts. Cee Lo, I want him over on your side of the Courts at least two days a week, working with you and Dirty Red, if anything goes wrong with him during this part of his training, I want to know immediately."

"Do yu wont'em ta start now?" Thin asked.

"No, his hours will be from two thirty til eight, Monday through Thursday, and from two-thirty til end of shift on Fridays and the whole shift on the weekends is over. He will start his training on Monday afternoon and if no one has anything that needs addressing, that's all for now. You all can go except for Thin."

Once the other four guys had walked away. She stepped up on Thin to make sure that they were face to face. And looked him straight in the eyes.

"I know whatever you had to say slick out of your mouth was directed towards my little brother. But you better thank your god that I didn't hear it because if I had, I'd make you use that raggedy-ass pistol that you carry. I'm going to advise you once. Leave my brother alone. I won't tell you again."

I was in awe at the power that Vik possessed. I'd never seen so much respect given to a person so young. Especially after seeing what had transpired between her and Thin.

"Damn my nigga," Juice whispered, interrupting my thoughts. "None of dem niggaz had it dat lax when dey first started out on tha tracks but Cee Lo. Dem muthafuckaz wuz gittin it out tha gate."

"If you say so. But wasn't that before Big Duke got knocked and went to the pen?"

"Yeah, I guess ya right. But dem niggaz wuz on some on tha job trainin type shit from the git."

"Butju been rollin on cruise control fa a long minute now."

"I got swagga like that," I said, laughing out loud at the look on his face.

"Bruh, who are those two females with Vik?" I asked, changing the subject before he could recover from my self-proclamation.

"I dunno fam," he replied. "I ain't neva seen'em befo. Unless dey live ova on tha otha side of tha Courts. I don't fukkk round

ova dere too tough. Cee Lo don't be feelin tha hot boy shit. So he calls it, dat I be doin."

Vik and the two females came to the car no sooner than Juice finished his statement. "Fury, Juice, this is Fayeth and Tieaa," she introduced. "They'll be staying at the house with you two for the weekend. I've got to go out of town."

"Stay ta tha house wit us, as in babysittin' us?" Asked Juice with a frown on his face. "Dat'll be wack as hell."

"No boy, to keep y'all company," she replied. "Neither of you will have a reason to be up here. So I thought that a little company would be nice. Besides, Fury's birthday is on Sunday. Y'all can start celebrating a little early if you'd like."

"Aight sis," he said, rubbing his hands together as lewd thoughts went through his mind. "We can definitely do dat, ain't dat right dawg?"

I was so caught up sweating Fayeth that I just said yeah, okay without actually knowing what I was agreeing to or looking his way. Fayeth was a five-star chick, standing at about five foot six inches tall. A petite one hundred and ten pounds that was in all the right places. She had long, black, curly hair and one of the most beautiful faces that I had ever laid eyes on. If there was such a thing as love at first sight, I had just discovered it. I walked up to her, took her by the hand, and led her to the passenger-side rear door. Opened it for her to get in and got it behind her.

****

Thin and Po Boy were standing two parking spaces away, leaning against Thin's caddy, watching and listening to the whole conversation between Vik and her brother.

"Damn dat's a lucky ass lil nigga," Po Boy said after Vik's car pulled away. "It won't surprise me if he don't take yo place one day my nigga.

"Vik ain't neva went outta her way ta lookout fa us da way she do with him. "Dat nigga ain't put in a real day's work since he came cross da street, and I betja dat she's already put ova ten bands in his pocket."

"And you heard da same thang dat I heard. So y'know he's gotta be crashin' at her crib, and we ain't even been invited ta a damn cookout out dere"

"Shidd! On top of dat, I been at dat freak Fayeth fa ova a year, and ain't got nowhere wit her. He comes along and gits unda Vik's wing. Vik spit at her and he snatch her ass right up."

"Tell me dat he ain't ah lucky ass nigga, or dat Vik ain't groomin him fa sumthin."

As Po Boy spoke; animosity, envy, and larceny crept into Thin's heart because he could see clearly what his man was talking about. But he refused to expose his hand. He couldn't let Po Boy know what he was feeling. He had to stay a certified goon to his boy.

"Nah my nigga," he said. "It ain't goin down like dat. Dere ain't no replacin me. I'm dat nigga on Franklin Street, and don'tju fa'git dat shit.

"Dat lil nigga is jus gittin prepped fa da dog track, dat's all. She's lettin'em sample da sweet life. And once he gits a mouthful, he's gon wont mo. Dat's when his young ass goes ta work full-time."

""Yeah, I can see dat now datju put it dat way. But I still say dat he's lucky as hell, cuz she's spoilin da fukkk outta da lil nigga in da process."

****

The weekend was off the chain in the beginning. Juice, the girls and I were all over Jacksonville and Orange Park. We even went over to the beach.

Fayeth and I were walking along the edge of the water holding hands and talking. I was really feeling her. I guess that it could be called my first crush, and I told her as much. She just smiled but that was about as far as it went before she released my hand and walked away. Not so much as a 'I got a man' or 'I spent the weekend with you as a favor to Vik'. Instantly, I realized that I'd made a mistake by exposing myself and that I should have been more like Juice was with Tieaa. Enjoying every moment and fucking the shit out of her anywhere and everywhere the opportunity presented itself but instead, I let

my guard down and tried to treat her like a lady and it backfired. She's beautiful and sexy. I can't take that from her but she's a real hoodrat through and through. She's more attracted to the world in which I now live and the material possessions that come with it then being treated with respect and like a lady.

About nine-thirty Saturday morning while everyone else was still asleep, I packed an overnight bag and caught a cab to St. Augustine, where I spent the rest of the weekend visiting the tourist attractions in the oldest city in America.

I got back home at about five o'clock on Sunday evening. Vik was back, sitting in the living room watching television with the others when I walked through the door. It was evident that Fayeth hadn't said anything about what had transpired between us because all eyes were on me when I entered the room.

"Damn nigga, where tha fukkk didju disappear ta yesta'day?" Juice asked.

"I don't owe you no explanation," I replied. "But if you must know, I took a cab to St. Augustine to get a piece of mind. Is that alright with you? Or do I need your permission the next time?"

"Chill sensitive ass nigga. I ain't the enemy. I wuz worried bout'cho ass, dat's all."

I turned to go to my room, then changed my mind. Instead, I turned back to where Fayeth was sitting on the loveseat.

"Fayeth, it's my bad that I ain't like other niggas, that I looked at you as more than just a piece of ass. Had I known that you were about living for the moment in the beginning, I wouldn't have wasted your or my time on Friday. I have certain principles that I live by and I ain't gonna go against them for nobody. You don't have to worry about me anymore."

"Fury, you didn't do anything wrong," Vik said, having heard every word that I'd said. "That's her loss, not yours. You just continue to be you."

She then turned to Fayeth. "I brought you in more or less because I thought that you were a thoroughbred by the way that you carried yourself. But I misjudged you and I was wrong. Not many niggas out there in them streets are on some grown man shit, or have a good heart and will treat you with respect. You just let one of the few get away. Instead of someone that's going to keep it real and treat you like a queen, you're on that thot shit and crave the attention of those like J.R and Po Boy who will call you every disrespectful thing but your name in public. The type of nigga that only desire to get between your legs, then pass you off to one of his boys. That illusion of a spotlight and material gains that you seek as the lady of a dope boy is going to be your downfall. And in the end, all you're going to end up with is a houseful of crumbsnatchers with different daddies, and on welfare. If not with the AIDS."

Vik looked from Fayeth to Tieaa who was sitting on the sofa with Juice.

"Nah gurl," Tieaa said, answering the question in Vik's eyes before it was asked. "Dis here is my nigga. We established dat befo I eva gave up anything. And I'll be damned if I'ma let the next bitch hold down my position."

CHAPTER: 6

The next nineteen months flew by. Dirty Fed, J.R, and Po Boy had shown me all of the spots where I'd be posted up on certain days and at specific times as well as what to expect and what I had to do. One Friday, I was on the opposite side of the Courts with Cee Lo. I was posted up on the corner of McKay and Jesse Street, being Dirty Red's lookout. There was so much traffic coming and going that on several occasions a customer would stop where I was sitting and ask me what's up. I'd always point them in the right direction, depending on how much they were spending. I'd radio ahead for them as if they were getting VIP service.

A customer had just pulled away from the curb when I saw a black and white turn onto Jesse Street coming towards me.

"A fox is in the hen house," I said on my walkie-talkie. "A fox is in the hen house."

"If it's car one eighty-six, it's Barney Fife. Give him the envelope that I gave you," Cee Lo responded, "and keep your walkie-talkie on so I can hear whatever is said during the transaction."
I stood up just as patrol car one eighty-six stopped in front of me and the officer let down the passenger side front window.

"What's up Barney Fife?" He asked. "How's business?"

Without saying a word, I took the envelope out of my back pocket and threw it in the window on the front seat. He then turned on his flashers to hold up traffic, does a three-point turn and goes back the way that he had come.

"All is clear," I said, once I was sure that he was gone.

"Good work," Cee Lo responded. "Pull up anchor and relocate."

I didn't know that Vik had been listening in on the transmissions all weekend until she came over the air.

"Fury, when you come in, I wanna holla at you about something," she said.

When I got back down in the projects, I went over to the park and sat on the bench. The whole time wondering what I'd done wrong and why did Vik want to talk to me. And why had she broadcasted it over the air for her whole crew to hear.

I looked up, just as she was coming across the street towards me. And for the first time, I really looked at her. She was about five-ten, extremely beautiful and sexy. She could have easily been a supermodel if she didn't have those gun holster hips and that nice, round, bubble ass, or those fools that do model

searches know what real supermodels were supposed to look like. Rather than those anorexic broads they choose. She is the epitome of true sexiness and beauty. On a scale of one to ten, Vik was off the chart, and under different circumstances, I may have tried to get at her.

"Hey Lil Daddy," she said as she took a seat on the bench next to me.

"What's good, boss lady?" I replied with a question.

"I know that you're wondering what I wanna holla at you about, that's why you're sitting on this side of the street by yourself. Instead of over in the projects waiting with Juice."

Damn! How did she know that went through my mind. Had I been that predictable?

"You can ease your mind. You're not in any trouble," she continued. "Fury, I've been watching and listening to you over the past couple of weeks out there on the tracks."

"You've proven to be a real asset to this operation and twice as smart as all of those fools," she said, pointing towards Thin and his boys standing at the project's entrance. "Not only are you self-made as far as what you will and will not do but you find a way to perfect whatever it is you do and make it look easy. I've wished that Thin was as sharp as you are, but I know that it's only wishful thinking and that it will never happen. He has trouble with authority, I think it's because he's a grown-ass man, and

I'm a nineteen-year-old female. And I'm in charge."

The astonishment at her being only about three and a half years older than me, and having so much clout, and getting so much respect must have shown on my face.

"Yes Fury, I'm nineteen," she said. "I started out here on these streets at the age of thirteen, pretty much the same way that you did."

I must have looked astonished again by her knowing more about me than I had revealed to anyone because she smiled at the look on my face.

"Yeah! I know about you too. I do my homework as well. The only difference is that you're much smarter and more attuned than I was at your age. You've stayed in school and you're doing exceptionally well to where I went to JU and got my G.E.D. Not only that but you've already started to stack your paper. You aren't gonna be out here on these streets forever like J.R, Po Boy and Thin. And when you do decide to step away from the game, you're gonna be straight. I admire that in you. No matter how much money you make or what you possess. Don't ever let it change who you are."

Juice came running across the street to the park with Vik's cell phone in hand.

"Yo Vik, Marco and Varis been blowin ya joint up," he said.

"Damn LaVale!" She snapped, using his government name to show her disapproval and agitation.

"Can't you see us talking?"

"Yeah, but tha last time dat Varis called. He said dat it wuz important, dat he holla atja. He says datju know whut it's bout."

"We'll finish this conversation later, Fury," she said, rolling her eyes at her brother before snatching her phone. She then stepped off a few feet to return the call.

Juice's interruption gave me a chance to stand up, stretch my legs and look around at my surroundings. Po Boy and Thin were standing by the Gunby Courts sign by this time talking, while J.R was serving crackhead Na'Sha out of building three.

"Damn my nigga, yu got alla tha bitches in tha projects dat ain't got no man and some of'em dat do wontin ta give yu tha panties," Juice said out of the blue. "Butju won't pay'em no 'ttention. Afta dat skeezah Fayeth did a one eighty on yu. Yo ass been strictly bout business. Like Vik toldju dat day, dat's her loss."
"Nah fam, it's not like that. I have an agenda, that's all. Besides, I don't want a broad that them fake ass niggas have been up in," I replied, nodding at Thin and his boys. "They're getting money too, so I'm sure that they're cutting their share."

"Nigga please, dem niggaz ain't gettin no pussy. Ain't no bitches chasing them fools. I bet dem niggaz ain't got half tha cheese datju got and dey've been out here on tha tracks fa years. Don't no bitches wont dem butta'headz, not no real bitches anyway. Dey ain't got nuttin going on. Maybe Thin, cuz he's one of Vik's lieutenants, and he's the head of his crew, which gives'em a little clout. But J.R and Po Boy, on the otha hand, nah nigga. If dem niggaz is gettin wet, it's on tha trick tip from dem crackheadz like Na'Sha or dem junkies like Birdlegs. Dem niggaz are toy souljaz, the whole clique of'em. Yu my brotha are on a whole new wave. Yu are tha truth. Dem niggaz wish dat dey could play in tha same ball park witju. Shidd! Dat fine ass Dominican broad, Lil Micki Ramirez outta building 6 fo told Tieaa dat she's gon have yu fa her nigga. No matta whut it takes. And alla dem fools, includin Thin been tryna cut her fa a long minute wit'out any success. Nigga, yu need ta get at some of dem bitches."

Vik finished her phone call, and the three of us headed back across the street to where Thin and his boys were posted up.

"Juice, did you handle that business for me that I told you about this morning?" She asked.

"No doubt sis," he replied. "Five o'clock tomorrow."

As we were approaching Thin and his boys, Vik took her car keys out of her pocket and handed them to me.
"You and Juice go and get the car, while I holla at Thin and his crew a minute," she said.

I took the keys and Juice and I kept it moving on up into the projects.

"See whut I mean dawg?" Juice said, once we were far enough away for no one to hear. "None of dem niggaz have eva drove any of Vik's whips, includin' Cee Lo, as loyal as he is ta her. And tha broads out here see dat shit. Dat alone let's 'em know dat yu're a real nigga, and dey wanna git in where dey fit in witju."

"How do you know all of this?" I asked. "Whenever you're not out and about doing your thing, you are stuck in Tieaa's ass."

"Right now, Tieaa is queen B out here in the projects unda Vik cuz she's my bae. So alla tha broads thank dat cuz yu my mans, dat she can put'em in the car witju. So dey confide in her."

When we pulled up on the corner where Vik was waiting, Juice got out of the front seat and into the back. I looked over at Thin and his boys, as Vik went around to the passenger side and got in. He was mean mugging me. I shook my head and smiled to myself because I found it amusing.

"Where to boss lady?" I asked, without looking around at her.

"The Avenue's Mall Lil Daddy," she replied. "We need some fresh gear for tomorrow."

"What? What's going on tomorrow?" I asked, looking around at her.

"Do you remember the first time that we saw one another over in the park?"

'How could I ever forget that day or the comment that you made' went through my mind. So I just stared at her without saying a word.

"My bad," she said, obviously reading my mind through the look in my eyes. "Anyway, what I'm saying is that we're having one of those soirees tomorrow and I know that you wanna have on some new gear."

* * * * * *

"What did I tell ya Thin," Po Boy asked when Vik's car pulled off. "She's fukkkin or groomin dat nigga fa sumthin beyond tha tracks, jus as sho as shit stank. Big Duke is Cee Lo's ol boy. So she can't do too much wit him, wit'out Big Duke's okay. Butju on tha otha hand my nigga. Yo ass is replaceable. Shidd! She ain't neva took up dat much time wit none of us, and we've held her down since Big Duke first started groomin' her at the age of thirteen. So eitha she's bout ta demote yo ass. Or yo ass is bout ta be put on probation fa bein short on dat last pak and he's gon take yo block til she decides dat she wanna brang yo ass back."

"Nah my nigga," Thin said, trying to deflect his inner turmoil. "I been down wit her fa too long. She ain't bout ta flip-mode on me like dat."

"Shidd! Tha fukkk yu say. Dat lil nigga is tha only muthafucka dat I eva seen pushin her Beama or any of her whips fa dat matta. Not even Juice has been behind tha wheel and dat's her blood."
Even though Thin played it cool, the seed that had been planted a little over a year back was beginning to sprout. He too had a feeling that something was amiss with the way that Vik was giving Fury the extra attention. But he couldn't let his man know that he saw things the same way that he did.

'I'ma check that lil nigga,' Thin thought.

"Damn dawg! I know datju ain't dat fukkkin naive," Po Boy went on. "Nor are yu blind. Yu see dat she don't even thank dat fine ass Fayeth is good enuff fa'em now. Yu need ta wake tha fukkk up befo yu find ya'self out in tha fukkkin rain."

"Fukkk dat shitju talkin bout Po Boy. I'm tha muthafukkkin backbone of dis muthafukkkin shit. If I don't move, ain't no money gon be made on dis side of the of the projects,"

"No doubt dawg, but even Stevie Wonda can see whutju pretendin datju don't."

CHAPTER: 7

Five o'clock Saturday evening found me out in the park across the street from the Gunby Courts Projects. It was jam-packed like it was the first time that I'd come over on this side of town. Only now, I'm not an off-brand and there seemed to be twice as many tight-ass whips as the first time, old and new school. As well as more fine-ass females than I could count, most of whom knew me by name whether I knew them or not.

A jam-up job had been done in preparing this event. There was a DJ who was killing the turntables, mixing the latest music with some old-school, food was all over everywhere.

I was standing at the end of one of the lines, waiting to get me a plate when, "Whut up Florida Gator?" referring to the white and orange number twenty-two Florida Gator throwback jersey I was wearing, came from behind me. I turned around to see Juice, Tieaa, and Lil Micki standing there.

"What's poppin' y'all?" I asked, greeting the three of them.

"Whutz really poppin witju daddy. Lookin all fly in dem Red Monkey jeans and dem white and orange Jordans ta match ya jersey," Lil Micki said, looking me from head to toe. "Can a real bitch get some time wit a real nigga?"

Instantly, my thoughts went to what Juice had said about Lil Micki wanting me for her dude and it made me smile.

"Yeah shawty, that's what's up. We can chill." I replied.

"Why ya standin at tha end of tha line?" She asked.

"I want something to eat, if it's okay with you."

"No doubt daddy, but yu ain't gotta stand in line behind nobody. Dis is yo party. It's all boutju today boo."

"Word Juice?" I asked, looking from Lil Micki to him because I had no idea that this was all about me,

"Yeah dawg, today is yo day," he replied. "Datz whut Vik wuz putin tha finishing touches on yesta'day befo we went ta tha mall."

Lil Micki grabbed my hand and led the way to the front of the line with Juice and Tieaa in tow. When we got there, a dude was about to take the next plate.

"Move nigga!" She said, pushing him to the side. "Fury is gon git tha next plate."

He looked around at Lil Micki's touch, to look me right in the face. Then at Juice who was standing next to me.

"Respect," he yielded, before taking two steps backward.

I was on the dance floor that had been constructed just for these type of outdoor events with Lil Micki, dancing to 'Get Low' by FloRida featuring T-Pain. Little momma had her soft round ass baked up on me working it. I had my hands on her hips, riding that thing as shorty got low, low, low right along with the lyrics. I'd never had or been to a party of any kind before this one but this first one was off the hook and I was enjoying every moment of it.

"Yo Fury, come up on stage and holla atja boy right quick." The DJ said over the mic as the song came to an end.

I excused myself from Lil Micki and went to see what was up. Once I was up on stage, the DJ turned the music completely off and got everyone's attention.

"This is my man, Fury," he said to the crowd, "most of y'all already know him, and the rest of you would do good to get to know him. He's as real as they come, the last of a dyin' breed. If you've got my man in your corner, you've got a real soulja and a loyal friend all wrapped into one. I know that if Big Duke was home, he'd be doing this himself instead of me. But today, we're celebrating my man's birthday and formally welcoming him to the Dirty Money family."

The crowd was frantic; clapping, whistling, and chanting: FURY, FURY, FURY. I got chills due to all of the attention that I was getting, as I looked out over the crowd of people. The people that were there to celebrate my first ever birthday party with me. It was so intoxicating because I felt like I'd finally become a part of something where I was actually accepted.

Off to my left, I saw Vik and Cee Lo making their way through the crowd, coming towards the stage, and she had a big ass smile on her face. When they got to the stage, Cee Lo stopped.

Vik on the other hand came on up the steps and did the unexpected. She hugged me.

"Happy birthday Lil Daddy," she whispered in my ear and kissed me on the cheek.

Getting the mic from the DJ, she turned to the crowd.

"Hey, my people," she said, hyping them up.

"VIK! VIK! VIK!" They chanted.

"Are y'all having a good time?"

"YEEAAAHHHH!"

Holding up her hand to quiet them down, she continued. "Those of you who have been to one or more of our soirees in the past know what time it is. But for those of you this is your first, I'll tell you. Every time that we have a soiree, whether it's celebrating a specific event like we're doing today or just giving back to the community, we invite all of the hustlers from around the city," she said, pointing to several tricked-out vehicles, parked in various places. "And we have a car show. The winner takes home five bands and the bragging rights trophy until the next event. Unfortunately, though it hasn't left home in quite some time, Cee Lo has been doing damage to

these niggas at every soiree for the past five events." She pointed to a money-green '92 Crown Victoria sitting on 24 matte black with green rivet insert Joker rims, with the incredible hulk crushing a replica of the car between his hands painted on the hood and the big bragging rights trophy sitting on the ground next to the driver's side door. "Like its name, Crushin' All Competition."

About that time, the joint 'Blowing Money Fast' by Rick Ross featuring Styles P could be heard. The whole crowd turned and looked towards Franklin Street to see where the music was coming from, to be heard so clearly but didn't see anything. A couple of seconds passed and a four-door tangerine orange '91 bubble Chevy Caprice with Lamborghini doors up on the front, Chevy symbols are ghosted into the paint around the bottom quarter panel and an angel hovering over a graveyard holding a smoking AK47 painted on the hood turned in. Last of a Dyin' Breed came pulling into the park, stunting on 26" Rich Evans 8 oz Stilettos.

Pulling up in front of the stage, Varis got out of the car and made his way up on the stage where Vik and I were standing.

"This is a gift from Vik," he said, handing me the keys. "Happy Born Day souljah."

The crowd goes wild again with cheering, clapping, and whistling. I was almost in shock at receiving such an extravagant gift. Mainly because I'd never really owned anything for the first thirteen years of my life. Now at the age

of fifteen, I'm my own crib away from more than the average thirty-year-old.

I turned to face Vik, and the crowd got quiet in order to be able to hear what I had to say.

"Vik," I began, "If it wasn't for you, I'd still be mowing lawns for pennies over on Magnolia Avenue. You alone have brought my life to where it is today. I am forever grateful and to show my gratitude, to you and the Dirty Money family, I vow my undying, never wavering loyalty and respect."

The attention on me had receded and the soiree had gotten back crunk. I was standing out by the street in the semi-darkness, taking a few minutes of solitude for myself, trying to absorb the festivities of the day and how fast my life had changed in the past two years. When Thin and Po Boy rolled up on me.

Juice having peeped the move, ran and found Cee Lo.

"Lo, Thin and Po Boy jus rolled up on Fury out by tha street," he said, knowing that it was about to be some bullshit being that he hadn't seen either of them before now. "And ya know dat Thin keep dat faggedy ass pistol wit'em and if he's lookin' fa some smoke, Fury ain't gon back down."

"You're right," he replied, getting his own stick from under the seat of his car. "Go get Vik and bring her out there."

"Whutz up lil nigga?" Thin asked.

I turned around just as he and Po Boy got within a few feet of me.

"Yu thank datja da shit round here now cuz ya Vik's pet don'cha?"

"What in the fuck are you talking about, Thin? You need to step off with that foolishness," I replied. "This ain't the time nor the place for it. Everyone here is trying to have a good time, and here you come with this creep shit. I been peeped the dirty looks that you've been giving me, and I found it kinda amusing. Because we're supposed to be on the same team. Why are you riding my dick anyway? I haven't done shit to you."

"You game real good lil nigga. At least ya thank ya do anyway."

"What the fuck are you talking about nigga?" I asked, getting agitated with his bullshit. "What the fuck I need to run game on you for? Nigga, you ain't got shit I want. But if the truth must be told, boss game recognizes all game, that's all. The sad thing is though, you ain't even on my level and you're a grown ass man. I knew that you were a sour-ass nigga the first day that we were introduced. I just didn't know to what degree."

Cee Lo got to the outside of the soiree just about the time as Vik and Juice. The three stayed in the shadows and crept up to within five feet of them without being seen. They were so close, that they could have easily been a part of the conversation had the other three known that they were there.

"Lil nigga, I'm da muthafuckin backbone ta dis operation," Thin said, pacing back and forth. "Wit'out me, dis shit don't prospa. And I ain't bout ta let no young punk ass muthafucka like yu. Who ain't even from our hood, brang yo bitch ass round here and ruin whut I've built. Nor take whut I got."

"Nigga please, you've been out here hustling these streets for years and ain't got nowhere. What the fuck do you have Thin

that I can take? I got as much as you've got, if not more and I just got in the game."

"Ain't no need in playin' dumb. I know dat Vik is groomin' yu ta take my place in Big Duke's organization but it ain't gon muthafuckin happen. Not as long as I'm breathin it ain't."

"Thin, what in the fuck are you talking about? Grooming me to take your spot. Nah dawg, you've got your personnel fucked up and your information twisted. Shidd! Po Boy can take your place dumb as he is, if he really wanted it. Not only have you been misinformed, but you've been the third wheel for as long as I've been on the team. And ain't no telling how low your position was before that. You got a little clout in the projects because of your affiliation with the Dirty Money family. I'll give you that, but backbone. Nah dawg, not even close." I said and laughed in his face. "Cee Lo is that nigga under Vik. He's the one that's got the juice, the real underboss. Cee Lo is Vik's field general. You on the other hand, is just a dumbass nigga with a dumber nigga for your yes man. You can't see me and you damn sure ain't built for the kind of trouble that you're campaigning for. So one last time Thin, step the fuck off and leave me the fuck alone!"

"Nah lil nigga, I ain't built fa tha hand ta hand combat datju talkin' bout. But yo ass ain't Supa'man eitha," he said, pulling his pistol out of his waist and pointing it in my face.

Cee Lo stepped out of the shadows at that moment with Vik and Juice in tow. And put his 40 cal to the back of Thin's head.

"Nah dawg, it ain't going down like that," he said. "Now drop that gat before I blow your damn brains out."

Before Thin's gun could hit the ground, I went to his ass. I hit him immediately with a three piece; left eye, ribs, jaw then grabbed his big ass and slammed him.

Someone must have spread the news of a fight because everyone had crowded around to see who was going to get their ass whipped. Tieaa and Vik had to physically restrain Lil Micki to keep her out of the fight. As I sat on Thin's chest, punishing him.

"You don't pull a muthafuckin gun on me, threatening my life and don't squeeze the trigger muthafucka," I said.

Juice grabbed and pulled me off of him at Vik's command. I snatched away from him and kicked Thin in the face before Juice grabbed me again. This time pushing me through the crowd and back towards my ride.

The fight had pretty much disrupted the soiree. Everyone was either getting in their rides and leaving or walking back across the street into the projects.

I was leaning against the car waiting for Lil Micki, holding my hand to my mouth. Thin had thrown a wild punch and managed to bust my top lip when Fayeth walked up.

"Hey Lil Daddy," she said, "happy birthday."

I didn't reply. I just stood there and looked at her like, 'this bitch got some nerves to even be in my face'.

"I've been thinking about you," she went on after I didn't respond. "About the things that Vik opened my eyes to and how I was such a damn fool to let you slip through my fingers." Realizing that I was holding my hand to my mouth. She moved closer to me and reached toward my hand. "Are you hurt? Let me see your lip. Is there anything that I can do to help?"

"Yeah," said Lil Micki, walking up behind her with a bowl of ice and a white washcloth in hand before Fayeth could reach me. "Keep it movin' befo I tax dat ass. He's off limits." Cee Lo, Juice, Tieaa and Vik walked up while Lil Micki was putting Fayeth in check.

"You a'ight Fury?" Cee Lo asked.

"Yeah fam, I'm good. Just got a busted lip. Thanks for having my back."

"Anytime fam, anytime."

"Lo, would that fool really have smoked me?"

"Hell yeah, especially if he thought he could get away with it, and keep your eyes open when it comes to him because his larceny for you just got full grown with that ass whipping that you served him tonight.

"If you slip, he's gonna take you up outta the game permanently. Even if he's got to shoot you in the back to take you out."

"No doubt boss. Thanks for the heads up."

"What are you doing here, Fayeth?' Vik asked as if just realizing that she was there.

"Tryna git beat tha fuck up," Lil Micki answered for her.

"Actually, I stopped over here to talk to Fury. To say happy birthday and to apologize to him for not having sense enough to be his boo thang. When I could've been his one and only here on the Eastside," Fayeth said, staring Lil Micki down the whole time that she was talking to let her know that she was not intimidated by her aggressive tone. "I've come to realize that you were right on point about everything that you had said to me that day at your place. But I can see now that I've fucked around and let the next bitch take my throne."

She looked over at her friend Tieaa who was standing next to Juice.

"Now datju know dat I'm his queen," Lil Micki said, "dat means dat he's off limits. And if I catchja round'em again tryna putja bid in again. Have ya boxin' gloves on cuz ya gon need'em. Yu already burned yo bridge wit'em, and I damn sho don't wontja on da one dat I'm tryna build wit'em."

"Vik, do you know if Varis is still around?" I asked, trying to detour the conversation between Lil Micki and Fayeth before it became physical.

"Yeah Fury, he was over helping Tyga pack up his equipment," she replied. "Why? What's up?"

"Will you hit him on your two-way and ask him to drive the bubble back to the house for me? I'm going to stay the night with Lil Micki."

"I can do that."

"I appreciate it," I said, handing her the keys.

"Dat's my dawg," said Juice, with a big smile on his face. "I know datja gon beat dat cat tha way datjs jus beat Thin's ass ain'tja?"

"Shut up LaVale!" Tieaa said, hitting him on the arm. "Tha only cat datju need ta be worryin' bout is mine."

"You keep your eyes open out in those projects, Fury. Especially tonight," Cee Lo said. "Just because you don't see Thin, don't mean that he's not out there somewhere."

"Dat's true," Tieaa says. "He's kickin it wit Milkeila Washington. She lives on the fifth flo of my buildin. Right above me and momma."

"In that case, I think that you should get a room," Vik said, handing him his keys back. "And take Juice and Tieaa with you, or drop them off to the house.

"I need to talk to Lo about something."

*　*　*　*　*　*　*

"Lo, do you think that we should keep Thin in the loop now that the animosity in his heart for Fury has spilled over into a physical beef between them?" Vik asked.

"I see that as a catch twenty-two or a lose-lose situation at this point," he replied, after a moment of thought. "You have Thin who knows a helluva lot about the operation from the track's perspective. But doesn't have the brain power to work his position to his advantage. He'd rather listen to J.R and Po Boy, who ain't going nowhere beyond a habit, knowing what they tell him usually gets him in trouble."

"Now that Fury has stepped on his pride by exposing his true position in the family before whipping his ass in front of a crowd, he's really full of animosity and feeling some kinda way. So, if you keep him, the beef between the two of them is only gonna escalate and get worse until one of them is eliminated altogether. And if you just drop him, you stand a chance of getting set-up to be knocked. Fury on the other hand is very valuable. Not only is he one of the realest niggas I've ever met. He's loyal, obedient and will listen to instruction without question. He has more courage than Thin and his clique put together and he's only fifteen. If you didn't notice when Thin

pulled out on him, he didn't even flinch. I'll even go out on a limb and say that the more he learns, the more valuable he's gonna become. I personally think that he's lieutenant material right now. He's smart both intellectually and street wise, alert and respected. Besides, I don't think that it would be a wise decision for him to work with J.R or Po Boy anymore anyway. Those are Thin's boys and his beef is their beef."

"Are you suggesting that I promote Fury to a lieutenant?"

"No. I'm just stating facts on what you asked me. You're the boss. So no matter what decisions you make, they're the law and I got your back."

"Let's say that I took your advice and promoted Fury. Are you going to train him?"

"No doubt. When he vowed his loyalty to this family. I became oath bound to him as well. Saying that, anything that he needs to know. I'll teach him."

"You said that you don't think it would be wise for him to work with J.R and Po Boy, then who will he work with? Even if I could get Juice to commit to the family. He's too damn wild to work with you. So you know that him and Fury would end up bumping heads before long. And we don't want that to happen on top of this bullshit that's already going on."

"Vik, you know that J.R and Po Boy are loyal to Thin, and once he's out, they're going with him. What if you allow Fury to recruit his own team. He's been in the family long enough to

know your laws and how things are done. This way, he can groom them the way that he wants."

"I can see that," she said, nodding her head. "But how do I drop Thin without it coming back to bite us in the ass?"

"Come on now Vik. Thin is a twenty-five-year-old man that just got his ass beat in front of the whole projects by a fifteen-year-old boy. You and I both know that his pride is hurt and he's gonna want some get back. So let him hang himself. Call everyone together in an attempt to squash the madness. You know that he ain't. When he doesn't, I'll handle it from there."

"That's what's up, Mr. Field General," sha said, mimicking Fury's words.

"Make sure that you spit at Fury about the promotion if you decide to give it to him. And I'll get with Dirty Red and let him know that he'll be working with Thin and his boys while I train Fury. This way, he can be our eyes and ears over on that side of the projects. I'll also make sure that everything is kept on the low low until his crew is solid and ready to go to work, and to keep them out of Thin's way to avoid an internal blood bath."

CHAPTER: 8

The following evening at eight thirty-five found me on 23rd and Fairfax at Joe's Pool Hall. Vik had called a mandatory meeting, and despite the ass whipping that Thin had taken and his face being all fucked up, he was there with his boys so was Cee Lo, Dirty Red and even Juice.

When she walked in, she had a don't fuck with me, I ain't bullshitting look on her face.

"Good evening," she said, as she took her seat at the head of the table with Cee Lo to her immediate right. "I called this meeting because I saw it necessary. The operation itself is running well, but there seems to be an internal problem of some sorts. Something that is very unnecessary, and needs to be addressed now."

"Thin, I'm going to start with you," she said, looking directly into his eyes. "Yes, you do run your crew properly and your side of the trap is making an ass of money. But it seems that you've forgotten your position. You are not the backbone of this operation. I am, in Big Duke's absences. If I don't move, then there's no money made at all. You don't have the resources that I have to run this operation. Or the juice to keep it on the level that it operates on. I don't approve of that junkie stunt that you pulled in the park last night. If we were in contention for the Courts, a rival could have easily eliminated us all last night. Thanks to your bullshit. I'm not having that kind of shit happening ever again. That jealousy or whatever

you're harboring, if you plan on staying a part of this family. You need to find a way to put it elsewhere or channel it towards stepping up your hustle game. If Juice wouldn't have pulled Fury off of you. There's no telling how bad he would've beaten you. The sad part about the whole thing, is that it was over absolutely nothing and you brought it on yourself. You're supposed to be more mature and in control of yourself then that. Instead of being a leader like you're supposed to be, you're acting like a damn clown. Whatever the beef is between you and Fury. Y'all better figure out a way to squash it, here and now. I don't give a fuck how y'all do it, jus do it. There won't be no more incidents like last night. Not and the instigator is still in this family, that shit is over. That was the first and the last, do I make myself clear?"

No one said a word.

"Do you have anything that you want to say for yourself, Thin, before I go to the next order of business?"

"Yeah Vik, I do," he replied. "Me, J.R and Po Boy, been down witja since Big Duke first started groomin' ya ta takeova at tha age of thirteen, if it eva came ta dat and yu ain't so much as invited us ta ya crib fa a cookout. Dat lil nigga comes along and ya turn tha game upside down fa'em. Ya treatin'em like a fukkkin king. You're spoilin' tha fukkk outta tha nigga and we're doin' alla tha fukkkin' work. Look at dat whip ya gave'em. In alla tha time dat we've been down witja, yu ain't gave us shit."

"So you're feeling some kind of way and this petty ass larceny that you've got in your heart, is more or less about what you assume my personal interests are or who you think that I'm fucking? Is that it? First of all, whatever I do is my

motherfucking business. You and no other motherfucker including Big Duke, is going to tell me who to spend my time with, how to spend my time or my money. Do you get that? That's my house, I bought it myself. And if I want Fury in my motherfucking bed, butt ass naked, seven days a week, three hundred and sixty-five days a year and pay him ten thousand dollars a night to be there. As long as it ain't affecting your pockets, you shouldn't say one goddamn thing. Besides, there ain't shit you could do about it anyway."

"This," she said, circling with her finger to each individual sitting around the table. "Is about business, about getting ahead. Not about what you assume. There's no place in this operation for that kind of bullshit. So either you get your shit together and play your position or find somewhere else to be a drama queen. Jealousy and envy are two of the major downfalls of an organization. And I'll be damned if what Big Duke has built and entrusted me with will fall because of the petty bullshit that you're feeling. Not on my watch anyway. Until Big Duke comes home or says differently, I'm the HNI motherfucking C and what I say is law. I will run this operation the way that I see fit and the way that I think is best for it. Therefore, whoever don't like it, the fucking door is right motherfucking there," she pointed. "Use it. I'm the boss and

Cee Lo is my right hand. It won't take but a split second to replace any one of you."

Po Boy looked over at Thin who had cut his eyes at Fury. He knew that the animosity in Thin's heart for Fury had started to boil anew because the accusation that had been made the night before about him being the third wheel had just manifested itself.

"Fury, you won't be working on the park side of the Courts for a while. At least until I can figure out what to do about this conflict between you and Thin," Vik continued. "J.R, you will be lookout and Dirty Red will be working with Po Boy and Thin. Fury, you will be working with Lo. And Juice, it's about time for you to make up your mind on what you're going to do. Either you're in or you're out. No more straddling the fence. Do you hear me?"

"Yeah Vik," he replied, "I gotja."

"Is there anything that needs addressing before I end this meeting?"

"I'd like to say something," I replied. She nodded her head. "Thin, I don't have no beef with you, and I never had. Whatever your beef was with me before it turned into what it did last night. I wish that you would've come to me like a man beforehand. I'm sure that we could've worked it out. I'm loyal to Vik, and what she says is law. But if you ever draw another gun on me, you better squeeze and take me all the way up out of the game right then. Or I swear to the most High that I will

kill you the next time. I don't take being threatened in any way lightly, especially the way that you put that gun in my face last night."

"Lil nigga, you betta be glad dat I got respect fa Vik's law ya'self. Or I'd murda yo muthafuckin ass right tha fukkk now," he said, pulling his Glock out, only to have Cee Lo's 40 Cal and Dirty Red's Calico 9 lock, loaded and aimed at him before he could put the gun on the table to show that he was strapped. "So don't get things twisted."

"I'm through talking about it Thin, and this is squashed like the boss lady says as far as I'm concerned. But be real about it and do the same before things turn graveyard ugly for one of us."

"Are you two finished?" Vik interrupted, not letting the irritation that she was feeling go unnoticed. No one said a word. "This meeting is over then. You all can go, except for Fury and Juice. You two sit tight."

"C'mon sis," Juice said, "I promised bae dat we'd go ta tha movies at 10 o'clock. Can dis wait til lata?"

"Yes, go ahead," she replied. "Fury can fill you in later. If you're ready to commit that is. So catch Dirty Red before he leaves and ask him to drop you off in the projects."

Cee Lo's cell rang just as Juice runs to the door to catch Dirty Red, which gave me enough time to try and figure out why Vik wanted me to stay put after the meeting had ended. She had already laid down her law. And even though I wasn't the one

who started the conflict, it still surrounded me. And with Thin having seniority over me, if anyone had to be exiled or put on extended probation. I'm pretty sure it would more than likely be me.

"What's up Vik, Lo?" I asked, once Cee Lo had finished his call. "What's this all about?"

"Last night after you left, Cee Lo and I had a long talk," Vik began. "We discussed you, Thin, the fight, the pros and cons of what's going on and what might happen in the future. In the end, I had to make a decision and Lo supports it one hundred percent."

My heart started to beat a thousand miles per minute, causing everything that she'd said during the meeting to be discarded. My only thought at that time was that I fumbled the ball by beating Thin's ass last night. But if that was the case, so be it. I'm a man before anything and what's done is done.

"The reason that you will be working with Cee Lo is because he and I have decided to promote you to a lieutenant. And after you finish that training, you will have to recruit your own team and train them on the same side of the Courts."

"What about Thin?' I asked, breathing a little easier now. "Won't he think that he was right all along about you grooming me to take his place and cause problems?"

"We've already thought about that," replied Cee Lo. "That's why you're gonna be on my side of the Courts with me. Thin knows that I ain't with the bullshit and he ain't gonna come

over there unless I have to alert the family due to an emergency. Honestly Fury, you and I both know that he's big mad and he ain't gonna squash the madness. It's only a matter of time before he rolls up on you again. You heard what he said when he was showing you that he was strapped, as well as what he said last night."

"He thinks that you're being groomed to replace him, and nothing beyond exiling or eliminating you is gonna change his mind about that. So, the best alternative for that is to groom you for his position. Once he starts the madness again, he's out and we know that J.R and Po Boy are going with him. Hopefully by then, you will have organized your squad and be ready to take over his block without missing a beat. If we have any problems out of him after that. We'll deal with them as they come."

"Say no more, whatever shots you and Vik have called, that's what it is."

CHAPTER: 9

"You've already gotten your education from the lookout standpoint of the game and you pretty much know who's who on that level," Cee Lo said on my first training day with him. "Even though Barney Fife keeps us informed on when a narc is gonna be sent in and we avoid him or her most of the time. They still manage to get in and make a crumb deal from the jits out here grinding late night every once in a while which makes this a weed and seed zone. You also know that we've got the majority of the clientele sewn up in the city. Very few in all of Duval County have the connections that Big Duke left behind. Therefore, a lot of the dope boys from around the city, and some of the jits that's got their weight up will come to you to cop their work. So, I'm gonna start your education in sales and distribution with terminology on weights. As well as show you on the scale what's being asked for. Let's start with coke. Dope Boys that are buying weight will never come to you to buy one ounce, which is twenty-eight grams. Unless they're just getting their feet up under them," Cee Lo said, showing a sack of powder first, then a cookie of crack. "Even then, if they ask for an ounce instead of an onion, a zone or a whole one, walk away. It's the man or a narc. If he or she ever ask for weight in ounces, regardless to how many they're trying to buy, walk. You identify real hustlers by how they come at you for the work. Meaning four and a baby or a big eight instead of four and a half ounces. A quarter instead of nine." Cee Lo showed me everything from a nickel hit in both powder and crack to a whole bird, explaining weights and prices as he went along.

"Never let the buyer set the price when you're selling them weight. Normally when this happens, they will set the price higher than it actually should be in hopes that greed will override your common sense and lure you into the trap. And when this happens, ten times out of ten, it's a setup and you will be selling to an undercover or a snitch. How much he or she gets for their money on the first transaction doesn't matter. As long as it looks kosher. Their main objective is in making the connect and the buys from you to make their case solid. There's never a need for long drawn-out conversations during a transaction either. No matter who you're dealing with, it's about doing business and moving on. The least amount of conversation that you have about what's going on, the better. That goes double for if you're out on the tracks doing some hand-to-hand transactions. In that case, it's always good to know your customers because there's always a chance that the car itself is wired with audio and/or video surveillance. The camera is usually in the sun visor pointing towards the driver's side door or in the passenger side door panel. To be able to get a good facial shot of the person and transaction. So, it's best to try and avoid direct exposure to them both."

"There's never a definite place for a wire if you're being recorded. Even walking customers could be wearing a wire. So, like I said, the least amount of conversation the better. This keeps you from incriminating yourself if the alphabet boys are listening on the other end while the transaction is going down and recording your every word. As well as keep you out of a possible conspiracy charge if the dope boy that you're dealing with is under investigation and his phone is bugged or he's working with them"

For the next couple of weeks, I worked every position on the block, from lookout to lieutenant. I got a thorough education of what the cocaine game is like from every aspect. More money went through my hands in that short period of time then I'd saved over the past two years and I've got close to a hundred stacks in the stash if not more.

"Damn Lo, we've been eating real good these past couple of weeks," I said one Friday night after we'd closed shop and was at Unique's counting the week's trap. "I knew that there was mad money being made but I never knew that it was like this."

"No doubt, Fury, that's why we can afford to work in shifts. Rather than be out here from sun up til sun down." He replied. "But don't get things twisted, it ain't always been like this and things are always subjected to change. When Big Duke and his partner Flex first put down over in the Courts, it was like the wild west out there. You had everybody and their mammie out there trying to put in work. The Jackboys were out there robbing the hustler and customer they caught out late night, niggas were shooting it out for the trap spot and jump out was out there raiding at least twice a week trying to gain control of the projects. It's pretty lax now so to speak, thanks to the work that Big Duke and his boys put in for us to be where we are today. But this is still hard work. No matter how much money you see on a day-to-day basis or who you work for, things could still go wrong. One false move or wrong decision and you're popped, jacked or dead. Besides that, there's still greedy ass Barney Fife who could flip on us at any minute and put the alphabet boys on us. The only thing that's keeping him accepting bay and not asking for a bigger piece of the pie than he's getting, Is he knows that we've got a video tape of him accepting payoff money out there in the Courts, from Big Duke before he got knocked and from Vik about a month ago. As an ace in the hole if he tries to flip. He knows how to identify our entire team and makes sure that we know where the duke boys are and that we aren't hit on his watch.

"Speaking of teams, have you recruited any souljas yet?"

"Juice and I are taking the girls skatin' tomorrow night. I've got a little something lined up then with some guys out of Sherwood."

"A'ght, handle that business and let's get them in training."

CHAPTER: 10

Juice and I, along with Lil Micki and Tieaa were sitting at a table near the arcade in Skate City when three guys around the age of eighteen approached our table with three girls in their company.

"Peace, loyalty and respect," one guy said, using the code that I had sent out as a means of knowing what the business was.

I nodded my head and stood up. "I am Fury, and this is my man Juice." I replied, pointing at him.

"I'm Trey, dis is my brutha Breeze and our cousin Zee," he said. "T Bone told us datju wuz lookin fa some real niggaz."

"That I am my man," I replied.

"Lil Micki, Tieaa, do me a favor and take them," I pointed at the three females, "out on the floor for a few laps or down to the concession stand for a soda or something and let us fellas talk a minute."

Lil Micki and Tieaa got up from the table without saying a word and turned towards the concession stand.

"Damn Fury! You must be dat nigga on yo turf," said one of the females as they got up from the table. "Ain't no nigga alive gon control me lie dat."

"Yeah! He is dat nigga and he's also my nigga," Lil Micki said to clarify her position and to avoid any violations on her territory. "So pump ya brakes and slow ya roll. Lookin' ain't no problem, but when ya start bumpin dem gums. Them ya askin fa trouble."

"Yo'Leeka, shut tha fukkk up and folla suit," Trey interjected. "So, we can talk business."

She rolled her eyes at him, before walking off behind the other four females.

It took about fifteen minutes for me to run down the basics of what I was looking for, and all three of them accepted. Timing it perfectly, we were just wrapping things up and my three new recruits were getting to their feet to excuse themselves when the girls walked up.

"Oh yeah!" I said, reaching in my pocket and pulling out my sandwich. "This is a little something to wet your appetites and to seal our deal." I gave them two one-hundred-dollar bills each. "I'll meet y'all at the Waffle House over on Dunn Avenue in about thirty minutes"

"A'ight, we'll be dere," Trey replied, and the six of them walked away.

Once they were out of sight, I called Cee Lo and put him up on the meeting and told him to be at the Waffle House on Dunn Avenue in about twenty-five minutes. So he could screen the recruits firsthand from the outside looking in before they went into training.

The six of them were just getting out of a cab when we pulled into the Waffle House parking lot. Not knowing who was in the car behind the limo-tint, just knowing that they liked what they saw. They were pointing in amazement at the car, as we pulled up and parked. When we got out of the car, you could really see the wanting on all six of their faces and the hunger in their eyes. Wanting for various things, for their own personal reasons. I personally knew the feeling because I'd walked in their shoes once myself.

They waited on the curb for us and we all walked in together. I spotted Cee Lo immediately sitting at the counter eating breakfast as usual. Juice and I nodded at him in acknowledgement as we took the large booth directly behind him.

"Damn Big Homie, dat's a fly ass whip ya pushin," Trey said. "How many stacks yu got invested in it? Dat muthafukkka is off tha meeta."

"None my man. It was a gift," I replied.

"Fa real nigga?" asked Zee. "Ain't no fukkkin way. Yu bullshiddin ain'tja? Ain't nobody gon jus give a nigga a fly ass whip like dat fa nuttin. C'mon dawg, everythang gotta price. 'Specially sumthin like dat."

"I don't lie my man. Like I said, it was a gift."

"A'ight, aight my bad dawg. I wuzn't callin yu no lie. It's jus dat, dat's tha tightest whip dat I've eva seen, and ain't nobody eva

gave me shit. It's kinda hard to believe dat somebody'll jus give a whip like dat away."

"I feel that, Zee. I've been there before myself but when the opportunity knocked. You've got to be ready to take it and run.

That's what I did. You spoke of a price. Everything in life does have a price. But not always the kind of price one would think. I got that whip as a token of appreciation for my obedience and respect, that went along with my hard work and my unwavering loyalty to my people. I'm offering y'all the same opportunity that was given to me. What you get and how much you get from here is solely up to each of you. I damn near got everything that a grown man could want right now. Because once I committed to this way of life. It became my way of life and I'm real with it. Depending on how deep your loyalty is and if you're real and dedicated to this. Each of you can have what I've got and more, sky is the limit. But there are some wannabes. Those who want to enjoy the spoils of this life, but don't want to put in their share of the work to get them. Or play their position on the team. I'm not going to front; you can't feed all niggas. Some just won't let you. They'll catch feelings because the boss is making more than they are. Regardless to how well they're eating. Evidently, they've forgotten where they came from or that the boss is the reason that they are doing as well as they are. I don't want those kinds of people around me. They only cause hardships. There's no place on this team for envy, jealousy, larceny or stupidity. If you're truly loyal and your brother's keeper. You will come up with no problem."

"If you have any problems and you can't find me, take them to Juice. If one of us got problems, then all of us got problems. We will put our heads together and try to solve the problem. If it's bigger than that, I've got people who can handle it for sure. Lastly, don't stress yourselves about being an outsider or trying to fit in. With you three being on my team, you will be okay. As long as you stay on our turf. At least until you're familiar with your surroundings and the people become familiar with each of you. You stress over your girls on your own time. Whenever we're putting in work, it's about business and business only. Do either of you have any questions?"

"I have one," said the bright-skinned girl, sitting next to Breeze. "Where do me and my gurlz fit in on yo team? We're bout gittin our grind on too."

"Ya don't," Lil Micki answered, then looked over at Fury because she knew that she had overstepped her boundaries for the second time in one night by interfering in his business.

Seeing the look on his face, she shut up and looked away.

"What's your name ma?" I asked, looking back at the girl who asked the question.

"Khadijah," she replied, "but I'd ratha yu call me Khandi."

"Khandi, I'm curious. Why would you want to be on my team? What could you and your girls possibly contribute to it?"

"I know a lil bit bout hustlin. Like I said, we're bout gettin our grind on too. Not only dat, I know damn near all of tha fiends

and junkies' ova in tha Forrest, thanks to my ol' boy. If yu put us down, and school us on whutju expect of us," she said, pointing to herself and the other two females. "Me, Camesha and Yo'Leeka can put down fa yu ova on our turf."

Mesha, Yoyo, the two females said simultaneously to their names being called.

94

"Dat way, yo turf and clientele expands ove ta Sherwood," she continued.

No sooner than she finished her statement, my phone rang. After looking at the number as if trying to see who it was which I already knew due to the ringtone, I excused myself, got up from the table and headed towards the bathroom to take the call.

"I heard what the broad name Khandi had to say," Cee Lo said, immediately after I answered. "Take her up on it."

"No doubt, I was thinking the exact same thing. As soon as she mentioned it," I replied. "But I don't want her to think that I'm over-eager to jump at the proposal."

"Understandable. Do your thing, that's your squad."

Back at the table, I spoke to Khadijah directly.

"Khandi, if I was to take you and your girls on. How do I know that y'all aren't going to stick me up for my money or cause problems between us?" Pointing from myself and Juice to

Breeze, Trey and Zee. "There are standards that you three would have to abide by when it comes down to business. And stiff consequences for the breaking of certain rules."

"First off, me and my gurlz are some real bitches," she said, bluntly. "I ain't neva had much, wit my ol' by bein strung out on dog food. But I still ain't neva stole nuttin'. Whuteva I ain't been able ta git from doin' hair or babysittin'. I jus didn't git. Besides, if I jus wonted ta jack yu. I'd git it outta Breeze instead of tyrna be down witja. If yu give me and my gurlz dis opportunity and let us really make some paypa like we wanna. I promise ya, datju won't regret it and yu'll be able ta see fa ya'self dat we're some real and loyal bitches."

Lil Micki was eyeballing Yo'Leeka the whole time that Khadijah was talking. She was still feeling some kind of way about her having said anything to Fury back at the skating rink. And the thought of her possibly spending any kind of time around him didn't sit well with her. She didn't want any of the females around him to tell the truth but he ran things when it came down to it and what he said was law.

'Damn, I hope he don't take these bitches on,' she thought. 'I'd hate to have to fuck one of them up about my man.'

"If I can say sumthin', Trey said.

"Go ahead my man, speak your peace," I replied.

"If dey git in dis business. Dey're on deir own when it comes ta business. Dey'll be responsible fa whuteva dey've gotta do.

Yoyo's my boo, and I'll die ta protect her. But I've made a commitment ta yu and my word is my bond."

"Dat's real," said Breeze. "I gave yu my loyalty when I took yo paypa back at Skate City. So if ya put'em on and dey fukkk yo bread up. Dey've gotta answa fa dat. I ain't gon go back on my word cuz Khandi wanna be cutthroat. 'Specailly now datju've opened some new does fa us and she don't hafta be."

"Alright then; Khandi, Mesha, Yoyo, y'all are in also. Everything that you've heard me tell the fellas apply to the three of you as well.

Whatever y'all missed back at the skating rink, you'll pick up along the training course anyway."

I reached into my pocket and gave them a yard fifty each. Knowing that they saw the two bills that I'd given to the guys. As my first test to see where their loyalties lay.

"I'll pick y'all up here at two fifteen on Monday."

When the three of them accepted the yard fifty without complaint. I peeled off another fifty for each. To let them know there weren't any indifferences on this team, and that I was only testing them by giving them less than I'd given the guys initially.

After they had left, Cee Lo came to the booth and slid into the booth beside me.

"What's good fam?" He asked.

"Everything is everything Lo," I replied. "I was about to get Juice's input on what he thinks about our new team."

"Our team?" He asked, with an astonished look on his face.

"Yeah bruh, I said our. You hauled ass from the meeting at Joe's before you found out what Vik wanted. So I waited until tonight to make sure that everything went right before I told you that I'd been promoted to lieutenant. And that I want you to be my sergeant if you're ready to commit to the family. I'm getting ready for a takeover, and I'm really going to need you as my right hand. Especially with the possibility of being able to expand to the Forest. Not many people take you seriously, but you've been my man ever since I came over on this side of town. Real recognize real, and I'll take my chances with you at my back over anyone else."

"I gotjo back den, my nigga," Juice replied. "I'm in, and whuteva yu decide, I'ma roll witja."

"That's what's up fam. Loyalty and respect."

"No doubt. Loyalty and respect."

"Lo, do you have anything to add?" I asked.

"Not really, this is your thang. But I do have a few questions," he replied. "How much money did you put out tonight for starters?"

"Why?"

"So I can reimburse your money like Vik said for me to do."

"It's not important. You don't owe me nothing. The hands of one are the hands of all. What I do need though, is two cars that can be tricked out. So they will have their own transportation. They caught a cab here."

"Yeah, I saw that."

"It will also let them know that this ain't no game. I'm also going to need the ice that identifies them as official members of the family."

"Hold on a minute," Cee Lo said, taking his cell out and dialing a number. The call lasted about two minutes before he hung up. "You got what you need. The cars will be in the Courts when you come home from school on Monday. The ice will be ready by the time your squad is ready for graduation.

"One last question. When your female squad is ready to be put to work. Who's going to be your underboss over in the Forest?"

"I don't know yet, Lo. Khandi seems to have the ability to lead, but who knows. When the time comes to decide, Juice and I will put our heads together and come up with who we think is best for the job."

The following six weeks were all business. I'd pick my team up at the Waffle House as planned and take them to the McKay Street side of the Courts. There we were straight grinding. The money was coming four times as fast as usual because there

were always four runners and two lookouts during their training. Khandi and the girls were absorbing street knowledge and the drug trade hustle game just as fast as Trey and the guys.

There were no complaints about anything. They embraced the game and their roles in it like they were bred to be hustlers. On several occasions, I have walked up on them talking about having money in their pockets every day. Something that wasn't happening before this opportunity knocked. I could see as well as hear in their conversations that they felt a part of something that was finally prosperous for them. I could relate to what they were feeling because I'd walked a mile in their shoes and that brought us even closer together as a team.

Things were looking good.

One Tuesday after shift, Juice and I were in the projects talking.

"Do you think that our team is ready, Juice?" I asked.

"Hell yeah! If yu ask me, yu picked a helluva team my nigga. 'Specially tha gurlz. Maybe we should hop ova ta tha Forest wit'em and let'em setup shop. See whutz really poppin ova dere while dey establish dere domain."

"I like that idea fam. What about the fellas? Do you think that they're ready?"

"Dey been ready fam but Thin ain't stepped outta bounds yet. So dey gon hafta stay put fa now."

"That's true. Let's run your idea by Lo and Vik about the girls going to work on their own turf. If they give us the go ahead, you get on that."

"A'ight."

Cee Lo and Vik walked up to where Juice and I were sitting on the hood of the car. "What's good fam?" She asked.

"Chillin' Vik, Lo," I replied. Juice, like Cee Lo just nodded his head. "We were discussing our team, that's all."

"Damn Fury! What have you done to my little brother?" she asked, looking over at Juice. "The nigga has matured to the fullest since he's been over here with you. You must really believe in him."

"No doubt, boss lady. Juice is my main man and I got mad love and respect for him. As well as I'm loyal to him. When you promoted me to one of your lieutenants and told me to recruit my own team. He was my first choice, but after I'd gotten my foundation together. I

100

asked him what was he going to do as far as the family goes. Once he committed, I made him my right hand. He knows that this business is serious and that there's no time for the bullshit when we're out here working. He has embraced the role he has to play and everything came together on its own from there. I know that he's got my back, just like he knows that I have his."

"I'm feeling that and I'm also feeling the unity. What about y'alls squad? How are things with them? Are they ready for graduation? A little exposure to their new lifestyle?"

"Fa sho!" Juice exclaimed. "We wuz jus talkin bout dat befo y'all walked up."

"I can hook that up for this weekend if y'all would like."

"No doubt sis. Me and Fury wuz also talkin bout tha gurlz puttin' in work ova in tha Forest. We wanna go ova dere and put'em ta work. See whut kinda security if any we gon need round'em and how dey git down on dere own

homefront."

"What did you say about that, Fury?"

"I actually liked the idea as soon as it came out of Juice's mouth. Once they graduate, it will be time to go to work anyway. So I told him that we'd bring it to you and Lo for the final say."

Vik looked at Cee Lo.

"I like it," he said. "I'd run with it." Vik nodded her head in confirmation.

"Have y'all picked squad leaders yet?" He asked.

"Yes, I'm going to roll with the guys," I replied, "and Juice is going to roll with the girls. 'Tis way, there won't be any animosity amongst them."

"Smart thinking. Who will keep the keys to the cars?"

"No one in particular. They all will have equal access to them. Honestly, they don't even know about the cars yet. They're for graduation.

"Speaking of cars. Juice, hit Varis up and tell him Saturday evening at five o'clock."

Without a word, Juice took out his cell and walked away.

CHAPTER: 11

J.R, Po Boy and Thin were sitting at Milkeila's dining room table putting their week's trap money together to be turned in to Vik and making small talk.

"Have y'all seen dat lil nigga Fury lately?" Po Boy asked.

"Nah, whutz up wit'em?" Thin replied, with a question of his own.

"I don't know dawg, but him and Juice been hangin real tight lately. In fact, Juice don't act at all tha way dat he use ta eitha. It's like dat lil nigga dun growed all tha way up or sumthin."

"I doubt dat shit seriously. Dat's jus tha way dat Cee Lo run his shit ova dere. Y'know fa ya'self dat he ain't bout tha bullshiddin."

"I don't thank so Thin. Nobody could control dat lil nigga befo but Vik, and she ain't been hangin round like dat lately."

"So whutju sayin is datja thank sumthin up ova dere?"

"Don't git me ta lyin cuz I don't know. All I can tell yu is whut I see, and dat's dat Juice dun changed."

"Tha first time dat I saw'em afta tha meetin at Joe's," J.R interjected. "Dem niggaz wuz out in tha park talkin wit Dirty Red. When dey bounced, I stepped ta Red and asked'em whut wuz up. Dat nigga didn't tell me shit."

"Yu shoulda known dat already J.R," Thin replied. "Dat nigga is Cee Lo's boy. He ain't gon go against his loyalty ta'em ta tell yu whutz up.

Ya see dat when we're out on tha tracks. He don't interact or say a damn thang ta us beyond doin his job. He put in work and bounce.

"Besides, need ta know info don't come ta me second-handed."

"Yeah dawg, yu right. But I thank dat dat's shiesty as hell tha way he acts. Being dat we're pose ta be on tha same team."

"I need ta catch dat lil nigga Fury doe," Thin said, changing the subjuct. "I owe his bitch made ass. Dat nigga shined on me and disrespected me in front of everybody at tha last git togetha,"

"Nah my nigga, dat lil nigga whupped yo ass," Po Boy said, with a big grin on his face. "I didn't thank dat he wuz eva gon git offa yo ass."

"Shut tha fukkk up scary ass nigga," Thin growled. "Yo punk ass jus stood dere and watched like I ain'tja boy."

"Thin, yu my man an all, and I'm loyal ta yu. But ain't no way in tha hell I wuz gon buck dat gat Cee Lo had. Yu know jus like I do dat dat nigga is trigga happy, as many muthafukkkaz as he dun already wet up round tha city. Nigga, I ain't got no S on my chest. On tha real doe dawg, yu need ta leave dat shit lone and let it slide. Vik told botha y'all ta bury dat fukkk shit."

"Fukkk whut dat bitch said. She ain't tha one who had ta walk round dis muthafukkka wit two blackeyes, lookin like a coon. Or had her face all fukkk'd up. Muthafukkkaz laughin' at her behind her back an shit like she's some kinda fukkkin joke. Dat nigga is gon pay fa humiliatin me the very next time I see'em. Y'all niggaz down wit me, or are y'all pussies?"

"Yu know dat I'm down witja," said J.R. "I been loyal ta ya eva since ya put me down wit Big Duke so I could come up. If yu wanna peel dat young nigga's cap. I gotja back."

"Dat's whutz up."

"Whutz up witju Po Boy? Yu gon ride wit us nigga or whut?"

"Yu know damn well dat I'ma ride witju nigga," Po Boy replied. "Yu didn't even hafta ask dat dumb shit dere. Me and yu been boys since James A. Long down in Paypa City. And yu neva had ta question my loyalty befo, so why now. It's an insult datju even tried me like dat."

"Yu right my nigga. Dat's my bad fa even comin atju like dat."

"Yu ain't gon blast tha lil nigga are yu Thin?" asked J.R.

"I should merk his pussy ass, but nah. I'ma eat dat lil nigga doe. As soon as I see'em, I'ma step ta'em and steal off on his punk ass. I'ma give'em whut he gave me. I'ma make his young ass feel Thin."

"True dat, true dat. And I got dat lil nigga Juice. I ain't neva liked dat slick rappin fukkk nigga no way."

Thin's cell rang, interrupting their conversation.

"Yeah! Who dis?" He answered like he didn't recognize the number.

"It's Vik. It's on this evening in the park."

"Whutz tha occasion boss lady?"

"I don't know. Breast cancer awareness," she lied. "I just feel like doing a little something and giving back to the community. Tell your boys to clean up their rides. One of y'all might actually stand a chance of winning because Cee Lo won't be competing."

"Word."

"Yeah nigga, that's word," she said, and hung up before he could say anything more.

"Whutz up Thin?" Po Boy asked, after he'd gotten off the phone. "Why yu smilin'?"

"Dat wuz Vik, she put a thang togetha fa dis evenin."

"Whut fo?"

"How tha fukkk should I know? I'm here witju nigga. All I know is dat she said she felt like given back ta tha community. She also said dat Cee Lo ain't gon compete in tha car show. So yu know whut dat mean."

"Yeah! Dat he prolly ain't gon be dere, and yu can git at dat lil nigga wit'out him gittin in yo way."

"Dat's fa damn sho," Thin said, still smiling. "Let's finish countin up dis money. So we can go clean up our whips. Today is definitely gon be a real good day."

CHAPTER: 12

"Fury, I neva really knew whut it's like ta be close ta anybody otha den Vik, since my mama died," Juice said, as we're headed to the house after having a late breakfast at Shoney's. "Since I've known yu, yu've become like tha brutha I neva had. I got mad love and respect fa ya and undyin loyalty fa'eva. Anytime datju need me, I'll be dere and I always gotja back."

"That goes without saying for me too bruh. The only nigga that I've ever been close to at all other than you, was my nigga White Boy. He was like my big brother, and I'll never forget him. I place you on the same level that he's on. I've been loyal to you and have mad love and respect for you, ever since the day we first met over in the park. If you ever need…."

The ringing of my phone disrupted the conversation.

"Fury," I answered, on the second ring. "What's good?"

"Whut up fam? Dis is Trey. Whutz on tha agenda fa today?"

"Oh snap! I was supposed to call you early this morning. You need to get up with the others, go to the mall and get some fresh gear. Then meet me at the spot at four-thirty. I got somewhere I want to take y'all this evening."

"Dat's whutz up boss. Is dere a dress code in effect fa where we're goin?"

"No, not really. Do you."

When I got off the phone, Juice was just hanging up his as well. "Have you checked on the cars lately?" I asked, looking over at him.

"Yeah, I wuz jus on tha phone wit Varis. He said dat dey're ready and he'll have'em in tha park befo everythang jump off dis evenin. Dey'll be unda tha tent beside tha deejay's podium."

"Good work my man. Real good work."

"Fury, will yu do me a fava?" He asked.

"No doubt bruh. You know that you've been my man ever since you kept Klint and his boys from shooting the blitz on me. Anything you need, if I got it or can do it, you got it."

"I been out here on dese streets fa a long minute, and I neva owned a whip. I thank dat I'm ready ta drop me one. But I don't know how ta drive."

"Say no more fam. I'll teach you without anyone knowing about it like Vik did me."

"I don't give two fux bout who know dat I can't drive Furk. I live fa me dawg. I jus feel dat it's time fa me ta have a whip like everybody else. So wheneva my boo thang wanna go, we ain't gotta call no cab or ask tha next muthafucka fa a ride."

"Say no more, I gotcha."

I got to the Waffle House on Dunn a little early. I was sitting on the first stool at the counter, talking with the waitress when my team's cab pulled up. I sat there and watched as the six of them got out. To my surprise, the guys were dressed in all-black Roca Wear and the girls were in all-white Baby Phat, just like Juice and I had decided to dress in black and white. For the exception that I had on all-white

108

Gucci and he had chosen all-black Coogi. They looked like a real elite team. The hands of one were definitely the hands of all.

I came out the door, just as Zee was paying the cabbie. "What's good fam?" I asked when I got to them.

"Loyalty and respect, boss." They replied in unison.

"I see that birds of a feather flock together," I said jokingly, with a smile. "I love the way that y'all are dressed."

"No doubt, handz of one are tha handz of all," said Breeze. "And we want people ta know dat we're rollin togetha."

"I can feel that but are y'all really ready for what's in store for today?" They gave me a quizzical look, as I stepped off the curb, heading to the car. "I hope so, because y'all have definitely earned it."

"Are we goin somewhere dat we need ta be on our toes at all times?" Trey asked.

"No fam, it's not that kind of place but it's always good to be on point. No matter where you are. Because anything could pop off, anywhere and at any time. Especially when you least expect it to. Take that white dude that killed those people in the church in Charleston, South Carolina for an example,"

"Yeah, I saw dat on tha news," Yoyo said. "One of tha people wuz a Senator, government official or sumthin' like dat.

"I always thought dat tha church was one of tha safest places ta be."

"Someone will always try to pull you down, with no real reason to."

"C'mon fam," Zee said. "Ya mean ta tell us dat as good a nigga as yu is. Dat even yu got niggaz hatin on yu ta dat degree?"

My thoughts instantly went to the altercation that I'd had with Thin. "No doubt. What makes me any better than the next man?"

"Nuttin I guess," he replied, hunching his shoulders. "Bein yu put it dat way."

"Not everyone wants to see the next man come up, or get ahead. There's always those who have the misconception that you're trying to knock them out of the box. And they'll do anything to try and tear your playhouse down. Even in your own camp, if there's no real loyalty to and respect for one another. Animosity, envy, jealousy and larceny are found in all niggas and broads who feel that you're getting more than you should or that you're getting theirs. No matter how much is out there to be gotten. Where there's internal beef, there's weakness. Where there's weakness, there's no loyalty and where there's no loyalty, there's destruction. I won't allow that to happen here. There's too much at stake. As a team, we're a family and family looks out for and are beyond loyal to one another. This goes beyond your intimate, personal relationships. It's about us as a unit. Blood bonds Breeze, Trey and Zee as relatives, but unwavering loyalty and respect will bond us together as a family. If any one of you have a problem with anything that I've said, let me know now and after today we can cut ties on a good note."

"Me and tha gurlz are in fa tha long haul," Mesha said, without a second thought. "Yu've dun mo fa us in tha past six weeks, den our own moms and pops eva have. Alla our loyalty and respect is yurs and Juice's."

"Dat goes doubly fa me and my peeps," Zee reponded. "Since yu put us on yo team. We can do thangz fa ourselves dat we couldn't even imagine befo. We ain't livin day ta day no mo, wonda'n if we gon have enuff ta eat befo we go ta bed."

"Yu gave us a new and betta life and we're loyal ta tha death of us. Death B4 Disloyalty." "Death B4 Disloyalty," the other five said as one.

When we pulled up into the park across the street from the Gunby Courts. All six of them were astonished and all eyes. I could only imagine the look on my face being the same way, the first time that I'd come across town and seen what was going on. I swear it made me smile.

"Whut tha fuck is goin on out dere fam? Mesha asked.

"It's a soiree in y'alls honor," I replied.

"A soir... whut?" Yoyo asked.

"A get together or a party for y'all."

"Look at alla dem damn people and alla tha tight ass rides," said Breeze. "Fam, dis shit ova here is sick. I hope dat we fit in and don't come off like off brands."

"Dis is so much different from our hood."

"No doubt, I felt the same way when I came over to this side of town for the first time. But don't stress over it, you'll be fine. So, get out and have some fun. You're amongst family now."

Juice must have been looking for us because him and Tieaa were waiting at one of the food stations when we walked up.

"Whutz poppin fam?" He greeted us. "Loyalty and respect. I hope dat'chall are in tha mood fa some dancin and fun, cuz dat's whut dis is bout."

Inside the soiree, the whole team pretty much stayed together because this was their first and they didn't really know any of the people beyond the few they'd managed to meet in the projects during their training. They were constantly pointing at various tricked out old and new school whips or commenting on this or that. They were blown away by the respect that many of the people that they encountered showed towards them upon introduction.

"I can really git use ta dis kinda life," said Trey.

"Yu might as well loosen up and git wit tha program den," Juice responded as if he was talking to him. "Cuz dis is only tha beginnin' ta y'all's new lifestyle. So eat, drink, dance, smoke a lil sumthin, talk shit and have some fun. Thank of it as a work day wit'out putin in no work. Mix, mingle and git ta know some of dese people, cuz dey're customaz of ours one way or anotha."

Breeze, Trey and Zee grabbed Tieaa and headed for the dance floor where Juice and Khandi had already disappeared. Mesha and Yoyo each grabbed one of my hands and followed suit. The soiree was all the way live, and the dance floor was packed. The girls were putting it on me to the 'Lose My Mind' joint by Young Jeezy featuring Plies, when Lil Micki rolled up on us.

"Whut tha fuck is dis, Fury?" She asked, stepping between me and Yoyo who was in front of me and put her hands on her hips.

"This is Mesha and Yoyo," I replied, pointing from one to the other in introduction. "They're a part of my team, and we're celebrating them formally joining the family. You already know who they are and what this soiree represents. You've been around long enough to know what time it is and you were right there with me the night that I recruited them."

"YEAH NIGGA! I KNOW WHO THA FUCK DESE BITCHES IS. SO DON'T PLAY ME DUMB," she said, getting loud. "Y'KNOW WHUT THA FUCK I'M TALKIN BOUT. WHO THA FUCK YU THANK YU PLAYIN WIT?"

"Not now Lil Micki," I replied, holding my hands up to my mouth like praying hands and without raising my voice. "Don't do this here because you're not going to like the outcome."

The people around us had stopped dancing as well and had formed a big circle around the four of us. To watch the show that Lil Micki was putting on.

"FUCK DAT SHITJA TALKIN NIGGA!" She continued and getting louder, once she realized that she was the center of attention. "YO BLACK ASS AIN'T SPENT A WHOLE DAY WIT ME IN DAMN NEAR TWO FUCKIN MONTHS. WHUTZ UP HUH? YU FUCKIN ONE OF DEM BITCHES IN YO CLIQUE NIE?"

I grabbed her by the arm and led her through the crowd, out towards Franklin Street. At that same moment, Yoyo went to find Juice and the others, while Mesha followed us outside of the party.

"Let go of my muthafuckin arm nigga," Lil Micki said, snatching away. "Yu're hurtin my fuckin arm."

'You're lucky I got your arm and not your neck goes through my mind'. "Lil Micki, what in the fuck is wrong with you? Why are you acting like a fucking hoodrat all of a sudden?" I asked, instead of saying what went through my mind.

"Nigga, don't play crazy," she replied. "Ever since dem bitches came along, my time has been limited witjo black ass. A bitch can't git no time, no dick, no nuttin. Shidd! My punanny needs ta be scratched jus like tha next bitch's. Yu s'pose ta be my man, and I ain't gon take a back seat ta no bitch. I don't give a fuck who she is."

"Lil Micki, you knew what kind of nigga I am and what you were getting yourself into from the start. But now you've got a problem with it all of a sudden. My word is my life and I'm loyal to my people. I was given a job to do, and that's what the fuck I was going to do. I explained all of that to you on the way from the Waffle House when I first recruited them. And here it is six weeks later and you're catching feelings like I've been out creeping. Instead of doing my job. Lil Micki, you ain't gave me shit but some pussy since I've known you, and I can get that anytime and anywhere I want. If your cat needs scratching so badly that you're willing to disrespect me in public the way you just did. You need to find a chump ass nigga who will let you slide with that bullshit, scratch it for you from this day forth. I'm done fucking with you."

"Is everythang kosha here boss?" Mesha asked as she walked up. "Do I need ta handle dis?"

"Why yu wanna know is everythang kosha bitch!" Lil Micki growled. "Dis is my muthafuckin nigga and whuteva's goin on between me and him ain't got shit ta do witju."

Ignoring her, Mesha kept walking to stop more in front of me than beside me. Before turning to face her and fold her arms across her breast.

"Bitch, yo ass must be hard of hearin," Lil Micki went on. "Dis ain't none of yo fuckin business. So ya need ta push on."

"Nah chick, I ain't hard of hearin," Mesha replied, stepping up in her face. "Yu jus ain't said nuttin worth listenin ta yet. Besides, I wuz talkin ta Fury, not'cho stupid ass. I ain't none of Yoyo bitch. I ain't wi alla tha lip service. So make up yo mind whutja wanna do and let's roll wit it."

114

Mesha's body language said what her words didn't and Lil Micki didn't want no part of what she read.

"Dis is tha bitch dat'cho ass is fuckin muthafucka ain't it?" Lil Micki asked. "Dat's why she's all up in my shit and poppin off tha way dat she is.

"Yu gon make a bitch fuck botha y'all asses up."

"Evidently Lil Micki, you misunderstood what I just said. So, I'll repeat it again. Slowly this time, so you can understand what I'm saying... I'm done fucking with you! Ain't not broad alive is going to try and make a scene or grandstand on me in public and still call herself my lady. Nah ma, you got the wrong nigga if that's what you're thinking."

"Oh hell nah nigga, yo ass ain't gon diss and dismiss Lil Micki Ramirez jus like dat."

"I just did Lil Micki Ramirez. Now step the fuck off."

"Whutz goin on here?" Juice asked as he and the rest of our team came up.

"It's nothing fam, just relieving myself of a headache. Everything is good now. Let's go back to the party and finish celebrating."

"Fury, didn't I jus say datjo ass ain't gon dismiss me jus like dat," Lil Micki said again, grabbing the back of my shirt as I turned to walk away. "And I ain't gon say it no mo. Brang ya ass nigga so we can settle dis."

I snatched away from her and Mesha stepped between us to face her, as did Khandi and Yoyo. "Yu need ta walk now bitch," Mesha said, "befo ya gitja ass whupped. He said at he ain't got no mo rap fa ya. So, ya need ta keep it movin, cuz if ya flinch wrong, it's on and poppin right here, right now. And I promise datja won't like tha outcome."

Not being a fool and knowing that she couldn't win, even with the straight razor she had in her back pocket. Lil Micki backed away.

"Dis ain't ova yet nigga. I'ma have tha last laugh," she said. "Yo punk ass is gon git yurs. I promise ya dat." She then walked across the street and went into the projects.

"Damn cuz, yo ass got punk luck like a muthafucka when it comes ta broads," Juice said with a laugh.

"I know, right," I replied, with a laugh of my own.

The party was dying down when I saw Cee Lo and Vik standing by the DJ's podium talking.

"Y'all come with me," I said. "I've got some people that I want y'all to meet." And walked away before they could respond or ask any questions.

"What's going on Vik, Lo? I asked once we were in their presence.

"Chilling fam and enjoying the day," Cee Lo replied. "What's good with y'all?"

"Everything was good until Lil Micki rolled up on us acting a donkey and causing me to dismiss her."

Vik never said a word. She just stood there observing the way that our team had more or less put a protective wedge between me and Juice and her and Cee Lo. As well as the way that the girls who didn't know who she was, were all on the side where she was.

"Vik, this is Breeze, Khandi, Mesha, Trey, Yoyo and Zee," I introduced, pointing to each as I called out their names. "The newest additions to the Dirty Money Family."

"Fam," I said, turning to the team. "This is Vik, the boss lady, and her right-hand Cee Lo."

The curiosity in the girls' eyes turned to instant admiration and respect. Not only because Vik was only a year or so older than them and was running things but they had never seen a heavy girl and now they were down with one. Loyalty and respect, each said in turn to her, then Cee Lo, who returned the greeting in the same manner.

"Fury, Juice, I see that you two have put together a very impressive team," Vik said. "I like that. How did y'all enjoy our little soiree?" She asked them.

"It wuz off tha chain," Yoyo said. "I've only seen dis kinda shit on music videos. I neva imagined dat people throw down like dis fa real."

"Yeah!" Khandi seconded. "Don't nuttin like dis happen ova our way. Ain't nuttin ta do ova dere but sit around and waste time. Cuz damn near everybody's on sumthin' dat'll keep'em doin' wit'out."

"We're glad that y'all had a good time," Cee Lo said, picking up a briefcase that was sitting on the ground at his feet and opening it. "Everything that y'all saw here today was to welcome y'all to the family."

"Welcome to the family," Vik said, taking a yellow gold link necklace with a DMB for the charm out of the briefcase and draping one around the neck of each of the new family members. "Y'all are official now."

You could see the pride swell in each one of them, as they accepted the official insignia of belonging to the family. It could be seen in their eyes that they knew that they had become a part of something that would make their lives whole.

"Do y'all remember our first meeting at the Waffle House? When I told Zee that I got Last of a Dying Breed as a gift for my respect and obedience, that went along with my hard work and loyalty?"

"Yeah," Breeze replied, cutting his eyes at his cousin. "He didn't believe ya."

"Well, Vik gave me that ride for staying true to who I am and what I believe in."

All six of them looked from me to her, and a brand-new form of admiration and respect grew for her in the girls. They knew now that all things were possible if they played by the rules of the game.

"Would y'all like rides like you've seen today?"

"Hell yeah!" Trey answered without hesitation. "A bucket is more den whut we got at tha moment. And it'll damn sho be betta den catchin a cab or tha city bus everywhere we gotta go."

"Fam, I ain't neva in my life seen so many tight ass whips in one place befo taday," Zee said. "Dese niggaz be ballin outrageous ova here."

"Shidd! Ova in tha Forest, dem niggaz ain't got shit but a habit. Dey'll po hustle no doubt, but only ta cop a bag of girl or ta smoke a dirty. But dat's bout as far as deir hustle is gon go. Ain't no real hustlin' goin on like it is ova here. Dey ain't on tha same level as y'all or bout tha fina thangs in life. Dat's beyond deir imagination. I'd love ta have a whip like one of dese to show dem niggaz how real hustlaz git down."

"How long do you think it would take you to be able to cop and fix up a whip like that?" I asked, pointing at a sour apple green '84 box Chevy Caprice with white leather guts, sitting on 24" chrome Phantom rims with Jealous Niggaz Still Envy painted on the side panels. "Or that one," pointing at a pearl white convertible '70 Buick GS455 with pink leather guts trimmed in white seams and buttons to match the paint, sitting on 22" floaters. The hood was covered up, but Ladies First was showing down the side.

"I don't know fam, cuz I don't know whut kinda paypa went inta puttin it tagetha," he replied.

"But yu've opened a doe fa me, ta where I can put in work til I can git right and drop me one. And only death is gon stop me from doin it or from showin ya datja got tha right nigga on ya team."

"I know dat's right Boo," said Mesha. "Dat goes fa alla us. We gon make sho datju know dat yu ain't make no mistake by putin us on."

"Well, Juice and I are gonna do for y'all what Vik did for me."

At that moment, Juice pulled the cover off of the Buick. A picture of Khandi, Mesha and Yoyo was airbrushed on the hood.

"Omigod!" Khandi exclaimed, stunned when she saw their picture. "Our own tricked out ride."

The three of them hugged me then Juice like little kids getting a new toy. Then rushed to the car. Halfway there, Mesha stopped and turned around. She had never been given anything of value in her life and here Fury and Juice were giving her a car.

"Is dis really fa us?" She asked, her voice full of skepticism.

"Yes," I replied, holding out the car keys. "Here are the keys. Welcome to the family."

Juice then took a remote on a keychain out of his pocket and pressed one of the buttons. The box Chevy's engine comes to life. He pressed another button and 'Cold' by French Montana featuring Tory Lanez, comes bumping out of the car's system.

"And dis is fa y'all fam," he said to Breeze, Trey and Zee, handing over the remote. "Welcome ta tha family."

"Loyalty and respect fa life," said Trey. "My word is my life, and I'll die befo I'll go back on it. No matta whut fam, I'll alwayz have y'all's back. Nuttin and no one could change dat."

"Dat goes wit'out sayin fa alla us," added Yoyo. "Like yu told us on tha way ova here. We're a family and family lookout fa and are loyal ta one anotha. Loyalty and respect ta yu and Juice til tha end."

"Handz of one are handz of all," Breeze said. "Jesus Christ himself couldn't come between me and tha vow dat I've made ta y'all. Like lil bruh jus said, I'll alwayz have y'all's back."

"Death befo disloyalty," the six of them said as one.

"Fury and Juice got their shit together, don't they," Vik whispered to Cee Lo.

"No doubt boss lady," he replied, smiling to himself. "No doubt."

CHAPTER: 13

The soiree was over by the time Thin and his boys decided to come over to the park. Juice, Tieaa and I were walking towards the project where I'd left my car at the curb. When they rolled up on us.

"Whutz poppin y'all?" said Juice, as they approached us. "Y'all a day late and a dolla short ain'tja. Tha git tagetha is ova."

Neither of them said a word in response. I could see the animosity and hatred for me in Thin's eyes as he eyeballed me. The closer they got to us, the clearer it became that it wasn't gonna be long before we bumped heads again or I'd have to take him up out of the game altogether.

"Whut tha fukkk is wrong wit dem clowns?" Juice asked me just as we were about to pass them.

"I don't know dawg. That kind of shit has become normal with them," I replied. "So don't..."

Before I could finish what I was saying. Thin caught me off guard and stole off on me. He hit me in the ear, ringing my bell, knocking me to the ground, and temporarily stunning me. Po Boy and J.R grabbed Juice before he could react, and punched him in the stomach in the stomach to knock all of the air out of his lungs. Causing him to double over in their grip. No sooner than the confrontation jumped off. Tieaa took off back the way that they'd come to go get the others.

Instead of Thin finishing me off while I was down. He chose to stand over me and grandstand.

"Yeah lil nigga, I knew datjo punk ass wuz gon be slippin bout dis time of tha day. When I first saw yu roll up and park. Dat's why I waited til now ta come cross tha street. It's my time ta shine now muthafucka, and I plan ta git all tha way off. I'ma teach yo bitch a real lesson, like where yo loyalty should really lay. Yeah nigga, Micki told us everythang, includin how yu disrespected her wit dem bitches in yo clique. Dismissing her like she wuz one of yo nickel hit trick bitches. She asked me ta fukkk yo pussy ass up fa her too, and it's gon be a pleasure. Cuz I neva liked yo punk ass no way. Like I toldjo ass befo, ain't gon be no replacin me. I'ma make sho of dat and finish dis shit now. I shoulda merked yo pussy ass tha first time we bumped headz and dis shit woulda been ova wit back den. But thanks ta Cee Lo , who ain't here ta save yo ass dis time. Yu got away," he said, drawing his foot back to kick me in the face.

"I wouldn't do that if I wuz yu fat ass nigga," Trey said, coming up at a run. "I don't thank datja wanna putja muthafuckin foot on my people. Not if yu value yo sorry ass life."

By that time, the rest of the family who were only steps behind Trey came running up as well. "Who tha fukkk are yu nigga, his muthafuckin bodyguard?" Thin asked, looking back at Trey.

"Do whutja got on ya mind fukkk nigga and find out tha hard way," he replied, "and yo soft ass booty buddies betta unass my man Juice to, befo all three of yu fukkk niggaz git fucked up."

Those few minutes of tongue wrestling and the time that Thin had spent trying to taunt me, was enough for me to gather my bearings.

"Lil nigga, I see datjo ass ain't tha only silly nigga round here dat thank he's bulletproof is ya," Thin said, more than asked as I was getting up off of the ground. Then reached for his gun.

Without hesitation, I hit him with a right cross, knocking him to the ground. Then kicking him in the stomach as hard as I could. At that same moment, while J.R and Po Boy's attention was on Thin, Juice snatched away from them and punched J.R square in the mouth.

Knocking out his two front teeth in the process of knocking him down as well. Po Boy reached for the gun he had tucked in his waist, only to find five others already pointed at him.

The word that there was a fight over in the park had gotten over in the projects and to the few stragglers that were left from the soiree. They had made a circle as usual around us to watch. Cee Lo leading Vik and Dirty Red, pushed the way through the crowd to the inner circle. To see who was causing all of the commotion.

"What the fuck! Never mind," Vik said, once they had gotten to the interior of the circle, and saw Thin and J.R laying on the ground, and all of the guns pointing at Po Boy. "I should've known. Y'all can put those guns away. It's over."

Being obedient, they did as they were told and went to stand with Fury and Juice.

"Thin, I knew all along that you were a stupid ass individual," Vik said to him directly. "But now, I can add suicidal as fuck to that description. You've been fucking with Fury ever since he first joined our family, a little over two years ago and what have you accomplished? You started the first fight between the two of you, and Juice had to pull him off of your dumb ass. But still, you couldn't leave well enough alone. You couldn't keep it gangsta and get money. So here you are again with your dumb shit, about to get yourself and those two fools," pointing at J.R and Po Boy, "smoked."

"Cee Lo and I knew that you were too fucking jealous-hearted and stupid to swallow your pride, let that dumb shit ride and handle business. Because you're too worried about what a muthafucka on the outside looking in is going to think about you. When they ain't got shit to offer you but a conversation. You came out your mouth whining like a little bitch, that I was grooming Fury to take your place. Nah nigga, he wasn't being groomed for that, but your dumb ass just gave it to him. You're done out here in the Courts and anywhere else we get down at. We don't need your bullshit around here. There's too much at stake for your petty ass animosity. And as I said at Joe's, I'll be damned if what Big Duke has built and entrusted me with will fall because of your foolishness. I'll have your ass bagged before I'll allow that to happen."

"FUKKK DAT SHITJU TALKIN VIK!" He screamed as he's getting up off of the ground. "I DON'T GIVE A FUKKK WHUTJU SAY, I'M GIT MONEY OUT HERE LIKE I BEEN DOIN. DIS IS ME AND MY BOYZ GODDAMN TRAP. YU AND NO OTHA MUTHAFUCKA IS GON STOP US FROM EATIN. PARK SIDE IS MINE, AND IT'LL BE A COLD DAY IN HELL BEFO I LETJA STOP US FROM GITTIN OUR MONEY OUT HERE!"

"Are you sure about that Kendrick?" Cee Lo asked, in the calm but deadly voice that he always spoke in. As he stepped around Vik and pulled his 40 Cal out of the small of his back. "Y'know that I ain't gonna play no games with your ass. I'll blow your muthafuckin brains out in the street right now. The only reason that you're still breathing, is because you ain't never stepped out of bounds before now. Vik says that it's over for you on our team and on our turf," he said, snatching the family insignia from around his neck, "and that's law. It is over for you."

"J.R, Po Boy, y'all need to make up y'all's mind right now where y'all's loyalty lay," Cee Lo said, turning to them. "Thin is done out here." They both snatched their necklaces off and threw them on the ground, before moving over to stand with Thin. "That's what it is then," Cee Lo went on. "If I see y'all out here putting down. It's gonna get ugly, graveyard ugly for the three of you. I ain't got no problem putting y'all's asses to sleep permanently."

"Not now, Lo," Vik said, putting her hand on his arm to stop whatever he had on his mind. " Let them go."

"DIS AIN'T OVA MUTHAFUCKAZ!" Thin screamed as he and his boys walked backward towards their rides parked at the curb. "Y'ALL GON FEEL ME. Y'ALL MUTHAFUCKAZ GON FEEL THIN. I HELPED BUILD DIS SHIT AND DIS IS HOW YU GON BETRAY ME FA DAT FUKKK NIGGA. I'M THA MUTHAFUCKA ROUND HERE, KENDRICK MUTHAFUCKIN BUTLER."

"LIL NIGGA, YU BETTA KEEP DEM GOONS WITJU AT ALL TIMES," he said, pointing his fingers like a gun. "BANG MUTHAFUCKA....YA DEAD!"

My mind snapped and I rushed him. Then all hell broke loose, as Juice and Breeze rushed J.R and Po Boy. Cee Lo gave us enough time to get all the way off before he squeezed off two rounds in the air to get things back under control.

Micki didn't know that Fury's team was so loyal to him in such a short period of time. She actually regretted getting in her feelings and showing her ass. Or ever going to Thin and telling him anything for that matter. As she watched the ass whipping that he and his boys were taking. She knew that if she didn't ease back over into the projects, she was bound to be the next victim, and she knew that she didn't want no part of what she'd seen in the broad Mesha's eyes.

'Damn! I fukkk'd up,' she said to herself, but out loud as she tried to ease her way through the crowd and back towards Franklin Street.

Mesha was looking around in the crowd for Lil Micki. When she spotted her, the people standing near her instinctively moved to one side. To make sure that she wasn't looking at them and to avoid becoming a victim of the next beatdown that was surely about to happen.

"Yo Lil Micki!" Mesha called out, stopping her in her tracks.

"Bitch, tha word is out dat fat ass nigga mouth is dat yu told him to fukkk my people up fa ya. But instead, his bitch ass is tha one dat got stomped." She said, stepping to Micki with Khandi and Yoyo to surround her. "Rememba dat night at Skate City when we first met and yo stank ass had alla dat rah rah bout Yoyo havin problems when she start bumpin her gums."

Micki looked around for an escape route to look right in the face of Jonee who had an amused smile on her face at Micki's discomfort.

"Well bitch, yo ass is tha one dat's got problems. Cuz yo dick sucka dun wrote a check datjo stank ass gotta cash right nie."

Mesha then punched her square in the mouth, before the three of them beat the clothes off of her. Not a single person, male or female intervened to help or break up the ass whipping that Lil Micki was taking. Until Cee Lo said to break it up. Only then did Breeze, Trey and Zee each grab their girl to stop them.

"Don't eva disrespect my muthafukkkin people again bitch," Mesha said, snatching away from Zee. To stomp on Lil Micki's head where she lay on the ground balled up in the fetal position.

"Unless yu want some mo."

CHAPTER: 14

The next six months went by smoothly, despite the fact that Thin had threatened us. Listening to Cee Lo and not laying down on Thin's threat, I used Vik's influence and contacts to buy eight bulletproof vests and some automatic weapons and got twin Ruger SR1911 .45's for myself.

Things were really looking righteous for us. Me and the boys had the park side of the projects jumping off the hook compared to how it was prior, and Juice and the girls had Sherwood on fire as well. We as a whole, including Cee Lo and Dirty Red's side of the courts and weight sales were making anywhere from a quarter to a half million dollars a week with ease. We were making so much money that everyone on my team had copped a new ride except for me and Juice. He was due to pick up his Mercedes on Saturday, and the new Infiniti Qx56 that I now drive was a gift from the car salesman over on Blandon Boulevard for bringing my team in and each of them purchasing a brand-new whip from him.

On several occasions, I've spoken with Vik about getting my own crib. Telling her that I knew that she needed her privacy, as well as her space. Or that Juice and Tieaa had already gotten their own spot out in Cumberland Forest. She would always brush me off and suggest that I stay put a little while longer and stack a little more bread. To buy a crib, instead of renting like Juice was doing. The only thing that I can figure from this, is that she wants me to stay with her until I can do things for myself legally without having to ask or rely on anyone else.

Technically, I've been on my own for over two and a half years, and even though I've got damn near everything I want. I still can't maneuver the way that I really want. So, I've stayed put and continued to stack my bread.

The thought of having been on my own, made me realize that I hadn't seen Big Momma or Poppa in over two and a half years. I took out my cell and dialed the last known number that I had to their apartment.

"Hello, can I speak to Big Momma?" I asked, when the phone was picked up on the second ring.

"Who is this?" Poppa's baritone voice asked.

"It's Fury Poppa."

"Boy, where in the hell have you been over the past two years or so? Big Momma has been worried sick about you.

"Where are you? Are you alright?"

"Yes sir, I am fine."

"You ain't in jail are you?"

"No sir, I want to come by to see y'all if it's okay. That's why I called."

"Yeah Fury, you can come by anytime you want. This is still your home. We'll be more than happy to see you."

"Alright then, I will be there in a couple of hours."

CHAPTER: 15

Thin and his boys used every spare moment they had after being exiled to plot, scheme, watch and plan their revenge. Their plan was to get at the DMB family for taking away what they felt was theirs, in whatever way they could. Starting with who they thought to be the easiest and weakest prey.

'Dem muthafuckaz is gon regret doin whut dey dun ta us," Thin said to J.R and Po Boy as they are heading back to his car after following their target. "Do y'all rememba exactly whut ta do? Or do I need ta go ova it again?"

"Nah dawg, we got it," replied J.R as he got out of the backseat of Po Boy's Acura and into the front after Thin had gotten out.

"Tha timin gotta be perfect in orda fa dis plan ta work. Y'all don't need witnesses seein whutz goin down and callin five-o. So y'all park somewhere so y'all can see her when she comes out. And yu clowns betta not fukkk dis up."

"And make sho dat'chall don't do nuttin stupid to harm tha bitch eitha cuz I ain't tryna go ta war wit dem niggaz if I ain't gotta."

Tieaa was just stepping off the curb into the parking lot of the Avenue's Mall when J.R and Po Boy rolled up beside her and stopped.

"Git in tha muthafuckin car bitch," J.R growled, pointing a semi-automatic shotgun out of the passenger side window at her. "And I ain't gon tell ya twice. If ya scream or flinch like ya gon make a break ta run. I'ma wet'cho ass up."

Tieaa was so terrified that she dropped her bags and purse. No matter how badly she wanted to break and run, she could not move a muscle. J.R hopped out of the car, leaving the door open, and physically   forced   her   into   the   car.

At that moment, Juice and Tieaa's next-door neighbor was coming out of the mall. Seeing J.R hop out of the car and grab Tieaa. She came   running,   trying   to   stop   him.

"Hey stop!" She screamed, "leave her alone!"

J.R jumped back in the car, and Po Boy punched the gas, burning rubber as he sped away.

She remembered Tieaa telling her to call Vik for her if there was ever an emergency that surrounded her or Juice. She picked up Tieaa's bags and purse and went to her car. There, she looked through Tieaa's purse until she found her cellphone, then looked up Vik's number and called.

"Hello, dis is Ashunta Littles, Juice and Tieaa's next doe neighba," she said before the answering party could say hello. "Can I speak ta Vik please?"

"This is her. How did you get Tieaa's cell?"

"She dropped her purse in tha parkin lot wit her bags."

"Slow down, Ashunta. What are you talking about?"

130

"I'm out ta tha Avenue's Mall," she said then explained what she had seen, describing the car and the guy on the passenger side of the car that Tieaa was forced into.

"Oh shit!" Vik said more to herself, but still out loud. "Okay, Ashunta, thank you for calling. I'll handle it from here. Do you need someone to come and pick you up?"

"Nah, I'm good. I got my own whip and don't worry bout Tieaa's stuff. I got it til she's back home or Juice comes ta get it. Matter-o-fact, I'll put it in her car and have my sista park it in tha driveway."

As soon as Vik was off the phone with Ashunta, she called Cee Lo and told him exactly what she had just been told by Ashunta Littles.

"I think that you should tell Juice immediately, before he hears it in the streets," Cee Lo said. "There's no guarantee that the broad that called you haven't already told or won't tell someone else about what she saw."

"You're right," she replied. "Why don't you swing by here? He's due to stop by in about an hour.

I'm going to call Fury also, if you think that he needs to be here."

"Yeah. Juice is his right hand and he's gonna want to be there with and for him. Actually, I think it would be better if the whole family was there.

"You call Fury and tell'em to get his squad together and meet at your place. I'll call Red, and we'll be there within the hour."
* * * * *

Twenty minutes after I had called, I was pulling up in front of my grandparents' apartment in the projects on Magnolia Avenue. Jesikah and Juleyka were breaking their necks to get to the front door. To see who had pulled up in the shiny black Infiniti SUV. I could only smile to myself when I saw the exasperated look on their faces and in their eyes when I got out of the truck and approached the front porch.

Big Momma and Poppa were coming out of the screen door when I got to the bottom step and stopped. They were actually sober, and from the look in their eyes they had been that way for a little minute.

"My word boy," Big Momma said, "come on up here and give your grand momma a hug. Where have you been all this time?"

"I would ask how you're doing, but I can look at how you've grown, the way that you're dressed, and at that nice truck you're driving and see that you're doing good. Who's truck is that anyway?"

"I'm doing good, Big Momma," I replied, "and the truck is mine."

"Boy, quit your lying. You're only fifteen and a half years old. You can't afford a fancy truck like that."

"He's got a red BMW too," Jesikah interjected without thinking. My thoughts instantly went back in time to when I had last seen her and Juleyka at Sabrina's hair salon over on Randolph Street and smiled. Vik's little prank with the car had actually fooled them.

"Ms Thang, how in the hell do you know that he has a red BMW?" Big Momma asked, giving her a sideways look.

When she didn't answer, Big Momma turned back to me. "Fury, where did you get that kind of money to buy those kinds of fancy cars?" Like Jesikah, I didn't say a word.

"Where do you live, son?" Poppa asked.

"On the East side."

"Where exactly on the East side, baby and with whom?" Big Momma asked.

"It's not important. I just came by to see if you had my mother's address and if you needed anything."

"I bet he lives with that chick we saw'em with on Randolph Street at Sabrina's." Juleyka said to Jesikah a bit louder than she intended to.

Big Momma turned and looked from one to the other. "You two wenches mean to tell me that y'all have seen your brother since y'all caused him to leave home and didn't tell us?" I've always known that you two bitches were trifling as hell, but not to that degree."

"We didn't think that it was important," said Jesikah speaking for both of them. "Being that he didn't live here anymore and it had been over six months since he'd left."

"Not important! Girl, bye, that's your goddamn brother. Why wouldn't y'all's seeing him be important?

"You two conniving bitches are scandalous.

"Fury, I'm sorry that I didn't believe you or give you a chance to explain when you tried to tell me that you hadn't had anyone here," she said turning back to me. "That's been a burden on my heart ever since I found out the truth."

"It was these two hot-in-the-ass heifers all the time. It wasn't long after you left that I caught them having sex in my house. That's when I found out that it was Curly Mae's boys Peanut and Thumper in here on the day that y'all had the fight. They told me what happened."

"Look at'em," she said, rolling her eyes in disgust, "both of them tramps are big right now."

I looked over at them instinctively when Big Momma said look. And sure as hell, both of them were pregnant. I smiled to myself, even though they saw it on my face. Because now, both the angel and the princess had become a badge of disgust and shame to their grandmother, and they knew that I knew it.

My cell rang, disrupting our reunion. Once I looked at the number, I excused myself and walked off a few feet to answer.

"Fury," I answered.

"Fury, I need you to the house immediately," Vik said. "It's very important."

"Okay, I'm on my way."

"Also call your team and have them come as well."

"Say no more. I'm on it."

Returning to the bottom step, I reached in my pocket and pulled out my knot. Jesikah and Juleyka both damn near choked when they saw it.

"I've got to go now," I said, peeling off ten one hundred bills and handing them to Big Momma.

"I'll call you later to see if you've found the address for me."

Within forty-five minutes, Vik's yard in Mandarin was full of vehicles. Everyone was out on the patio, either watching the NBA finals or shooting pool, while we waited for Juice to come by. Neither Vik nor Cee Lo had spoken a word to anyone about the reason for this emergency meeting or what was so important. But I could tell that something was wrong by the worried expression that was on her face.

My thoughts were all over the place at once, trying to figure out what the problem could be. Being that the whole family was required to be here. By her not having said anything yet, I could only assume that whatever it was, it affected him more than the rest of us. Unless her patience was running thin and she only wanted to go over it once. What puzzled me though was that the look in her eyes was deadly.

About thirty minutes passed before Juice walked through the door. When he did come out on the patio he had a frown on his face as if something had already gone wrong before he got there. Seeing the look on his face, I got up out of my chair and waited as he approached me.

"What's up bruh? What's got you all frowned up?" I asked, when he was in front of me.

"Nuttin maja fam. I'll holla atja bout it lata," he replied. "Whutz goin on here? Have I missed sumthin?"

"Nah, Vik called this meeting, but she hasn't said a word yet. I think that we've been waiting for you to get here."

He got a puzzled look on his face all over again. "Whut tha hell is goin on?" He asked, talking to himself but out loud all the same.

"I don't know fam, but being that you're here now I'm sure that we're about to find out."

He walked over to the mini bar where Cee Lo and Vik were sitting. "Whutz poppin, sis Lo? Is dere sumthin wrong?"

Vik looked around first to make sure that everyone was on the patio and was giving her their undivided attention before she spoke.

"Yes Juice, there is something wrong," she said, looking him straight in the eyes. "J.R and Po Boy kidnapped Tieaa from the Avenue's Mall a couple of hours ago."

"Whut! Nah sis, don't play like dat. I ain't in tha mood fa jokes and shit."

"Do I look like I'm fucking playing, LaVale? Would the entire fucking family be here if I were playing around with you? Do you see a smile on my face?"

Knowing that she only called him by his government name when she was serious, he looked around for the first time and realized that the whole family was in fact there.

"Do you know a chick by the name of Ashunta Littles?"

"Yeah, she's my next...." He never finished. It had finally sunk in that this wasn't a joke because Ashunta and Vik had never met.

"Well, she called me from Tieaa's cell and told me that J.R pulled a gun on her and forced her to get in the car with him and Po Boy."

"MUTHAFUCKA!" Mesha exclaimed. "I shoulda killed dat son of a bitch when I had tha chance ta." Her face had transformed into a mask of pure unadulterated hatred as her thoughts escaped her mouth. "When I run up on his bitch ass tha next time doe, I'ma blast his pussy ass fa sho."

"Fam, boss lady, Lo," said Zee, "wit all due respect, we slipped when we let dem niggaz walk up outta tha park afta dat confrontation. Sumthin kept tellin me ta merk Thin when he said dat it wuzn't ova. But bein dat I'm obedient, when tha boss lady said to let'em go. I fell back.

"But as soon as we got lax, took whut he'd said fa an empty threat. Dey took action and now one of our people might be seriously hurt or even dead.

"We shoulda erased all three of em dat day."

"FUCK DAT SHIT!" Juice said. He was so mad that tears are running down his cheeks. "Dem muthafuckaz wanna go ta war, den dey betta be ready ta kill me tha next time dey see me. Dey've picked tha wrong niggaz bitch ta fuck wit."

"I'ma murda dem niggaz real slow and very painfully."

"I understand how you're feeling, Juice," Cee Lo said. "I would be out of my mind right now if it was Moet or Cordelia they'd taken, but we've got to get Tieaa back if we can before we erase them. She's what's most important, and we've got to do it right when we hit them if we're going to stay out of jail. That's why we're all here."

"I know Lo," he replied. "I know datja right and all, but tha thought of dat nigga puttin a gun in my baby's face or one of dem faggot muthafuckaz puttin deir grimy ass hands on her is drivin me crazy."

"I can feel that but let's put our heads together and come up with a plan. If they're still in the Ville, it won't take us long to locate her. Vik and I both have a lot of contacts around the city but we've got to execute perfectly once we locate them."

"You're driven by pure emotion right now. You need to calm down so you can think. To avoid making a mistake that might get you or her killed."

CHAPTER: 16

Over on the west side, in the San Juan projects, J.R and Po Boy took Tieaa to apartment 19A where Thin was waiting for them. When they walked in, he was sitting in a chair facing the door with a Heineken in one hand and a blunt in the other. He had a sick, sadistic-looking smile on his face as he looked her up and down.

"Bitch, make thangz easy on ya'self and take off dem clothes," he snarls, putting the beer and blunt on the table before getting up out of the chair. "Or gimme tha pleasure of tearin'em offa ya. Eitha way dey're comin off."

J.R and Po Boy looked at one another when he said that because they knew that this was not a part of the plan. But neither of them said a word to him to question his intentions.

"I been wontin some of dat good, hot pussy fa a long minute anyway. Butju thought datja wuz too good fa a nigga like me."

"I ain't takin off shit nigga," she replied, swallowing her near panic. "If yu wont'em off, ya gon hafta tear'em offa me. And dat ain't gon be as easy as ya thankin. I promise ya dat. If ya do git some of dis pussy. I'ma be dead when ya do. And when LaVale find out bout dis shit, he's gon murda yo fat stank ass."

"Shut tha fuck up bitch," he said, punching her in the mouth and nearly knocking her down. "Dat lil boy ain't gon do shit. He don't wont none of me."

The punch hurt like hell and she could taste blood from her lip being busted but she refused to let him know or to let him see any weakness. "Dat's all yu got fat ass nigga?" She taunts. "Yu hit like tha bitch yu are. My baby sista hit harda den dat and she's only six."

138

"If ya punk ass didn't have ya do boy holdin dat gun on me, I'd git on yo pussy ass right nii fa disrespectin me wit dat weak ass shit."

"Didn't I say shut tha fuck up bitch!" He said a second time, grabbing the front of her blouse and ripping it down the middle to To expose her perky, perfectly round titties.

In a panic, she attacked him. Fighting for her life, she ran into him full force, pushing with all of her strength until he went over the chair behind him. She goes over with him, landing on top of him just as his head hits the concrete floor, temporarily disorienting him. She punched him anywhere that her fist could land a blow before she heard someone come up behind her and everything went black.

When she came to, she had a splitting headache and was tied to a bed butt naked, face down in a spread eagle position. All she could think about was that she'd never see Juice's smile again, that her life was over. She was going to die there in that apartment naked and alone. When she lifted her head to look around the room, she saw J.R, Po Boy and Thin standing there naked, stroking themselves to life. Thin still had that same sick, sadistic smile on his face that she had seen when J.R and Po Boy first brought her into the apartment.

"Hey Sexy," Thin said in a mocking voice, like everything was kosher. "I been waitin fa ya ta wake-up. It wuz hard ta keep dese two niggaz from indulgin demselves in some of ya goodies wit'outja bein woke.I had ta threaten'em ta keep'em offa ya."

He could see the fear in her eyes as the three of them moved closer to the bed, and it fanned the flames of his lust into a raging inferno. When he sat on the bed beside her, he let his eyes rove over the length of her flawless, naked body and licked his lips.

"Yo skin is so beautiful," he said, putting his hand on her shoulder and rubbing his way all the way down over her soft, plump ass. He felt her cringe at the touch of his hand, and it nearly made him blow his load. "Damn I wont summa dat," he said as he rubbed his fingers down between the cheeks of her ass. Then down between her thighs to her moist pussy. There, he put two fingers inside her. "Oh yeah baby! Yu're wet as a muthafukkka. Yu been wontin ta fukkk me ain'tja?"

Not being able to restrain his lust any longer, he climbed on top of her and entered her from the back.

"Lord god no!" She screamed into the gag that's in her mouth as tears poured from her eyes and a pain like she had never felt before went through her body. He ripped her virgin asshole open in one hard thrust.

"Dat's right bitch. Scream," he said pulling her hair as he slammed deep into her again and again. "Dat lil boy datja fukkkin can't satisfy ya like a real man can. Can he bitch?"

The pain was so excruciating that she almost passed out from it. Closing her eyes, she bit down on the gag and began to pray for death. She didn't want Juice to see her like this. She knew that he wouldn't want her anymore after being used like this, and she could not imagine her life without him.

Once Thin shot his load and pulled out of her, shit and blood was all over his dick and between the cheeks of her ass. Her rectum was tore up and burning like someone had poured gasoline inside of her and set her on fire. He picked up her torn blouse off of the floor and wiped himself off. Before throwing it on her back like she was a junkie or a trick and walked out of the room.

Before Thin could get out of the good, Po Boy's nasty ass had already climbed on top of her and started the assault all over again.

* * * * * *

Once we had a plan of action together, we sat back and waited. Juice was impatiently pacing back and forth like a caged lion, all the while holding a chrome 357 automatic.

Vik got on her phone and started calling her contacts. She called Peaches on the Northside, One Nine in Emerson Arms, Bezo in Moncrief Village, and Ladybug on the Southside. None of them had seen Thin or his boys in weeks.

At the same time that Vik was on the phone, Cee Lo was on his. He calls Miami's bar over on the Westside, and Milkman answers the phone.

"Yo, this is Cee Lo. Where's Miami?"

"Whutz up, Lo?" Milkman responds. "Dat nigga's gon ta tha barba'shop. Gigi dropped his lil man bitchin bout him needin a haircut.

"Y'know how my sista can git sideways at times."

"No doubt. He did the right thing to move right then," Cee Lo replied, with a laugh. "Have you seen Thin or his boys over on that side of town? I called him but his phone went to voicemail."

"Yeah! I saw J.R and a broad in tha car wit Po Boy, goin towards tha San Juan projects bout two minutes ago.

"Ya wont me ta send Mook round dere and see if dey in tha projects?"

"Nah bruh, that's alright," Cee Lo replied. "Po Boy is probably over there running errands with his baby's mama. I can wait until they come back over on this side of town."

"How's business over there?" He asked, changing the subject to get Milkman's mind off of Thin and his boys so he wouldn't inform them that he was looking for them if he bumped into them.

"Not like tha DMB, but we still eatin good."

"Nigga, you have always cried broke. Knowing damn well you're not. Besides, word is y'all have opened up a fentanyl hole."

"Sumthin like that," he said with a laugh. "It seems tha mo muthafukkkaz tha Fentanyl kill, tha mo customaz we git."

"You know that shit carry a murder case if they can link a overdose to y'all right?"

"No doubt, but tha money is comin like when crack first hit in tha 80's. Besides, alla tha illegal shit out on dese streetz will send a muthafukkkka ta tha pen."

"True," Cee Lo concedes. "What about them Jaguars, are you still betting on that garbage?"

"Nigga y'know I am. Ya seen how we spanked Derrick Henry's ass last week."

"Y'all did that, but you still need to find yourself another team before your ass go broke for real," Cee Lo joked.

"Not in this lifetime my nigga. It's DUVAL til tha end."

"Alright pimpin, tell Miami to holla at me."

Everyone was staring at Cee Lo when he got off his cell.

"They're over on the westside," he said. "Milkman said that he saw J.R and a female in the car with Po Boy going towards the projects on San Juan Boulevard.

"Do y'all have your gear with you?" He asked.

"All tha time," Breeze said as he, Trey and Zee head for the door to go to their rides.

Mesha pulled her glock out of her purse and dropped the clip to make sure that she had a full clip. So does Khandi and Yoyo, following her lead.

"Sorry little sisters, but y'all won't be rolling on this mission," Cee Lo said when he saw what they were doing. "Stay here with Vik."

"Like hell we won't be goin," Khandi said defiantly. "Handz of one are tha handz of all wit us. Juice got a problem, goddamn it, den we got one too."

"We can hold our own," Mesha said, speaking for the three. "So eitha yu let us roll witja ta support our family or we're gonna folla ya. It's yo choice, but eitha way we're goin."

Before he could protest any further, the fellas came back in with their vest.

"Dis is jus like we prepared fa durin trainin," Breeze said. "Only dis time it ain't no game. So putja vest on now."

"When we roll on'em, y'all cover our backs and secure tha area once we're on tha inside.

"If dere's any gunplay, shoot ta kill. Don't give'em a chance ta shoot atja twice."

Cee Lo looked over at Vik for some help because he knew that she could deaden the whole thing if she said for them to stay put. But despite the circumstances, she only shrugs her shoulders and smiles due to the loyalty that this crew had to Fury and Juice.

"We'll take Zee's Escalade and Yoyo's Yukon," Cee Lo said instead of debating any further.

"Two vehicles won't draw much attention to us when we roll up in the projects.

"Vik, we'll call you as soon as we find her."

"C'mon Lo goddamn it!" Juice said, his frustration and impatience finally spilling over into words. Yu're wastin time. Let's fukkkin move."

CHAPTER: 17

J.R was sick on his stomach from the stench of shit and blood that permeated the room, and any desire that he may have had to indulge himself in the degrading of Tieaa was gone. Not that sodomy and rape was how he got down anyway. It was supposed to have been a simple intimidation thing, that they had taken too far. He had four sisters who he loved and would protect with his life from what Po Boy and Thin had done to Tieaa. He put his clothes back on and walked out of the room, leaving Po Boy doing his thing.

After Po Boy had satisfied himself, he climbed off of her, leaving her in more agony and bleeding worse than before. He walked out of the room naked and into the bathroom to wash himself up. When he comes out, J.R is standing there with his arms folded across his chest waiting for him.

"Whut we gon do wit her now Po Boy, bein dat'chall changed tha original plan?" He asked.

"Ask Thin," he replied.

"He ain't here, but his whip is still out in tha parkin lot. So I'ma assume dat he walked down ta tha Aamaco on tha corna."

"He'll tell us whut ta do wit her when he git back," Po Boy said, "bein dat he's tha one dat changed tha plan.

"Yu ain't gon gitju none of dat hot ass befo wa do whuteva wit tha bitch? I'm pretty sho dat we gon hafta kill her. Thin ain't gon take no chances on lettin her live. Not afta whut we've dun ta her."

"Yu and me both know dat dem niggaz is gon be out fa blood if dey find out dat we even got her. And I ain't ready ta die."

"Yeah, I know dat, but nah. I ain't gon mess wit her. I ain't inta rape my nigga."

"Yo bitch ass dun got scared nigga? Or are yu a fukkkin faggot?"

"I ain't no muthafukkkin faggot nigga, and yu betta watch yur fukkkin mouth befo I go in it" J.R growled, stepping up on him with his hands balled up into fists. "Yu come outta yo mouth like dat one mo muthafukkkin time nigga, and I'ma show yu jus how much muthafukkkin faggot I am."

"Calm down sensitive ass nigga," Po Boy said trying not to show how uneasy he had become. "Shidd! It ain't dat muthafukkin serious. All I'm sayin dawg is dat dat's some good ass and yu gon let it go ta waste wit'out even gittin a sample."

Po Boy stroked himself. "I thank I'll go bump me a few lines, den see if dat pussy is as good as dat ass. Since yo punk ass won't."

"Do yu nigga, but like I said, I ain't inta rape."

* * * * *

The San Juan projects entryway sat a few feet off the corner of San Juan Boulevard and Highway 17. Zee made the left off of San Juan onto Highway 17. Then the immediate right into the entrance of the projects, with Trey, who was driving his girl's whip right behind him. They spotted Po Boy and Thin's rides immediately, parked in front of building E.

There were two Hispanic girls standing on the sidewalk in front of the cars, when the two vehicles pulled up and stopped behind them. Yoyo got out of the Yukon and walked between the two cars to approach the two.

"Hey chicas. Hola a todos? Yoyo said.

"Bien gracias," the taller of the two replied, looking from her to the two SUVs.

"¿Todos ustedes hablan inglés?" Neither girl said a word. Yoyo reached into her pocket and pulled out four fifty dollar bills. ¿Hablas ingles?" She asked a second time.

This time they looked past her at the SUVs instead of saying anything. Following their eyes, Yoyo looked back and understood their reluctance to reply instantly.

"Oh no, son buenas personas. Ellos están conmigo," she said.

"Yes then, we do speak English," the taller of the two said in almost perfect English. "Have yu seen tha guys dat drive dese two cars?" She asked, pointing to Po Boy's Acura and Thin's Cadillac.

They looked at one another. Then at the money that Yoyo had in her hand. She could tell that they knew something by the way that they had looked from her to the SUVs full of blacks when she first approached them. But they were reluctant to say. She handed them two Grants each and asked about Po Boy and Thin once again.

"Second floor, apartment 39," said the same girl, pointing to the building that they were in front of before hurrying down the sidewalk.

"Lock and load," Cee Lo said. "Don't kill nobody here if you can avoid it. Now move."

Him, Juice and Zee took off at a sprint for the back of the apartments. Breeze, Trey and I went through the front. Ten seconds later, Dirty Red and the girls did the same routine to cover the perimeter, with him and Mesha sprinting to the back and Khandi and Yoyo holding down the front.

Inside the apartment, J.R was sitting in the living room, absentmindedly watching The Woman King and drinking his third beer. His thoughts were more wrapped up in Thin having changed their original and having raped Tieaa than it was on what was on the set. He knew that he wasn't the kind of monster that Po Boy and Thin were and he wondered how he'd ever allowed himself to get caught up like that.

"Somebody's gon die in tha worse way behind dis shit when Juice find out bout it," he said thinking out loud. "Ain't no way I wanna be on tha receivin end and go through whut dey're gon do ta a muthafukkka when dey catch-up wit'em." A cold chill ran up and down his spine as he imagined the slow, painful death that was coming.

A knock on the door brought him back from his reverie, thinking Thin had probably locked himself out. He was going to question him about changing the plan without considering what he or Po Boy thought about it. He got up and went to the door. Without even bothering to ask who was there or to look through the peephole, he opened the door.

"Damn my nigga," he said, losing his words in mid-sentence. As he looked down the barrel of Juice's gun. Surprise and panic simultaneously showed on his face. He wanted so desperately to slam the door and call out a warning to Po Boy upstairs in the bedroom with Tieaa. To let him know that the grim reaper was at the door. But his hands nor his vocal cord would work, and he knew that if he moved a muscle or made a sound, it would be the last thing that he'd ever do.

Trey snatched him out into the hallway and slammed him face first on the concrete floor. Busting his nose, top lip and knocking out one of his front teeth on impact then duct taped his hands and feet immediately.

"Boy oh boy are yu gon regret datjo molly head ass pointed dat gun in my baby's face," Juice squatted down and whispered to him. "And yo bitch made ass betta pray dat she ain't hurt, cuz if anythang is wrong wit her. I'ma make yu cuss ya mammy fa sellin tha pussy tha night she conceived yo fukkk ass."

Tears welled up in J.R's eyes because he knew that his fate had been sealed. He was a dead man. He could almost see the death of him in Juice's eyes, and feel it in the tone of his voice.

Fear shook him so badly that he pissed in his pants.

"I-I-I diddn't- didn't t-t-touch

her," he stammered. "I swe-e-ear I didn't."

"Shut tha fukkk up punk ass muthafukkka," Mesha growled, kicking him in the side. "Yo bitch ass is still guilty."

As the guys entered the apartment, the girls guarded the two entrances, and J.R. Mesha, having the pleasure of guarding him, tortured him mentally with the straight razor that she had taken out of her pocket. Squatting down beside him, she put the back of the razor on his forehead. Then slowly drug it down across his right eye, over the bridge of his nose, to his left cheek.

"Y'all picked tha wrong fukkkin family ta fukkk wit," she said. "I promise ya a real slow and painful death muthafukkka. I might jus cutja all ova and watch ya bleed ta death."

Inside, everyone fans out to take a room and do a clean sweep of the place. I opened the door to the bedroom at the top of the stairs, and saw Po Boy naked on Tieaa's back riding her hard. He was so wrapped up into what he was doing, that he never heard me open the door nor enter the room. Instantly, flashbacks of the life that I'd lived through in the Magnolia Arms projects flooded my mind's eye and my blood ran cold. I started to push his wig back on the spot, but I remembered Cee Lo's orders not to kill anyone here. I rushed over to the bed and hit him on the back of the head with my gun, as hard as I could. Knocking him off of her and opening a two inch gash in the back of his head at the same time. Not realizing that I had my finger on the trigger. The impact caused me to squeeze and my gun discharged. Within seconds, everyone that was inside the apartment, was in the room with their guns ready to kill whatever the threat may have been.

When Juice sees Po Boy laying naked on the floor and the condition that Tieaa was in, still tied to the bed, he lost it. He ran across the room and grabbed a fistful of Po Boy's dreads and pistol whipped him with blind rage. Cee Lo had to grab him to stop him from killing Po Boy on the spot.

"Not here and not now Juice," he said, shaking him to get him under control.

"Fukkk dat shit Lo. Lemme kill dis muthafukkka!" Juice said, as silent tears of pure unadulterated hatred runs down his cheeks. "Look whut he's dun ta my Tieaa. She ain't neva hurt nobody."

"He'll get his soulja, just not now. You can have him to yourself and make him pay however you want. But right now, we need to move quickly. Tieaa is what's most important right now anyway." I cut Tieaa's bonds and took the gag out of her mouth. She looks to be hurt pretty badly and needs to be cleaned up before we try to move her.

"Breeze, Trey, Zee y'all trade places with the girls. So they can clean Tieaa up some before she goes to the hospital." I told them. "One of you, call Vik and let her know what's going on here and where to meet us."

Mesha comes into the room first. When she sees the condition that Tieaa is in, she almost goes mad. She pulled the straight razor out of her back pocket and walked over the where Po Boy is sitting on the floor, with his back against the wall bleeding profusely from gashes in his head and face. She squatted down in front of him and grabbed a handful of his filthy dick and balls and put the razor's blade to the base to castrate him.

"Mesha! Not now." Cee Lo called out, having seen her before she could finish the job. "Help Khandi and Yoyo get Tieaa cleaned up, so we can move."

She obeyed but not before kicking him as hard as she could in the groin, flattening his balls and causing blood to squirt out of the head of his dick. He screamed out in pain, as a pain like he'd never felt before surged through him and exploded in his brain. She then squatted down in front of him again. This time putting the blade of her razor to his right eye and cutting into his eyelid.

"Yu're gonna die in tha worse way, yu maggot muthafukkka," she said, "and dat lil dick datja violated my sista wit. Yo punk ass gon eat it befo ya die nigga. Dat's my word."

She stood back up, and kicked him again.

Everyone worked fast and together; the girls cleaned Tieaa up and put her on a 2x-large man's T-shirt and a pair of boxer shorts that they had found in the dresser drawer. They used extra wash cloths as padding for her torn up rectum, to catch the blood and feces that was still running out of her.

By the time that Tieaa was ready to be taken to the hospital. The guys had already duct taped Po Boy's naked ass and put him and J.R in the trunk of his Acura.

Where in the fuck is Thin? I said thinking out loud. His whip is outside, so he's got to be around here somewhere.

"We'll catch him later Fury," Cee Lo said as if he'd been asked the question. "Tieaa needs medical attention now."

"Alright," I replied.

"Whoever has the keys to Po Boy's whip, drive it back to the house and put it in the garage. The rest of us will be at the hospital with Tieaa."

Juice scooped Tieaa up in his arms and we moved out. Trey and Zee had the trucks already turned around and the engines running, when we came out of the building. Breeze and Khandi jumped in Po Boy's Acura as we loaded up, and we rolled out.

On the road heading for St. Andrews Hospital, Tieaa broke down right there in Juice's arms.

"Bae, I'm so sorry fa alla dis." She said looking up into his eyes. "When dey rolled up on me in tha mall's parkin lot, and J.R pulled dat shotgun on me. It caught me off guard and I froze up. I know dat I shoulda been on point cuz anything might go down anywhere here in tha Bang'em or at least I shoulda ran. But my feet wouldn't move and I forgot dat I had my fie in my purse. I was so shook, dat I couldn't thank."

"I tried ta fight once dey got me ta dat apartment, but eitha Po Boy or J.R hit me on tha back of tha head wit sumthin and knocked me out. When I woke up, I wuz tied up ta dat bed tha way dat'chall found me." She shuddered and started to cry.

Juice closed his eyes to fight back the silent tears that rolled down his cheeks. As the pain that he heard in her voice gripped his heart like a vise and squeezed nearly driving him insane.

"Dat ain'tjo fault ma." He whispered in her ear as he stroked the knot on the back of her head, and trying to comfort her. "We slipped when we let dem niggaz live. Even afta Thin had made his threats against us.

"Please daddy, don't hate me." She said, crying hysterically and as if she hadn't heard a word that he had said. "I know dat I'm dirty now afta whut dey did ta me, but please baby don't leave me."

"I love you Tieaa," he replied, hugging her tight, "and I ain't goin nowhere. I'ma be right here witju ta make sho datja well taken care of from now on."

"Please rest nw Sugga. Nobody's eva gon hurtju again. Dat's on GOD."

"Gurl, yu ain't dun nuttin wrong, and ya still alive," said Mesha from the front passenger seat. "It ain'tjo fault whut dem low-life son of a bitches dun ta ya. So hold yo head up. Everythang is gon be jus fine. Whut we gon do ta dem muthafukkkaz is gon make'em cuss tha day dey forceja in dat damn car."

"What about Thin, Tieaa?" I asked, from the very back seat. "I saw his Caddy, but he wasn't in the apartment. Was he there with y'all?"

She physically trembles in Juice's arms as her mind's eye replayed the rape she had endured and she held onto him as if her life depended on it. For Juice to see the fear and pain in her eyes, on her face and to hear it in her voice filled him with unadulterated hatred.

"He's tha one dat initiated tha whole thang," she replied, after a brief silence. "When J.R and Po Boy wuz takin me ta dat apartment, all dey talked wuz takin deir cut of tha ransom money and leavin tha state fa good.

"I thank dat Thin changed his mind once we got dere, cuz he said dat I wuz gon pay fa tha day dat him and his boys got exiled fa tha rest of my life." She cringed as she felt Thin's dirty hands and sweaty body on her all over again. "He said dat I'd neva fa'git him and neitha would y'all."

"Okay Tieaa, we'll take care of them. But in order for us to be able to handle this the right way, I need for you to do one thing for us. When the police question you about whether or not you knew the men that attacked you. You've got to tell them no."

"You've got to give them enough information to make your story believable, but without them being able to put a positive ID on anyone in particular.

"Can you do this for us?"

She nodded her head to say yes.

"Good fam, we got a real special treat for all three of them."

CHAPTER: 18

When Thin walked up the backstairs into the apartment building, he was rolling a blunt and singing to himself. As he approached his destination, he paused outside the door just long enough to lick and stick the strawberry-flavored Swisher Sweet, light the blunt and take a deep drag.

"Damn! Dis Jungle Runtz is tha shit," he said looking down the blunt as he holds the intoxicating smoke in his lungs.

Exhaling a few seconds later, he opened the door and went inside. The living room was still empty the way it was when he decided to go get a blunt. He goes into the kitchen to get a beer to go with the blunt then back in the living room and sat on the sofa.

"I know yu niggaz ain't still up dere muttin dat bitch are y'all?" He asked, over his shoulder. "Y'all need ta hurry up, cuz as soon as I finish dis blunt and beer. I'ma git in dat ass one mo time befo I go back cross town."

"Y'all niggaz hear me up dere?"

Puzzled by the fact that neither J.R nor Po Boy came out of the room or answered that he had only gotten silence in return. After putting out the blunt, he sat the beer on the coffee table, got up and went up the stairs to the bedroom door.

"I know yu niggaz heard me," he said opening the door. To his surprise, they weren't there and neither was Tieaa.

He walked out of the room, down the stairs and over to a window that's facing the parking lot. Po Boy's Acura is gone.

"Where in tha fukkk is dem dumb ass niggaz wit dat bitch, he said, talking to himself. Dey saw dat my ride is still out dere. So dey shoulda known dat I wuzn't gon too far. Eitha one of dem simple ass muthafukkaz coulda hit me on my cell ta see where I wuz. Or ta tell me dat dey wuz gon bounce and take tha bitch wit'em. Dey shoulda jus kept deir stupid asses here til I got back. Sometimes, I wonda bout dem fools."

He searched his pockets for his phone, then remembered that he had left it in his car. He went out of the apartment, ran down the one flight of stairs to the outside and went to his car. Taking his keys out of his pocket, he pressed a button on the keyless entry remote and the passenger side door popped open. Sitting in the passenger seat, he opened the center console and takes out the cell. When he looked at it and saw that there weren't any messages or missed calls, he pressed 2 to speed dial Po Boy's number. When his voicemail picked up after the third ring, he left a message.

"Where in tha fukkk are yu dumb ass niggaz at wit dat bitch? Y'all fools know dat we gotta git rid of her and y'all out ridin around wit her like everythang is kosha. Hit me back dumb ass nigga when ya git dis message, witja stupid ass."

He closed the door and got over in the driver's seat. As soon as he crank the car up, he remembered that he hadn't locked the apartment up. He jumped out of the car, leaving it running, the car door open and ran back up into the building.

* * * * *

At the hospital, Vik was waiting outside the emergency room entrance when we arrived. Her and Juice took Tieaa inside while the rest of us waited out in the parking lot.

156

After about fifteen minutes or so, she came back out.

"Y'all go on back to the house and wait," she sa. "Juice and I will be there as soon as she's admitted."

She must have read my thoughts or my facial expression, questioning her decision.

"If we're all here when the cops come, it may draw too much attention and hinder Tieaa's story. We don't want the slightest hint to be given that Tieaa may know her attackers, and stop us from serving real street justice on them maggots without any repercussions," She went on, before I could say anything.

"Load up," Cee Lo said. "We will be at your crib waiting on y'all, and don't hesitate to call if you need us."

She nodded her head in agreement before turning around and heading back inside the hospital.

* * * * *

When we got back to the house, Breeze and Khandi were sitting on the back patio watching television and eating pizza. As soon as they saw us come in, both of them were on their feet coming towards us with concerned looks on their faces.

"How is she?" Khandi asked.

"We don't know what condition she's really in yet," I replied. "We won't know anything more than she's going to be admitted at least for tonight, until Juice and Vik get here. So in the meantime, all we can do is be patient and wait."

"No doubt," Breeze said, heading back to his seat. "Khandi orda'd some food from Pizza Hut. Why don't'chall try ta put somethin on ya stomach while we're waitin fa fam and tha boss lady?"

"Breeze, what did you do with J.R and Po Boy?" Cee Lo asked, after everyone had sat down to eat and wait for some news to arrive on Tieaa's condition.

"In tha trunk of J.R's car. In tha garage like fam orda'd."

"Good job you two," he said, "real good job all of you. We got in and out without drawing any unwanted attention, and we got Tieaa back. A little hurt but still alive, which is most important."

"We missed Thin's fat stank ass though," Khandi said. "Dem two clowns in tha garage are only do boys fa dat nigga.

"He pull deir strangs and dey dance ta his beat."

"Don't misunda'stand whut i'm sayin, cuz it don't make'em less guilty fa whut part dey played in whut dey dun ta my gurl. But dey're too damn stupid ta have thought ta violate her demselves."

"Fam, rememba Tieaa sayin dat J.R and Po Boy wuz talkin bout leavin tha state wit deir cut of tha ranso money dey wuz gon demand in exchange fa her?" Yoyo said more than asked. "She said dat Thin musta changed tha plan once dey got her ta dat apartment, cuz he violated her first."

"FUKKK DAT SHIT!" Mesha exclaimed, throwing her slice of pizza back on her plate. "Po Boy no good ass didn't hafta folla dat fat low-lifed muthafukkkaz lead. His punk ass raped Tieaa cuz he wanted ta. He helped degrade our sista on his fukkkin own. So stop tryna make excuses fa dat nasty muthafukkka. I don't give a fukkk who wuz pose ta be in charge!" Mesha, who very seldom showed any emotion beyond her love for Zee or her loyalty to the family, was so mad that she was physically trembling and tears of unadulterated hate were running down her cheeks. "Shidd! J.R - Swore dat he didn't touch her, and he's mo of a fukkkin follows den Po Boy . So don't gimme dat do boy bullshit!"

"Chill ma," said Zee while going to her and putting his arms around her to comfort her. "We gon fix'em all up real good. So stop stressin ya'self."

"I ain't tryna make excuses fa no muthafukkkin body," Khandi said getting up from her seat. "So don't even much try ta play me like dat. I wuz jus statin whut Tieaa said. Shidd! I wanna murda tha fukkk nigga jus as bad as yu do."

"Thin raped her cuz he wuz gon kill her," Breeze said in a voice as if he was trying to talk through a problem. "He neva planned on holdin her fa ransom. Dat wuz jus game dat he ran on his boys. To get dem ta roll wit tha plan."

"I've heard every word that each of you had to say," Cee Lo interjected to calm things down, "and I agree one hundred percent with all of you in one way or another."

"J.R and Po Boy were Thin's do boys, maybe they both are even a little bit stupid as hell. Yet, like Mesha said, they're responsible for their own actions. But more so, I know that Breeze is right. Thin's intentions were to kill Tieaa, that's exactly why he raped her. He knows our code of honor. He knew the moment that they took her, that his life was forfeit. So he was going to degrade her before he took her life.

"Trust me though, they're going to pay in the worst way for their sins. No matter how minute their part was, they won't be going to the hospital in the end.

"As for missing Thin, we'll catch him. By him not being there was just a minor setback. But I'll bet my jag against two dollars that his dumb ass is over in the projects right now at Milkeila"s crib, wondering where J.R and Po Boy are with Tieaa."

Trey jumped up out of his seat. "Let's go git dat sour ass nigga den fam," he said. "I wanna see tha look in dat muthafukkkaz eyes when we roll up on his soft ass."

"Me too, soulja. Especially this soon after they'd taken her. But Vik said to wait here for her and Juice and that's law."

Trey sat back down.

"I promised Juice that he could erase Po Boy himself when it was time to serve justice," Cee Lo went on. "Do any of you have any objection to that?"

"I jus wanna cut dat lil dick of his off dat he violated my sista wit and make'em eat it like I promised'em," Mesha said.

"And I want to do Thin," I replied. "This started because of me, and I want it to end with me. I have something special in mind for him. It's going to be much worse than killing him right away."

"Fam, Lo," interjects Breeze. "I'm loyal beyond loyal ta tha botha y'all, and If eitha y'all orda'd tha execution of Milkeila, and make Thin watch while she screams. It would be carried out immediately wit'out question. But honestly fam, Lo; I thank dat Juice should be tha one callin tha shots here.

"No matta who did whut, dis goes beyond business fa him. B'cuz of who it happened ta. It's personal fa him"

"We are a family dat looks out fa one anotha, and justice is gon be served regardless. But let's leave it up ta him how it'll be dun."

"I hear you, but what happens if his emotions get the best of him and he gets careless?" I asked. "He may get himself killed which we don't want to happen. Or kill some innocent person due to his personal feelings clouding his judgement."

"That's where we come in," said Cee Lo. "We can keep him from getting careless or reckless.

"There's no doubt that he's full of hatred and wants some revenge. Any of us would if we were in his shoes. But he's disciplined and we'll have his back if needed."

About that time, Juice and Vik walked in. We all stood up, waiting for them to come out on the patio. One look in Juice's eyes and I could tell that his whole life had changed. There was an evil look, a hatred in his eyes like I'd never seen before.

"Loyalty and respect," Mesha said stepping forward first when they came out on the patio.

"How's my sista?"

"She will be alright with time," Vik replied. "She's a little bruised physically and emotionally and she had to have a few stitches, but she will be just fine."

"When the police came to get their report, she did very well pretending that she didn't know who kidnapped and violated her. Street justice can be served to the fullest,"

"We wuz jus talkin bout dat, jus befo y'all came in," said Breeze. "I know dat'chu got tha last say, but I suggested dat Juice call tha shots on dis one.

"It's closa ta him den any of us. Tieaa is his girl."

"What did Cee Lo say about your suggestion?"

"Tha pros and cons wuz weighed, but in tha end, he wuz down wit it." She looked over at her enforcer, and he nodded his head in approval.

"That's what it is then," she concedes and takes a seat at the bar.

Juice stood there for a long minute in silence, as if lost in another world or trying to collect his thoughts. "I 'ppreciate y'all havin faith in me on dis," he finally said, "but I can't trust myself right nie ta do whutz right."

"I got too much hatred in my veins at dis time. All dat I can thank about is killin somebody real close ta alla dem muthafukkkaz. I wont'em ta hurt like I'm hurtin or tha way dat Tieaa is hurtin."

No tears came but the hatred in his heart spoke volumes in his words.

"If I had my way, I'd kill all three of deir fukkkin families like animals and make'em watch."

"If y'all only knew whut I felt when I saw my baby tied ta dat bed, and suffa'n tha way she is. None of y'all would wanna be in my shoes right now and yu'd unda'stand whut I'm tryna say."

"I wanna take care of Po Boy. I saw whut he dun, whetha he wuz first or last. I saw'em and I'll do him myself. I'll trust in y'all ta make tha otha two pay."

"Say no more fam. We gotcha," I replied. "Now everybody listen closely, I got a plan."

CHAPTER: 19

Thin is sitting at the window in Milkeila's living room bright and early the next morning. His mind was all over the place because he knew that J.R saw his car when he came and picked up his truck. Especially with him having parked right next to it.

"Whut tha fukkk is wrong wit dem dumb ass niggaz?" He said, talking to himself. "Dey hall ass on me yesta'day wit'out callin and dey rturned none of my calls. Now J.R comes his stupid ass right out here and don't say shit, jus git in his whip and bounce."

He picked his cellphone up off of the coffee table and dialed J.R's number. When the voicemail picked right up, he left a message.

"Where tha fukkk are y'all dumb ass muthafukkkaz at? Y'all bounced on me yesta'day and don't call or return any of my calls. Den yo stupid ass sneak out here in tha middle of tha night and gitja ride wit'out sayin a fukkk thang. If it wuz too late fa yu ta come up ta tha crib, alls ya had ta do wuz leave me a message on my cell."

"Y'all niggaz betta git'chall asses ova here ta Keila's crib like now. Y'all know dat Vik got dem goons out lookin fa dat bitch by nie, and if dey catch'chall wit her. Dey're gonna murda y'all's asses on tha spot. Call me as soon as yo dumb ass git dis message."

Fifteen minutes later, his cell rang. His heart almost jumped out of his chest when he saw the number.

"Yeah," he answers.

"Thin, dis is Juice."

"I know who tha fukkk it is nigga." He snapped, feigning irritation from the call. "Why tha fukkk yu callin me? I ain't part of yo muthafukkkin clique no mo."

It took every ounce of Juice's willpower to stay composed and focused in order to carry out his task.

"Chill sensitive ass nigga," he replied. "I ain't the one who putjo soft ass in exile nigga. Yu did dat all by yo muthafukkkin self. But it ain't bout dat.

"I called cuz I jus got home from Daytona and Tieaa ain't home."

The mention of Tieaa's name made his heart skipped a beat and he damn near dropped his phone .

"I saw ya boyz at tha beach, and when I didn't see yu wit'em. I figga'd datju wuz atja gurlz and maybe ya seen Tieaa ova in tha projects at her ol' gurlz crib. Bein dat dey live in tha same buildin an all."

"What in the fuck are them dumb ass niggas doing in Daytona at the beach, and where in the hell did they leave the bitch," went through Thin's mind.

"Naw nigga, I ain't seen ya bitch," he replied. "Why didn't ya call ova ta her ol' gurlz crib ta see if she wuz dere?"

"I did, but ain't nobody answer'n. Jus tella dat I'm home fa me, if ya see her befo I do. If ya don't mind."

Thin was so nervous when he got off the phone that he started sweating. Why did dem niggas skipped town on me, he said, thinking out loud. Did dat bitch get away from dem at thea apartment and dey hauled ass? Nah, dey woulda called me by now, if dat wuz tha case. Maybe dey're gonna leave me ta deal wit Juice and dem goonz by myself, when dey find out what went down. Nah, dat ain't it eitha.

No sooner than the conversation with Juice and his contemplations had passed from his thoughts, his cell beeped with a message alert. He picked it up to checked. TEXT FROM J.R; Thin, Po Boy and me are in Daytona at the White Hall Hotel on A1A, in room 345 on the 17th floor. You need to get your ass down here, so you can tell us what to do with this bitch.

"Damn!" Thin thinks, "that lil nigga really don't know where his woman is do he. Too fucking bad he ain't gonna see her alive again. And why the fuck is this nigga texting me instead of calling."

Instead of calling himself, he sent a reply text.

"A'ight, y'all sit tight. I'm leaving now."

Juice, Zee and I were parked seven parking spaces down from Thin's car, outside of building 6. Watching and waiting as Thin exited the building and jogged to his car. No sooner than he made the right turn out of the projects, onto Franklin Street, the three of us were out of Zee's truck, heading for the building's entrance.

Outside of Milkeila's apartment door, we put on ski masks and gloves. I tried the door to see if it needed to be jimmied. Surprisingly, it was unlocked. Thin had been in such a rush that he didn't even bother to lock it behind him. So we went in and took our time, moving silently from room to room. We found what we were looking for, laying so peacefully in her bed asleep.

Sensing that someone was standing over her, Milkeila sat up wide-eyed and confused at seeing three masked men in her bedroom.

Before she could orient herself enough to scream, Zee and I had already grabbed her for Juice to duct tape her mouth, wrist and ankles.

Once she was subdued, Juice let his eyes rove over her beautiful, flawless, naked body as she lay there helpless. To see the fear in her eyes behind the tears that fell was somewhat of a relief to him. But as he stood there watching her, he wondered if she was half as scared as his Tieaa had been. Then he shuddered as the image of her being tied to that bed in the San Juan projects flashed before his eyes. He shook his head to clear his mind and got back to business.

Reaching in his pocket, he pulled out some works and a half-gram of uncut heroin. He took his time, making sure that she saw his every move. As he cooked up and filled a syringe with what was to become her new god, before tying her off and shooting her up.

Her body went into a miniature seizure as the addictive drug polluted her body for the first time. No sooner than the tape could be taken off of her mouth, her stomach emptied and she vomited then went into a junkie's nod.

I searched her closet and found her some clothes while Zee cut the tape off of her ankles and wrist, and Juice cleaned up the vomit. We dressed her and moved out with her, leaving everything as close to normal as it had been when we first entered her apartment.

* * * * *

An hour and a half after he had left Milkeila's, Thin pulled into the White Hall Hotel parking lot.

He saw Po Boy and J.R's vehicles immediately and pulled into the parking space next to J.R's Expedition. He was so caught up in his own thoughts of what he was going to say to his boys for their stupidity that he never noticed the black and silver rollback tow truck that had been following him since he entered the Daytona Beach city limits on A1A.

He hopped out of his car and went into the hotel. On the elevator, he was planning what to do with Tieaa and how to cover it up so him nor his boys will go to jail.

"Dese niaagaz betta be ready and not bullshiddin," he said, thinking out loud. "Cuz if dey ain't got tha room in eitha of deir names we can knock tha bitch off in tha room and go out tha back way."

The elevator stopped on the 17th floor and the door opened. The third room to the left of the elevator was the place. When he walked up to the door, he could hear the television on and a woman laughing.

"Whut tha fukkk are doze dumb ass niggaz doin wit dat broad?" He said, as his thoughts escape him orally. Do dey realize dat dey can git an ass of time fa whut we've dun ta her?

He knocked on the door, and a blonde wearing only a G-string opened it. Then turned and walked away without saying a word. Puzzled by this, he hesitated instead of following her inside. "What the fuck are these idiots doing?" He thought. "Why is a snow bunny here with these dumb ass niggas? I'ma have a talk with these fools."

"Are you going to come in, or are you going to stand out there in the hallway all day?" The broad asked from inside.

Once inside, he noticed that there were only white females in the room. All of them were butt naked, except for the one that had come to the door.

"Where tha fukkk is J.R and Po Boy?" He asked.

"Who in the hell is Po Boy? And why would you be looking for a dude up in here? I'm the one

that called you for the girl."

"Bitch! Whut tha fukkk are yu talkin bout?" He asked. "I came up here ta meet my boyz."

"You've got the wrong fucking room then buddy. If you've got some blow to sell or snort with us, come on in, and get paid, fuck, suck and have some fun. Otherwise, you need to get the hell up out of here."

*   *   *   *   *

Juice, Zee and I took Milkeila to the Hollybrook Projects where two loyal customers; Ghost and Trina, were waiting for us.

"Listen good Ghost," I said, once we had her inside their apartment. "She's only going to be here for about three days, including today. So you're gonna have to stay on top of this job."

"There is enough boy in these bundles that I'm giving you, to do the job that we talked about properly and for you and Trina to get off without short changing what I want you to do. But, don't fuck this up either by rushing and O.D her, just turn her all the way out.

"If you fuck this up, I'ma make sure that Vik cut y'all off completely. As well as use her influence to make sure that y'all can't get served anywhere in the city. On the other hand, if you handle this business properly, I'll double this when we come back for her on the third day."

"No matter how many questions she ask, don't tell her anything that pertains to how she really got here."

"I gotja boss," he replied. "She'll be ready ta sell pussy ta a preacha durin Sunday mornin service when y'all come back fa her, she'll be so far out dere."

"That's what I want to hear. Make it happen."

My cell rang as soon as we got back in Zee's truck.

"Fury," I answered.

"Fam, dis is Yoyo. We're all in Daytona right now," she said. "Lo says fa y'all ta come straight here afta y'all take care of dat business. Thin has taken tha bait and is up in tha hotel as we speak."

"We're on the way now," I replied, and hung up.

"That was Yoyo," I told Juice and Zee. "Everyone is in Daytona, including Thin. Lo says for us to come down there asap."

*　*　*　*　*

Walking up out of room 345, Thin's mind goes into overdrive. "Whut tha fukkk is goin on here?" He said, thinking out loud once again. "Dese niggaz must be tryna set me up fa tha enemy." He took his cell out of his pocket and dials Vik's number to see if he could lie up on some information.

"What nigga!" She answered in an irritated but exaggerated tone of voice on the first ring.

"Hey Vik, dis is Kendrick." He said, in a calm voice.

"Hey Vik, dis is Kendrick." She mocked. "I know who the fuck you are nigga. What do you want? I'm busy."

"Calm down ma," he replied. "I talked ta Juice dis mornin. He said dat when he got home from Daytona, his girl wuzn't home, and asked me wuz she out here in tha Courts ta her ol' gurlz crib. He asked me ta hit'em up if I seen her."

"I hit his cell," he lied, "but it went ta voicemail. Is he home?"

Vik knew that he was lying, trying to get some information because Tieaa was sitting there in the living room with her. But she played her part to a tee.

"How in the hell would I know if he's home or not sour ass nigga? He doesn't live here. And why the fuck would he be calling your fat, grimy, nasty as anyway? All of the people out in those projects he knows."

"Get the fuck off of my motherfucking line nidda, and don't ever call my phone again. We don't fuck with your kind," she said before hanging up in his face.

Just before he got off the elevator on the ground floor. A cold chill ran over him and the elevator seemed to be closing in around him.

"Sumthin ain't right," he said, talking to himself. "I know dat I shoulda stuck ta tha original plan and everythang would be kosha now. Whut tha fukkk have I got myself inta wit dem two dumb ass nigga?"

Out in the parking lot, he noticed right away that he had been tricked into coming to Daytona Beach. All three of the vehicles were gone, and he was stranded.

WHUT THA FUKKK! He exclaimed, throwing his hands up in the air in an exasperated gesture. Being that he still had his cell in his hand, he pressed # to speed dial J.R's phone. It picked up on the first ring but no one said a word which made him think it was J.R because that's how he always answered his phone.

"Why tha fukkk y'all niggaz playin muthafukkkin games wit me?" Thin yelled in his phone. "Y'ALL GOT ME WAY DOWN HERE IN MUTHAFUKKKIN VOLUSIA COUNTY WIT DIS FUKKK SHIT! I AIN"T WIT DAT BULLSHITAT ALL, AND Y'ALL BETTA BRANG MY MUTHAFUKKKIN WHIP BACK BEFO DERE BE SOME MUTHAFUKKKIN PROBLEMS!"

"IF Y'ALL CLOWNS ARE TRYNA SET ME UP FA JUICE AND HIS GOONZ TA GIT AT ME. I'MA SMOKE BOTHA YU MUTHAFUKKKIN NIGGAZ IF I LIVE THROUGH IT!"

Just like it was answered, J.R's line hung up without a word which puzzled Thin even more. Being that J.R was always the type to want his approval on everything or was always trying to explain if he felt that something went wrong. X

CHAPTER: 20

That night, Thin was still in Daytona at the Peter Pan Motel, stressing over the way things had started to unfold. He felt like his deeds were trying to catch up on him with the help of his so-called boys.

"Damn! I made a foolish mistake by lettin my dick do tha thankin and changin tha damn plan," he said talking to himself. "I need ta find J.R and Po Boy's dumb asses wit dat broad befo Juice find out whut time it really is. I know dat it's gon git real ugly fa sho if he find'em first, and she's my only bargainin chip."

When he got out of the shower, he turned on the television then reached on the nightstand beside the bed and got his cell. He pressed 1 to speed dial Milkeila's apartment but no one answered.

"Damn!" He exclaimed, "I leave tha fukkkin crib fa a coupla hours and she's got her ass out in tha damn streetz already."

He hung up and threw his cell on the opposite side of the bed, then picked up the television remote before laying back on the pillow, turning the television to channel 2. A breaking news report came on as soon as the channel was tuned in.

"Moments ago, a Duval County man was burned alive in his sports utility vehicle, just outside the Ormond Beach city limits, on A1A in Volusia County," said the reporter. "Authorities believe that JayShaun (J.R) Robertson of the Brentwood projects in Jacksonville, Florida has been murdered as some sort of retaliation."

At the mention of J.R's government name, Thin sat up and was fully alert, giving the news his undivided attention.

"As you can see behind me, the vehicle is still smoldering from the deliberate torching."

"When the firefighters were finally able to extinguish the fire and get the charred remains of the victim out of the vehicle, both his arms and legs had been broken and he had been buckled in his seat to make it impossible for the victim to escape the painful death."

"Witnesses say that the tormenting screams of the burning man were so horrendous that it sent chills through their body."

"Evidently, this method of elimination was a message to someone other than the victim," she said as she and her camera crew move to the speed limit sign a few feet behind the vehicle. "Here as you can see is spray painted; street law: DEATH B4 DISHONOR. As well as the driver's license of the vehicle's occupant is glued to the sign so he could be easily identified."

Thin was so nervous that he began to talk to himself.

"Tha scene where J.R wuz jus merked is less den five miles from here," he calculated out loud.

"If dey saw J.R and Po Boy here in Daytona, I know dat dey got'em both. So where tha fukkk is Po Boy? Why didn't dey kill'em both? And even if he wuzn't wit J.R when dey got'em, he still couldn't've go far."

"Damn! Dat means dat dem niggaz know bout whut we dun ta Juice's bitch, and dey've known all tha time, Thin continues, trying to talk it through. Why didn't I figga dat shit out in tha beginnin? When I thought dat J.R and Po Boy had hauled ass wit'out holla'n at me yesta'day."

He got the phone book out of the nightstand drawer. Using the room's phone, he called an Uber.

"I gotta git tha fukkk back ta tha Bang'em," he said, still talking to himself. "I'ma sittin fukkkin duck up in dis muthafukkka, and ain't no tellin where dem muthafukkkaz at right now." As soon as he hangs the phone up, his cell beeps with a message alert. TEXT FROM PO BOY:

Thin dem niggas got J.R and burned'em alive in his whip. Nigga, I'm goin ta tha police station and turn myself in. I ratha be doin time den tryna face dem fools. Dey ain't playin no games bout whut we dun and I ain't ready fa no dirt nap.

Thin was so shook by what he saw on the news that the prior thought of why J.R had texted him instead of calling had escaped him to ask Po Boy the same as well as to ask him where he was, before he sent a reply message.

"How did dey git J.R and not yo ass too?"

A few minutes later, Thin's cell beeped again. TEXT FROM PO BOY:

"I wuz comin outta room 345 where a room full of snow bunnies wiz havin a coke party. I needed sumthin ta calm my nerves. Anyway, I saw dem niggaz goin up in our room where J.R and tha bitch wuz. So I ducked back in tha room wit tha white bitches and went out tha hotel tha back way. Dey didn't see me, but dey did git my whip. And if yo ass is still in Daytona now, dey might already know where yo ass is ta merk yo ass next. Dem niggaz are playin fa keeps."

Thin sat there contemplating the message for a minute. As his thoughts instantly went back to the room full of naked snow bunnies

174

at the White Hall hotel. The message sounds about like the truth because all of the information was on point. And he knew that he would not have been told that they were looking for him if it was anyone other than Po Boy so he accepted the message for what it was and sent one last message.

"Do whutju thank yu gotta do. I ain't bout ta become no niggaz bitch in tha joint cuz of a rape charge. Ain't no muthafukkkin way! So I'll see ya when I see ya."

When the uber driver came, Thin gave the cabbie the address to Milkeila's crib in the Gunby Courts. "No" he thought, "if they're really looking for me, they'll be expecting me to go home." Then he changed his mind and gave the driver the address to his aunt's crib in Palatka.

Once they were on their way, everytime a vehicle stayed behind them for more than a mile, Thin started to get paranoid and look back, trying to see if the vehicle was following them.

"Is there something wrong dude?" The driver asked, looking at him through the rearview mirror, after seeing him freak out more than once. "You keep looking over your shoulder every time another vehicle gets behind us, like someone is after you."

"I'm good," Thin replied. "I jus git noid when I ain't got my gat wit me, dat's all. Don't pay me no mind, and speed tha fukkk up."

"Why do you need a gun? You seem like a pretty nice guy."

"Why alla tha goddamn questions? Jus drive tha fukkkin car, take me where I wanna go and mind yo muthafukkkin business"

"I'm just trying to make the ride a little more comfortable for the both of us. Besides, all of that fidgeting and looking back you're doing is making me nervous."

"Turn on tha radio or sumthin," Thin said. "Anythang ta gitja mind offa me."

Thin took out his cell and called home once again. Unlike the first time, when he didn't get an answer, he left a message.

"Bitch, I don't know where tha fukkk yo ass is at, butja ain't been home all fukkkin day. I'm goin ta my ant Shannon's crib in Palatka. Some muthafukkka stole my Lac while I wuz in Daytona. I'll be home as soon as I find out sumthin bout my whip. If ya need ta stay atja sista's crib while I'm outta town, do dat."

Thin was so paranoid and busy looking behind them, that he totally ignored the silver Dodge Charger that rode long beside or slightly in front of the Uber. All the way to the foot of the Memorial Bridge in East Palatka, where the driver of the Dodge let off the gas to allow the car to pass and pull a good following distance ahead. Then follow them all the way to the Alhambra Trailer Park on St Johns Avenue.

Passing the Uber at the curb, the driver goes to the store and makes a phone call from a pay phone.

"Cee Lo," the receiving party answered, on the first ring. "Where are you Red?"

"I'm in Palatka at Kmart. Thin is here in tha traila park behind tha store on St. Johns Avenue."

"Good work fam, get back on the East Palatka side of the bridge and wait for us at the Siesta Inn. We're on the way."

Thin was awakened by the sun shining in his face through the partially opened curtain and the sound of the midday channel 2 news coming on. He laid on his aunt's sofa with his eyes closed for a few more minutes, praying that what had happened in Daytona was just a dream.

"Good afternoon, ladies and gentleman. The second brutal murder in less than twenty-four hours has the 7th Judicial Circuit Authorities baffled," said the news reporter on location. "Vontavis (Po Boy) Allen of Clay County's Green Cove Springs was found brutally murdered at the River Crest Inn here in East Palatka."

At the mention of Po Boy's name, Thin's eyes popped open, and he sat up. Fully awake and giving the television his full attention.

"Some time last night, the Putnam County Authorities were called to this motel room where they found the victim tied to this bed." He pointed to the blood stained bed as he reported his story. "Naked, face down in a spread eagle position where he had been sadistically sodomized with a Grey Goose vodka bottle, beaten beyond recognition and shot in the back of the head at point blank range."

"When authorities arrived on the scene, the bottle which was used to violate the victim had been crushed inside his anal cavity, with only the neck visible from the outside. He had also been castrated and his penis and genitals had been stuffed into his mouth, it was a horrifying scene."

"Authorities are led to believe that this murder is related to the Ormond Beach murder, that it's some sort of retaliation, as well as a warning. Due to the message left behind at this scene as well." The reporter said, as he and his camera crew exit the room, and he points to a silver Acura TSX that's parked outside the room's door. "Spray painted here on the hood in black is; STREET LAW: NEVER FUCK WITH A MAN'S FAMILY, and the victim's driver's license are glued to the hood."

"This is pretty much the same method that was used to leave the warning in Volusia County." Thin was so shocked that he began to have a panic attack and started talking to himself as he stared blankly at the television.

"Dem muthafukkkaz can kill me anytime dat dey wanna. Dey've been toying wit me, ta lemme know dat dey knew my every move, dat dey have been in control dis whole time. Dey been knew whut we dun ta Juice's bitch. Dey merked my boys right unda my nose in two different counties, ta prove dat part. FUCK! Who are dey gonna kill next…. He jumped up off the sofa and got his cell as his girl ran through his mind."

CHAPTER: 21

By eleven o'clock Saturday night, everyone except Cee Lo was at Vik's house in Mandarin. He was out using his connections to sell Thin's car and all of the audio equipment that had been taken out of the other two vehicles. Whatever he gets for it, also the five bands that was taken off of J.R and Po Boy will be given to Tieaa for her medical bills or whatever she wants to do with it. A contribution from Thin and his boys.

While we were waiting for him, I decided to call Ghost and check on Milkeila. Trina picked up on the second ring.

"Hello," she answers.

"Hey Trina, this is Fury. Is Ghost around?"

"Yeah! Hold on a minute and I'll go git'em fa ya."

"Whut up boss?" Ghost asked a couple of minutes later.

"Hey Ghost, is she ready?"

"Hell fukkk yeah! She's mo den ready Tha bitch is a certified freak wit it."

"Shidd! She's already put in some work and everythang. And she like tha taste of pussy jus as much as she like tha dick."

"What do you mean by she's already put some work in? You put her out on the block?"

"Nah boss, she did it on her own. She asked me fa a fix ta git tha mornin monkey offa her back. I lied ta her. I told her dat we didn't have no mo, and dat I didn't have no mo money ta go and cop. Ta see how much mo work I needed ta do ta git tha job done."

"She got ta fiendin real bad. So she walked up on tha block where dem jits be gittin money. Y'know she's a dime and dem lil niggaz ain't gon pass up a chance ta smash her. No matta how much it woulda cost'em."

"Anyway, she came back in tha car wit three of'em and served all three of'em at once. I'm talkin bout dick in her ass, mouth and pussy all at tha same time."

"Don't do that, Ghost. Don't lie on her like that."

"Don't insult me like dat, Fury. I'ma junkie, not a liar. Tha broad is all tha way out dere already bruh. She's even freaked wit Trina a time or two when dey've were gettin on. I don't know where yu got dat shit yu gave me fa dis job, but it hooked her ass like hooked on phonics. She'll do anythang ta control dat monkey dat'chu gave her once it gits ta apin. Do yu wont me ta put her on tha block?"

"No, this was for personal reasons. You can drop her off in the Courts tomorrow. Then meet me at the fish market on Davis at twelve o'clock and I'll straighten you."

"A'ight boss, dat's whutz up. I'll see yu tamorrow."

Cee Lo walked in a couple of minutes after I got off of the phone. He talked with Vik and Tieaa for another minute or two before giving Tieaa a big wad of money. Then we got down to putting part two of our plan in action.

"Everyone knows that if we fail to plan at this phase of the game then we've already planned to fail before anything else can jump off. And we all may end up in jail real soon," I began. "All of us know that Thin is grimy, and by us eliminating J.R and Po Boy, he's rolling solo for now. By the street laws that we've left behind, he should have figured out by now that we know about what they done to Tieaa. He may even be running a little scared, but Milkeila and his pride ain't going to let him stay away too long."

"By him moving up here from Palatka, and we know that's where he is. He may bring some of those goons up here with him to try and get some get back. Or even try to jack us. He know that Vik runs a pretty tight ship, and in this case consistency is predictability and predictability is weakness. Something I know he'll rely on in an effort to catch us slipping. When he does come for his revenge."

"By him knowing what kind of paper we make, my guess is that they'll try to fob us first. Despite that, we're gonna go back to work like nothing ever happened so keep your shirts on and a full clip at all times. Including you and your team as well, Juice."

"Whenever you're out on the tracks, be more than ready for anything that may go down. Especially now that he's number one on the enemy list. If anyone sees him or an unfamiliar vehicle comes through, get on your walkie talkie and alert the family so everyone can be on point. But as long as he's not posing a threat, or trying to put down, let him do him. We want him to think that it's over, that J.R and Po Boy have paid the price for what they did when we caught and erased them. We're going to get him where it hurts the most first, meaning with Milkeila. She's his kryptonite and he's a maniac when it comes to her."

"Speaking of Milkeila, just before Lo came in I was on the phone with Ghost. The plan to set her out and make her into a junkie has been aced. She's certified, tricking an all. Ghost said that she'll do anything to keep that monkey from aping. He's dropping her off in the projects in the morning. If any of you see her out there fiending and she don't have any money, put them jits that like to trick on her. Let's turn her all the way out. It will humiliate Thin dramatically, when he finds out that his goddess is a junkie and a trick."

* * * * *

Thin searched his contact list for a few minute before he found the number he was looking for. Using his aunt's landline, he dialed the number.

"Yo, who dis?" He answers immediately.

"Whutz up Nookie, dis is yo cuzo nigga."

"Thin, whutz up fool? Damn it's been a long minute since a nigga heard from yo ass. Big tyme city nigga like yu dun fa'got where home is ain'tja?"

"Nah cuzo! I won't eva fa'git where I come from. Shidd! I wuz born and raised on Eagle Street in tha white projects. Paypa City will alwayz be my home."

"Why yo fat ass ain't been down dis way ta see yo people since Christmas den?"

"I'm atja ol gurlz crib right now nigga. I stayed here last night."

"Word nigga."

"Yeah nigga dat's my word. Yu don't recognize ya own mama's numba?"

"Dat's fukkk"d up yo. Yu shoulda rolled through 11th Street. I wuz up dere sittin in my whip, blowin one wit Pokey and her homegurl in Dee Dee's parkin lot."

"It wuz late when i got dropped off."

"Dropped off? Whut tha fukkk is a nigga datz clockin tha kinda bread datju be gittin doin gittin dropped off?"

"My Caddy got stole in Daytona yesta'day."

"Where wuz ya boyz?"

Thin was silent for a couple of seconds.

"Cuzo, botha dem niggaz got merked. It wuz on tha news."

"J.R got hit up in Ormond Beach at first dark yesta'day. He wuz burned alive in his whip from whut tha news report said. And Po Boy wuz murda'd ova in E.P sumtime late last night at tha River Crest motel.
"I don't know whut dem niggaz wuz inta afta Vik kicked us ta tha curb," he lied. "But whuteva it wuz, it got botha dem foolz merked in tha worst ways."
"Did I jus hear yu right?" Rock asked, having tuned out everything else. "Didju jus say datju ain't a part of dat git money clique no mo?"
"Yeah nigga, yu heard whut I said."

"Whut tha fukkk didjo dumb ass do ta git cut off? Y'all niggaz wuz gittin maja paid."

"It's a long story fam, but check dis doe. If yu and yo boyz are down wit it. I can putja up on dat lick and we can really git paid."

"Wit it! Nigga I wonted ta hit'em up when yo ass wuz gittin money wit'em. Yu wuz tha only thang stoppin us afta dat nigga Big Duke wouldn't take us in.
"So y'know dat I'm ready ta put in dat work now. Lemme git up wit my niggaz and we'll meetja ova at tha village tomorrow and make arrangements."
"A'ight cuzo, I'll be dere bout twelve."

*　*　*　*

No sooner than Milkeila walked into her apartment with Ghost and Trina in tow, the phone rang. "Y'all come on in and have a seat," she said as she went to answer the phone.
"Hello," she answered.

"BITCH! WHERE THA FUKKK YO ASS BEEN FA THA PAST COUPLA DAYZ?" Yelled Thin.

"I should be askin yo fat, bitch ass dat same muthafukkkin question nigga," she replied in a soft but mocking voice.

"If yo ass woulda been in place ta answa tha damn phone or check ya damn messages. Instead of out runnin tha fukkkin streetz, Yu'd know where tha fukkk I'm at."

"Whut tha fukkk yu wont Thin? I got company waitin on me. So say whutja gotta say so I can go."

"WHUT BITCH! WHO THA FUKKK YU GOT UP IN MY MUTHAFUKKKIN CRIB?" He yelled. "YU

KNOW DAT I DON'T PLAY DAT SHIT!""

"Yo crib?" She asked with an amused giggle. "Boy bye, if dis wuz yo crib, yo fat, funky ass would be here instead of whereva tha fukkk yu are nie. So drop dat yo crib shit."

"I'm in Palatka ta my ant Shannon's crib. Some muthafukkkin body stole my whip friday night when I wuz in Daytona."

"Yu'd know dat already if yo ass woulda been in place instead of out in tha damn streetz."

"Yo ant Shannon's crib huh? Somebody stole yo muthafukkkin ride, and yu end up in Palatka instead of comin home."

"Nigga please, don't insult my fukkkin intelligence wit dat weak ass bullshit. Yo punk ass is right down dere witja ugly ass baby's mammie muthafukkka and yu know it."

"Who tha fukkk yu thank yu playin wit?

"I gotta go, I got company. And yu can take ya time bout coming ta gitja shit," she said "It'll already be packed and waitin fa yo no good ass out in tha hall when yu git here." Then hanged up in his face.

"KEILA! KEILA!" He screamed into the phone. "FUKKK! FUKKK! FUKKK! I don't know who tha fukkk dis bitch thank she's playin with," he said talking to himself as he slammed the receiver back into its cradle. "I'ma stomp a mudhole in her ass when I git home."

CHAPTER: 22

After his meeting with Rock and his boys, Thin caught an Uber back to Jacksonville. As the car was pulling up to the entrance of the Gunby Courts projects on the Franklin Street side, Thin sees Fury and his boys standing on the sidewalk talking with some of the project girls. His train of thought instantly went into panic mode as J.R and Po Boy's murders flash into his mind's eye because he knew that they were responsible for them in one way or another.

"Turn in right here," he said to the driver, "and drop me off in front of buildin 6."

Instead of turning into the projects as instructed, the driver pulled over to the curb about twelve feet from where the small crowd was standing.

"I'm not permitted to pull up into public housing unless it is raining or for the elderly," he replied, looking at Thin through the rearview mirror. "Too many robberies or passengers jumping out and running without paying their fare."

"Damn yo! I'll give yu an extra fifty spot if yu do me dis one fava," Thin said trying to bribe the driver into pulling up into the project so he could avoid Fury and his crew.

The driver turned around in his seat so he could look in the back seat at Thin then put his hand out. "Money first, your fare plus the extra fifty then we will move up into the projects."

"I got my cab fare on me but tha extra fifty is up in my crib," he lied, knowing that he never intended on giving the driver anything extra.

"Too bad homeboy. I've heard that a million times over. You could've done better than that, that's the oldest trick in the book. So pay your fare and get the hell out of my car. I have work to do."

"Damn! I need my gat," Thin said to himself looking back at the entrance where Fury and his crew are standing before he paid his fare and got out of the car.

The whole crowd looked back at the sound of the car door closing. Thin's heart almost stopped when he made eye contact with Fury because he knew that they wanted him dead for violating the street laws, and he was an easy target out in the open like he was. Then confusion took over the place of his panic when he realized that they didn't even give him a second glance after the initial look. He hurried across the projects' courtyard towards his destination. Looking back over his shoulder every few steps until he was inside the elevator, heading for the fifth floor.

No sooner than Thin was out of sight. A phone call was made from the entrance to the other side of the projects.

"Yeah," Cee Lo answered.

"Lo, this is Fury. Thin just got out of an Uber and is heading for Milkeila's."

"Did he see you?"

"Yes, we're out here on the block rapping with Bria and her girls. He looked spooked, maybe because he knows that it's only a matter of time before he has to pay the piper like his boys did."

"When we looked back at him after he closed the car door. I thought he was going to jump back in the car, when we made eye contact.

But on the same note, I know that he's thrown by the fact that no one made a move on him."

"Alright fam, I'll call Vik and you call Juice. Let him know that he's back in town, and to stay ready for anything."

"Whut tha hell is goin on," Thin said, thinking out loud once the elevator doors were closed behind him. "Why didn't dey take me out, out dere? I knw dat dey're tha ones who merked my niggaz. Unless dey've satisfied deir blood lust wit tha horrible ways dat dey executed dem."

The indelible thought of the way J.R and Po Boy must have suffered before they died gave him an attack of claustrophobia inside the elevator. Especially the thought of how J.R's truck had become his fiery casket as he burned to death in it. Thin closed his eyes until the elevator had stopped on the fifth floor and the doors opened. He then stepped off, and leaned against the wall in the hallway to try and clear his mind.

It didn't take him long, as his mind tuned itself in on the upcoming caper that he had put his cousin up on. The timing, place of the hit and the escape route after the hit was what mattered the most to him. The success or failure of how and when everything would unfold was in his hands and fully relied on how accurate his information was at the time of execution. The only way that he could get paid is if everything went perfect.

"We gon knock Big Duke's organization's dick in tha dirt fa whut dey dun ta y'all," he vowed to J.R and Po Boy. "Y'all didn't die fa nuttin, or in vain. I'ma make sho of dat."

He stopped in front of Milkeila's apartment door. He had a flashback of the phone conversation that they had had the day before, and he got mad all over again. "Dis bitch betta not have anotha nigga up in my shit, or I'ma fukkk'em both up," ran through his mind. The mere thought of another man being inside with her or even close to her had him so uptight that for a long minute after he unlocked the door, he couldn't go inside of the apartment.

"MILKEILA," he called out, as he entered. The apartment was quiet and appeared to be empty.

"MILKEILA," he called out again, as he walked through the living room heading for the bedroom. It was also empty.

"Where tha fukkk is dat damn woman," he said, thinking out loud. "It ain't like she didn't know dat I wuz comin home."

Thinking that she would come home while he was in the shower, he took a longer shower than normal to get his thoughts together. He was going to have a long conversation with her about the way she popped off at the mouth on the phone. When he finally got out of the shower, there was still no sign of her. So after getting dressed, he got his extra gun out of the bottom dresser drawer and tucked it in his waist. Then a couple of dollars out of the top drawer to replace what he'd spent over the past couple of days before heading back out of the door. He left the living room light on, on his way out. This way, she will know that he had been there if she comes back before he sees her.

Out in the hallway, he decided to take the stairs to avoid another attack of claustrophobia in the elevator. As he comes out of the stairwell on the third floor, he swears that he could hear Milkeila laughing through one of the paper thin project walls. Walking over to the apartment directly across from where he had come out, he stood there for a few seconds and listened. Sure enough, it sounded like her. Getting uptight all over again because he knew who lived there, he forgot what he was on his way to do and knocked on the door.

A short light-skinned dope fiend named Y'onda comes to the door. "Yeah," she answered as she swinged the door all the way open for her man to see who was at the door. Immediately, Thin sees his woman sitting in the living room with Junkie Fred, and walks right past Y'onda into her apartment without even acknowledging her.

"Damn nigga! Yo fat is gon jus walk up in a bitch's crib wit'out bein invited in?" She asked, following in his wake.

Thin was so beside himself now that he went straight into the living room without even looking back to see if she was behind him or to care that Junkie Fred was sitting on the love seat adjacent to Milkeila. He had tunnel vision and Milkeila was all he could see. He grabbed her by the arm, and snatched her up off of the sofa.

"BITCH! Whut tha fukkk are yu doin down here wit dese muthafukkkin junkies?" He asked.

"Nun of yo fukkkin business nigga," she replied, snatching out of his grip and putting her hands on her hips defiantly. "I'ma grown ass muthafukkkin woman. I do whut tha fukkk eva I wont. When tha fukkk eva I wanna muthafukkkin do it."

"Yu need ta take yo fat ass back down ta Palatka where ya punk ass been layin up witja bitch, fa tha past three days and leave me tha fukkk alone."

"And don't eva put'cho muthafukkkin dick beataz on me like dat again."

Ignoring everything that she had said, he grabbed her by the arm. "Brang yo ass on her gurl befo I stomp a mudhole in yo ass, right here," he said, yanking her towards the door. "And I ain't gon tell yu no fukkkin mo."

"Hold on my man," said Junkie Fred, getting to his feet. Despite him being a heroin addict, he was not a small man. If you didn't know him, you would assume he played professional football or he was a bodyguard. "Ain't gon be no muthafukkkin fightin up in here, unless I'm tha one dat's doin it and I don't hit on women. So unass dat woman and ease yo ass on up outta here befo yu piss me tha fukkk off."

Thin pulled the 9mm glock out of his waist and pointed it at him. "Nigga shut tha fukkk up and sitjo bitch ass down befo I splatta yo muthafukkkin brains all ova tha fukkkin wall."

Milkeila was so mad with Thin that she didn't say a word despite his ranting and raving until they got behind the closed door of her apartment.

"Nigga yo ass got some fukkkin nerves," she said, turning on him and getting up in his face. "Jus who tha fukkk do yu thank yu are? Yo punk ass go down ta Palatka and lay up witja ugly ass baby's mammie fa three fukkin days. Den brang yo pussy ass back here and try ta put down on me like I'm yo lil nappy head ass daughter."

"Disrespectin and humiliatin me in front of people, by putin yo muthafukkin hans on me like it okay. Yu know dat I ain't wit dat shit dere."

"And I know datju don't thank yo ass is gon stay up in my shit. Ain't no muthafukkkin way. Not afta yu jus acted a damn donkey on me. Yu gotjo bitches mixed tha fukkk up. I ain't dat stupid bitch ya jus left. So whutja need ta do, is gitja shit and go back where ya been fa tha past three fukkkin days."

"I ain't goin no damn where Milkeila," he replied. "Dis is my muthafukkkin crib. I pay tha cost ta be tha boss up in dis bitch. Shidd! If it wuzn't fa me, yo ass would be livin offa welfare."

"Nigga bye, dis is tha fukkin projects. Tha little bit yo ass do, I can give a jit some of dis good pussy," she rubbed herself as she spoke, "and he could do jus as much if not mo. I don't need yo fat, funky ass fa shit. Fukkk yu nigga."

"Watchcho mouth Keila."

"Whuteva nigga, I dun said whut I had ta say and I meant whut I said." She turned to walk away.

He grabbed her by the arm and turned her back around to face him. "I ain't finish talkin ta yu gurl."

"Yu might as well be, cuz ya wastin my time and yo muthafukkkin breath. Yu need ta save dat shit fa Oprah or some talk show that wanna hear dat shit, cuz I ain't tha one."

"Right now, yu need ta fukkk fight or git light, cuz I'ma go take me a showah and lay down. I ain't got time fa yo bullshit." She turned and walked away without saying another word.

"Whut tha fukkk dun got inta dat damn woman since I been gone? Her attitude dun did a complete one eighty," he said as his thoughts escape him orally, and he goes into the bedroom behind her where she was already taking off her clothes to get in the shower.

"Milkeila," he said, after he'd gotten his rocks off and is laying beside her. "I love yu gurl, and yu know dat I'm jealous as hell when it comes ta yu. God ain't created a bitch yet dat can hold a candle ta ya, and I got problems witja bein round otha niggaz. Jus ta thank dat anotha nigga has touched yu makes me crazy. I can't help it, dat's how fukkk'd up yu got me."

"I ain't got no problem witja havin friends, but not Junkie Fred and his bitch. Why wouldja wanna hang wit dem dope fiends anyway.

Besides, yu represent me out here in dese projects and I don't wont nobody talkin bad bout my gurl."

"Hold on one got damn minute Kendrick," she said, sitting up. "First off, I give less den a fukkk bout whut a muthafukkka has ta say bout Milkeila Washington, cuz none of dem bastards feed, fukkk or finance me."

"Secondly, yu and no otha swangin dick is gon pick or dictate who my muthafukkkin friends can and can't be."

"I ain't neva had shit ta say boutja hangin round dem two got damn butt'head faggots datja called yo boyz, did I? So yu can save dat song and dance."

"And how tha fukkk can yu afford ta be jealous anyway? When yo fat ass been down in Palatka fa tha past three fukkkin days witja baby's mammie, and now ya tryna catch feelin's cuz I wuz down stairs? Do yu nigga, and I'ma damn sho do me."

She got off the bed, grabbed her purse and goes into the bathroom. Slamming the door, she locked in behind her to keep him out.

*   *   *   *   *

When Milkeila finally came out of the bathroom, she was feeling a sickness coming on and she was seriously feening. The little fix that she had had in the bathroom was just enough to wake the joneses up inside of her. She looked over at the bed where she'd left Thin prior to going in the bathroom. He was laying on his right side in a deep sleep.

Not bothering to put on any underclothes, she hurriedly put on a pair of loose fitting shorts and a Jacksonville Bulls t-shirt. She didn't care how she looked at the moment. She had to get out of the apartment and get what she needed before she became physically ill. She went back into the bathroom to get her purse. Looking inside, she had only a couple of dollars. "DAMN!" She swore to herself, throwing the purse on the floor. "Dis ain't enough ta git me shit," she mumbled, putting it in her pocket. Agitated with the lack of money to get what she needs to cure the sickness that was slowly creeping up on her, she forgot that she had thrown her purse on the floor as she turned out the light and walked out of the bathroom.

Trying to think of how she could get the money she needed without having to turn a trick, she saw Thin's pants laying on the floor next to their bed. She knew that he always kept at least two bands in his pockets at all times.

"No, I won't, I can't," she said, talking to herself as she eyeballed his pants, and the monkey on her back started to take control. "He won't miss a coupla dollaz. He'll thank he spent it."

Slowly, she walked over to where the pants were laying, watching him with every step. The closer she got to the pants, the queasier her stomach got, she needed a fix now. When Thin didn't stir, she got down on the floor where the pants were. Looking back over her shoulder every few seconds to avoid being caught going through his pockets, she searched until she found what she was looking for. She peeled off the top four bills and put the rest back. Hoping that he wouldn't miss the eighty dollars she'd taken.

The money in her hand only intensified her jones. She was feening so badly by that time that she only took enough time to put her feet in her shoes before heading out the door.

CHAPTER: 23

Sunday morning, a knock on my bedroom door woke me from a fitful sleep.

"Fury, its Vik," came through the door.

"Come in, it's unlocked," I replied, sitting up.

She opened the door and came in. She was already dressed as if she was just coming in after a night out on the town. "Good morning, Mr. Brown," she said with a smile.

"Hey Vik," I replied. "What are you smiling about this early in the morning?" I looked over at the clock. It was 7 a.m. "Why are you up so early this morning anyway? Today is Sunday."

"Get up, Mr. Brown, we've got a long drive ahead of us." She said instead of directly answering the questions.

"What's with the Mr. Brown crap and the "we" and "drive" in the same sentence? You're in a real playful mood early this morning. Did somebody get their coochie popped last night?"

"Boy please, I'm waiting on you for that, but you're dragging your feet," she replied, still smiling.

"Seriously though Fury, you and I are going to Coleman today."

I closed my eyes to collect my thoughts as Coleman went through my mind because I knew that I'd heard of the place before or seen it written on something. When it dawned on me that Big Duke was in federal prison in Coleman, I opened my eyes and stared at her.

"You guessed it," she said, reading the unasked question in my eyes. "We're going to see Big Duke today. He wants to meet the ingenious Fury face to face."

"Okay, get up out of here then so I can get out of bed and get in the shower."

Forty-five minutes or so later, we were on the road heading south. I was sitting on the passenger side of Vik's BMW, lost in my own thoughts. When she tapped me on the leg. "What's on your mind, Lil Daddy?" She asked. "I've been talking my ass off, and you haven't said a word?"

I looked over at her. "I'm sorry, I wasn't actually ignoring you. I guess that I was caught up in my own thoughts and didn't hear you." She gave me a sideways glance but didn't say anything. "I was thinking of how it's been over three years since you welcomed me into your circle, and I never said thank you."

"My whole life has changed since you gave me this opportunity and I am forever grateful."

"I can remember the first day that we saw one another. You must have truly thought that I was homeless."

"Not exactly," she replied, taking her eyes off the road just long enough to look me in the face. "Despite the fact that you were a bit dirty and that I'd gotten sarcastic. I figured that you had been in a fight by the wild look in your eyes, and the blood that was on the front of your shirt. Once you turned around to look at me, after my smart remark."

"Vik, why did you take to me so easily when you didn't really know me? You had only seen me sitting over in the park."

"Do you remember the day before your birthday when we were sitting in the park talking? When I told you I started out on the streets at thirteen years old, pretty much the same way that you did."

"Fury, I was you, only the female version. My mother died from a heroin overdose when I was thirteen and Juice was nine. I had to do something to take care of my brother and me, and to avoid going into a foster home and possibly losing my little brother forever so I dropped out of school and went to Big Duke. He was basically the only father that we'd ever known anyway by him being our mother's man. He took us in, and schooled me in street knowledge while teaching me the drug game."

"Pretty much the same way that you've done me huh?"

"No. You were holding your own without me. Even though I had no idea how well you were holding your own before you had to move out of your spot. But prior to that, I saw the realness in you, and I wanted that in my circle. I only offered you an opportunity to make more, and you being as sharp as you are, took it."

"It took Big Duke some time to teach me about the streets. I guess because I didn't want anything to do with the dope game after drugs had killed my mother, I had to conquer my fears before I could catch on. To where it just came to you as we went along, like it was second nature."

"Why am I the one you invested your time and money into the way that you did? I know that you have told me and shown me things that I doubt that anyone else knows about. Not even your brother, and he's your blood."

"That's true. I'm a pretty good judge of character most of the time, and you're real. Real niggas are rare these days no matter how much one claims to be."

"After our first talk and business deal at the Ice Cream Station, I knew that you were one of the rare. I could give you the whole game the way that it was given to me, if you wanted it and without it coming back to bite me in the ass."

"Look at Thin and his boys for an example. He made the statement that if he don't move, don't no money be made. Unlike Cee Lo who is beyond loyal and knows everything, if Thin knew half of what you know, his fat, grimy ass would have more than likely tried to knock me and Cee Lo out of the box a long time ago and take Big Duke's organization over for himself."

"I'd seen how disloyal he was and I always knew that he was a cutthroat. By the way, he played with the money. That's why his involvement and knowledge of, as well as his in the organization was limited beyond the tracks. He had been recruited by Flex before I ever went to Big Duke for help. By him portraying loyalty to Big Duke, I couldn't remove him without his permission or Thin doing something to jeopardize the organization as a whole unless I was going to have him erased."

"I understand all of that, but I still ask why. Why have you invested so much in me? More than in your own brother?"

"Honestly Fury, because I know that I can trust you, that your word is your bond, that if I give you an assignment it's not gonna be questioned and nothing will get in the way of you getting it done. Not only that, you're a thinker. You're not gonna rush into anything without a plan and get caught slipping or blind-sided. Besides, real recognizes real, and I knew that the more you knew about the game, about the organization, the more valuable to the organization you would become."

"You naturally give and demand respect without even opening your mouth. That in itself will get you a long way in this game. Not only that but you're a natural born leader. Look at your squad, if you were not a part of my team or you decided to go rogue, we couldn't compete with y'all. They're very disciplined and loyal to only you. If you wanted me out of the picture, to take the operation for yourself, all you would have to do is open your mouth to them, and they would hand it to you without a second thought or asking you why."

"Then there's Juice. You said that I've shown and told you things that he doesn't even know. As I said, that's true, but more so by his own volition. I have tried on several occasions but he was a freelancer at the time. He was getting his money but on his own accord. Not as a part of the family. No one, I mean no one other than our mother had ever been able to control him. No matter how others assumed that I could. You came along, y'all bonded and he gets right into compliance and commits to the family. If you choose, you can give him the knowledge that I've given to you."

"Why did I invest so much in you? Because you were the missing piece that made the family circle complete, that's why."

"Why does Big Duke want to see me, Vik?"

"I don't know, but you will be able to ask him for yourself in a few minutes. This is our exit."

* * * * *

Fifteen minutes later, Vik and I were sitting in the visitation room of FCI Coleman. We were making small talk when Big Duke walked in through the inmate's visitation door. All six foot four inches of him. He had on a pressed forest green khaki uniform with white on white Nike AirMax sneakers. He looks to be in his mid to late-forties and in good physical condition. I could see the power that he possessed radiating off of him in the way that he carried himself and in the way that the guards, as well as the inmates acknowledged him as he walked by them. Despite my cool demeanor, I was nervous as hell.

Vik and I both stood up as he approached the table.

"Hey, Baby Girl," he said, hugging and kissing her on the cheek. "It's good to see you, as always."

"Hey yourself," she replied, with a warm smile and returning his embrace.

Releasing her, he looked over at me and she introduced us.

"Loyalty and respect," I said, using my own way of greeting him.

He stood there for a long minute without saying a word, just staring at me as if he was turning my words over in his head or searching for a response of his own.

"Loyalty and respect to you to souljah," he finally said, opening his arms to embrace me. "It's good to finally meet you, Fury. I've heard a lot about you."

I looked over at Vik as we took a seat who was still smiling because she knew she had been talking about me to him.

"The things that I've heard about you are very impressive," he went on, skipping all of the small talk. "Especially the fact that regardless of what business demands of you, you're still going to school and making remarkable grades. Very few can balance and excel in both worlds at once."

"I've heard so much about you until I feel as if I've handpicked you myself. I can see your demand for respect without a single word coming out of your mouth."

I looked over at Vik once again because she had basically said the same thing on our way here.

"Your demeanor demands it and I can appreciate that quality in you. It shows your inner strength but not in a threatening manner. That will get you a long way, not only in this business but in life as well. It will show the people that you come in contact with that you are not a pushover but you are also approachable."

"Vik told me that you are top notch when it comes to dealing with pressure or strenuous situations, that you are a thinker. That too is very impressive because normally the average fifteen year old is either overly aggressive or a sap when it comes to the streets. Thinking doesn't usually come until after a catastrophe or two."

"She has also told me about the two confrontations that you had with Kendrick. I apologize to you for his stupidity. His jealousy for whatever reason caused him to lose sight of what was most important. Forgetting your place is the dumbest move that anyone trying to get ahead can make."

"That's in the past boss, and I held my own," I replied. "You don't owe me any apology for what he brought on himself."

"Call me Duke," he said, "and I know that you held your own against him both times that if you would have said the word, he would have been erased right there in the park, during the second altercation. But your loyalty to Vik and Cee Lo let him live."

"I also know that you hold your own when it comes down to business. I really appreciate that."

"Tell me something though Fury. If I would've told Vik that nothing was to have been done to Thin or his boys for what they'd done to Juice's lady, and dire consequences would have been handed down for disobeying my orders. Would you have followed my orders?"

"Honestly Duke, no," I replied without hesitation.

Duke sat there silently for a long minute staring.

"Why not?" He finally asked.

"From a business perspective, I'm a firm believer that the hands of one are the hands of all. If one of us has a problem then all of us have a problem. It's that simple.

"I've instilled that in my team and I won't go against it. To violate one of us in any manner is like violating all of us. I live by that code and I won't deviate from it."

Big Duke nodded his head in approval as he remembered Cee Lo telling him of how Khandi openly defied him when it was time to get Juice's lady back.

"On a more personal note, Juice is my main man and he was before I ever became a part of your organization. Tieaa is his everything, and if I would have sat on the sideline and done nothing, I would have went against my word which I will never do. My word is my bond, and I gave him my word that I would always have his back.

"I'm loyal to my word Duke."

"Besides, this is my family that he attacked. If there would have been some repercussions behind defying your orders. So be it, we would have faced them and died together."

"Why then haven't you finished that order of business yet?" He asked, not hiding his surprise in the last part of the answer. "Or used some of my people to bring you his head?"

"Because that's not me. Not the way that I do things. Besides, how can you trust a person whose loyalty has a price tag on it? For the right price, they'll even betray you. Other than that, it's not time for the fatal blow yet."

"What happened to J.R and Po Boy were personal for Juice because he saw Po Boy's work firsthand and they were meant as a distraction to get Thin's attention at the same time. They served their purpose and got what was coming to them, all at the same time.

"No one living outside of the family except Thin knows the real meaning behind the hits. I seriously doubt that he'll go to Johnnie law because it will all lead back to what they did to Tieaa to set the whole thing off. In the meantime, we're doing to him what he intended to do to the family. "

"And that is?" He asked.

"From what Tieaa told us when we found her, Thin did what he did to her to humiliate the family for cutting him and his boys off."

"That sounds about like him. So, what have you done so far to him personally in retaliation?"

"Other than let every weight hustler in the Ville know that he ain't to be trusted, and if they're getting their work from us, and dealing with him. They will be cut off as well?"

"Thin is hung up badly on a chick named Milkeila Washington in building 6 out in the Courts. The once respected, sexy lady of the Gunby Courts projects is now a certified fiend and a trick. I had

Ghost and Trina out of Hollybrook turn her out on the dog food, and according to what Ghost has told me, she will do anything to satisfy that monkey once it gets to aping.

"Only the selected few that are loyal to Tieaa know what happened to her. But when it's all said and done, everybody in the projects and on the Eastside will know about Milkeila Washington's heroin addiction."

"Thin will feel the humiliation that he intended for us to feel, and taste the fear that Tieaa felt before he meet his maker. In the end, I'll be his personal executor because all of this started with me."

"You're sharp Fury, real sharp," he said then turned to look at Vik. "Babygirl, you have picked a real one for our family."

"Thanks," she replied. "I learned from the best."

"Speaking of real," he said, looking back at me. "I hear that you have a real elite squad of your own."

"No doubt, thanks to Vik and Lo."

"Why thanks to them? What did they have to do with your squad?"

"Well, when they decided to promote me to lieutenant. They allowed me to recruit them myself."

"And how did you become such an elite squad?"

"My team and I have more in common with one another outside of business, and it made our bond that much stronger. We understand, respect and are loyal to one another because we all came from nothing, living in the projects."

"I shared with them the education that I'd received from Lo and Vik from my own perspective. All the while letting them know that business comes first. I vowed my unwavering loyalty to and respect for them, and they to me. Each one knows her or his respective position and that each member is equally valuable to the team if things are going to work. We are a family."

"No doubt about that, Fury. We are definitely a family," he said, "and I like the way that you think. You're every bit as real as I've been told you were. Other than Cee Lo and Dirty Red, you're the first young real nigga that I've crossed paths with in quite some time. Stay that way."

I looked over at Vik, and her chest was swollen with pride.

"Thanks, but I don't consider myself as being real. I'm just me. Like I told you, I live by this code. I also have personal rules that I live by, and being me is something that I will never change. I stand for and die by what I believe in."

The more we talked, the more relaxed I became in the presence of one of the most powerful drug lords in Jacksonville, Florida.

"Fury, I'm sure that you know that there is a downside to what we do," he said.

"No doubt, I know that it's illegal. Not being disrespectful but look at you for an example. You're the big dog of the east side drug trade. You control all of the action on your turf, and money is not an issue for you. But you're still doing time."

He nods his head in acceptance of the answer.

"Do you have any money put away for a rainy day?"

"Yes, quite a bit."

"How much do you have?"

I didn't answer. I just sat there and stared at him instead because that information was none of his business.

"Good answer soldier," he said when he realized that I wasn't going to reply. "Never completely expose your hand to anyone."

"I asked that question though because the game does not guarantee you anything. Nor does it last forever. There are always greedy muthafuckaz like Barney Fife, who's on the take but you still end up getting knocked. Or cutthroat ass niggas that turn informant after they've gotten knocked on a misdemeanor charge and the jackboys. Who are always trying to take your grip. No one is untouchable."

"Not only that, whenever you're hustling and living for the material gains and the limelight, it's all in vain. The glamor of having been a small part of the game is your reward. In the end, if you get knocked, you ain't even got bond money, and a criminal record is all that you got to show for all of your hard work. So, whenever you are ready to clean up your stash, just say the word. I got some people who can handle that for you."

Despite me nodding my head in understanding, this visit still didn't really make any sense to me. He already knew almost everything about me, and I know that he didn't want to talk about the little bit of money I have compared to what he makes. So to satisfy my curiosity, I asked.

"Duke, why did you really want to see me today? It's evident that you already know everything about me. Are you just satisfying your curiosity and putting a face with the name?"

"Not exactly," he replied." I trust Cee Lo and Vik in every way. Their word, is more precious than gold to me."

"You're a real soldier Fury, and as Vik has said, you are a real asset to this operation. I can see that you are intellectual, street smart, loyal and that your dirty work shows a trace of sociopathic tendencies, when circumstances require it."

"I wanted to see you because there's one more step for you to take in order for you to fulfill your true position in this family. I had to see you face to face, to be able to see with whom I'm dealing with before I could allow it."

He stopped in the middle of his explanation and looked up, looking behind me before he stood up. Vik and I both stood up as well, out of respect. Before we looked back to see Cee Lo heading towards the table.

"Sorry I'm late Pop," Cee Lo said, as he and Big Duke embraced, "I had to drop Moet and Cordelia off to her mom's."

"It's all good," he replied. "How are they? And your mother?"

"Everyone is fine."

"Your being late gave me time to get acquainted with Fury. You and Vik have done a jam up job with him."

"He made it easy, by being sharp already."

I looked from Big Duke to Cee Lo, and a pop went through my mind a second time because in all of the time that I've been a part of this organization, not once had Vik mentioned that they were father and son. Nor had Cee Lo or Juice. In fact, Cee Lo called his ol' boy Big Duke like everyone else.

When I looked over at Vik, the puzzle that was going through my head must have shown on my face.

"Yes Lil Daddy," she said with a smile. "They're father and son. Look at them."

"Any questions that you have in that area will have to wait until another time," Big Duke said before I could say anything more. "Time is running short for you and Vik, and I haven't answered your question."

"Vik, Lo, I can see everything in him that y'all have told me. Y'all did well when y'all decided to promote him to lieutenant. He has everything that it takes to be a leader and more."

"Anyway, our next shipment comes in on Tuesday night. Dante` and his boys will meet with y'all at the Blue Goose in St. Augustine. I want Fury taken along for the pick up, get him familiar with that area. Better yet, let him handle that business. Experience is the best teacher."

* * * * *

Fifteen minutes later, Vik and I were back on I75 heading home. I still had a thousand questions going through my head. By the way she sat with her back to the passenger side staring at me, it was evident that she knew that there was a lot going on in my head.

She patiently sat there waiting for the questions to begin.

"Vik, why didn't you tell me that Big Duke was keeping tabs on me?" I began.

"This is his operation, Fury," she replied. "He keeps tabs on all of us. The same way that he talks with me about you. He does the same thing about Lo and with Lo about everyone in the family. Once you're old enough to come visit him by yourself, he'll check on things through you the same way."

"He has a lot invested in this operation so it's normal for him to want to know what's going on. If he loses, he loses big. Put yourself in his shoes and in his current position. What would you do? This operation is worth at least seven million."

There was no need for me to answer her question because I knew that if I had that kind of money tied up in something outside of my control, I would be doing the exact same thing without a second thought about it.

"He has to be impressed with what he's found out about you though because in the five years that he's been down, not once had he sent for Thin or his boys and they were with him before me."

"I doubt it seriously if Thin even knows who Dante is or what he looks like for that matter. Not even Dirty Red has been recommended by Big Duke to meet Dante and he's beyond loyal to Cee Lo like your squad is to you."

"You could've at least given me the heads-up that he wanted to see me to tell me about meeting with one of his suppliers?"

"I didn't know. He called me last night after you had gone to bed, and said to bring you to see him today. No more, no less.

"I didn't even know that Lo was going to be there."

"Speaking of Cee Lo, why are you the boss in Big Duke's absence instead of him? It seems to me that by him being Lo's ol' boy that he would have left his son in charge."

"I see that you still have quite a bit to learn about the hustle game. Especially on a scale as large as ours," she replied. "I know that Cee Lo is beyond loyal and would never rip his father off. But what if by chance, he would have been the shiesty one instead of Thin. Big Duke would have been totally against any sort of retaliation that would have harmed his only child. Deadly serious repercussions would have come behind disobeying his orders. He would have wanted to deal with him himself."

"On the other hand, I am expendable. Even though Big Duke more or less raised me as his daughter, it would be much easier for him to sacrifice me than his own seed. Sometimes in certain situations you have to be ruthless to prosper or to survive even with flesh and blood. It takes a real cold-hearted person to erase their own child.

"So how do you avoid having to ever make a decision that you may later regret? You don't give total control of or too much power in such a large organization to family members unless you're passing the torch."

"Treason or betrayal on my behalf would mean death. For Cee Lo, it would be exile or extended probation due to his love for his son. In which case could come back to haunt the organization as an end result. Not only that but Lo has less patience and lower tolerance than I have which could also jeopardize the operation as a whole or come back to bite him in the ass as well."

"Let's take the day that I exiled Thin and his boys for an example. If it would have been left up to Cee Lo, he would have erased all three of them right then and we can't afford to kill people just because they're stupid."

CHAPTER: 24

The ringing of the phone woke up Thin who laid there a few extra seconds to gather his bearings before rolling over to answer the phone.

"Whutz up cuzzo, dis is Nookie."

"Whutz up wit dat B I we talked bout nigga? Me and my boyz are ready ta feed."

"Damn nigga! Lemme wake tha fukkk up befo yu start wit alla tha damn questions."

"Whut tha fukkk yo ass doin in tha bed dis time a day anyway? How tha fukkk we gon git money witjo ass in tha bed? Yu act like yu got bankaz hours or sumthin."

"Whut time is it?" He asked, talking more to himself than his cousin as he rolled over to look at the clock on the wall. "Damn! I've slept tha whole day away."

"Cuzzo, gimme a coupla dayz ta put dat business in effect. I'll hitja back when everythang is everythang."

"A'ight fam, handle dat business and let's git paid," Nookie said and hung up.

"Milkeila!" Thin called out as he got out of the bed, and headed to the bathroom. "Where in tha hell is dat damn woman?" He said, thinking out loud.

In the bathroom, he saw her purse laying on the floor which made him think that she was still in the apartment somewhere. He picked it up, and put it on the back of the toilet without looking inside. Had he done so, he would have seen why she was down on the 3rd floor to Junkie Fred and Y'onda's apartment.

"Milkeila!" He called out a second time to be answered by silence once again. He hurriedly washed his face and brushed his teeth. Thinking the whole time that he was going to catch her downstairs at Junkie Fred and Y'onda's after he had told her that he didn't want her around them. He wasn't going to play with her this time. He was going to whip her ass good if she was at their crib.

Out in the hallway, he went straight to the stairs. He was too wound up and did not have the patience to wait the few seconds it would take for the elevator to arrive. Determined to catch her, he half ran, half jumped down the two flights of stairs to get to his destination. When he came out of the stairwell, he goes over to Y'onda's apartment and knocks hard on the door. When no one answered, he tried the door and it was unlocked. He stepped inside to look for his woman, and found Junkie Fred and Y'onda both sitting on the living room floor, in the dark, butt ass naked in a junkie's nod.

He stepped over them and searched the entire apartment looking for Milkeila. When he didn't find her, he went back out of the apartment. Now, he was really pissed off because he didn't know where else to look for her off hand.

"Fukkk her fa now," he said, thinking out loud while walking back into the stairwell. "I gotta scope dis business out so we can git paid."

His mind was so preoccupied with his part in the upcoming caper that he almost walked right past the two jits and the broad having sex behind the stairs on the ground floor. The three of them were naked, laying on the floor. The jits made a sandwich out of her. She was riding one and the other was in her asshole from the back. To see them freaking like that actually turned him on, it reminded him of how he and Po Boy had freaked Monkey Jo at Palatka High School in tenth grade.

"Damn lil niggaz," he said after a couple of seconds of watching and not being able to stand seeing them get their freak on and he couldn't. "If y'all gon trick. Y'all shoulda at least went up ta her spot or rented a room from Junkie Fred and Y'onda. But instead, y'all niggaz gon jus mutt tha bitch right here behind tha stairs like she in't shit huh?"

"Shut tha fukkk up fat, hatin ass nigga and mind yo own damn business," said the jit on her back when he looked up at the sound of Thin's voice. "She ain't stressin ova where she's at. So why tha fukkk are yu? Yo bitch ass ain't paid fa dis trick no fukkkin way."

"So ya need ta mind ya own fukkkin business and keep it movin."

Looking closely at the tramp stamp on the broad's lower back, Thin noticed that it was Milkeila that the jits had in the two piece and almost lost his mind right there. Flying into a rage, he grabbed a handful of the jit's dreds and snatched him up off of her and slammed him against the wall then grabbed her by her hair and pulled her up off of the other jit.

"BITCH! WHUT THA FUKKK ARE YU DOIN?" He screamed, and slapped the shit out of her.

"HAVE YU LOST YO GODDAMN MIND? HOW THA FUKKK YU GON DISRESECT ME LIKE DIS?

"WHY THA FUKKK IS YO ASS OUT HERE TRICKIN ANY FUKKKIN WAY?"

Thin was so irate that he hadn't noticed the pistol laying on the pile of clothes, or that the second jit had gotten up off of the floor and put his pants and shoes on.

"Thin," said the second jit, cocking his own pistol.

Thin was in such a rage that he didn't hear him call his name. When he did turn to look in his direction, the jit had the pistol aimed at his forehead.

"Big man, yu need ta walk and let us finish handlin our bidness," he said in a calm but deadly tone. "We ain't got no beef witju, but we paid dis trick fa whut we're gittin and we're gon git ours."

"I DON'T GIVE A FUKKK WHUTJA PAID FA MUTHAFUKKKA !" Thin screamed. "DIS IS MY MUTHAFUKKKIN BITCH, AND Y'ALL THANK DAT I'MA JUS STAND BY AND WATCH'CHALL STICK YA NASTY DICKS IN HER SOME MORE? YOU TWO NIGGAZ SERIOUSLY GOT ME FUKKK'D UP FA REAL!"

"Nigga, dat ain'tjo bitch. She's a fukkkin junkie and a trick bitch," saidi the jit that he had slammed against the wall after he had put on his clothes. "She's fukkkin community property dumb ass nigga, and yu're tryna wife her. Nigga please."

"Do yu know how many niggaz dick yu don kissed when yu be kissin dat bitch?"

Thin reached for his gun.

"Don't even thank about it bitch ass nigga, or I'll blow yo fukkkin brains all ova tha fukkkin wall," said the jit with the pistol.

"Pimp git dat niggaz burna and whuteva else he's got in his pockets fa fukkkin up our groove. He ain't unda Dirty Money's protection no mo."

"Whateva he's got in his pockets will make up fa whut we gave his bitch as he calls her."

"I hope yu niggaz know dat it's gon be some repercussions behind dis shit y'all jus pulled," Thin said after his gun, cash and jewelry had been taken. "Alla dat da'chall jus got, jus growed a tail."

"Nigga please, yu're tha last muthafukkka in tha world I'd worry bout. Yo coward ass ain't gon do nuttin but whutju doin now. If I even thoughtja wuz a threat, I'd murda yo fat ass right now. Besides, who's gon come ta yo rescue? Yu lookin fa J.R and Po Boy ta walk through tha doe?"

"Yeah right, bitch ass nigga. Don't fukkk round and catch up wit'em on tha otha side."

"We'll catchja on tha rebound Ms Good Booty and finish up dis bidness," he said as the two jits go out of the building.

"Milkeila, whut tha fukkk is wrong witju?" Thin asked, turning back on her once the jits were out the door. "Are yu reall on dat shit like dat lil nigga jus said?" He grabbed her arm looking for tracks.

"Hell no nigga!" She lied, snatching her arm out of his grasp. If he would have known where to look, he would have known that the jit was telling the truth. "I wuz jus gittin back at'cho ass fa goin down to Palatka and layin up witja bitch fa three fukkkin dayz."

"Yu jus caught me doin me, dat's all."

"Why tha fukkk wuz y'all behind tha muthafukkkin stairs on tha fukkkin flo den? And why tha fukkk didja have two pf'em in yu at one time, if yu wuz only tryna git back at me?"

"Who tha fukkk yu thank yu're talkin to? A muthafukkkin idiot or sumthin?"

"I wuz gittin mine down here, cuz yo ass wuz upstairs in my fukkkin bed fa one. And fa two, I had two of'em inside me at once cuz a bitch like a dick in her ass and pussy at tha same time every now and den, jus like tha next bitch."

"Yeah, dem lil niggaz paid me ta git me off. I ain't gon front. Shidd! Ain't nuttin free in dis world no way, and any bitch dat wuz tryna git her freak all tha way on and could git paid to woulda dun tha same fukkkin thang."

"So, if dat's whutja mad bout, den goddamn it, it is whut it is."

"I can't believe datju jus stood dere and said dat shit ta my face like dat. Yu and me been togetha fa ova three years, and yu ain't neva let me fukkk yu in tha ass. But now all of a sudden yu like a dick in yo ass like tha next bitch. Ain't no fukkkin way."

"And yu know fa ya'self dat I ain't neva lied ta yu bout shitja eva asked me. If I woulda been ova ta Sha'Vonna's crib when I wuz down in Palatka, I woulda toldja dat dat's where I wuz. Yu shoulda called ta my auntie's crib. Yu know tha numba, jus like yu know dat she ain't gon lie ta yu or fa me."

"I love yu Keila, and ya know dat I do, and dis is how yu gon play me? Bitch! I betta not even catch'cha tlkin ta anotha nigga, or I swear on my seed dat I'll kill yo muthafukkkin ass tha next time."

If she would have listened a little closer, she would have heard the genuine hurt that was in his voice and knew that he meant every word that he had said. But what he felt was the last thing on her mind. All she cared about at the moment was getting rid of him, so she could get what she needed to satisfy the jones that had welled up inside of her.

"Yu ain't gon do shit to Milkeila Mo'Eisha Washington muthafukkka but git tha fukkk outta my face," she said, putting her hands on her hips and rolling her neck as she spoke. "Dis is my ass muthafukkka, and if I wanna give it ta tha Pope, goddamn it, I'll do jus dat."

"And ain't a damn thang datju or any otha muthafukkka can do bout it, but accept it. I'm my own muthafukkkin woman."

He knocked her on her ass right where she stood.

Still naked, she bounced right back up off of the floor, with her hands balled up into fist. "OH

NO MUTHAFUKKKA!" she growled. "DIDN"T I TELL YO PUNK ASS NOT TA EVA PUTJO MUTHAFUKKKIN DICK BEATAZ ON ME AGAIN? I AIN"T DAT BITCH IN PALATKA. YU AIN'T GON PUTJA MUTHAFUKKKIN HANDZ ON ME WIT'OUT A FIGHT."

She threw a right jab that landed square in his mouth, busting both his top and bottom lip, before running into him like an NFL linebacker. They went through the exit doors, and out into the courtyard. Her titties and ass were seen by everyone as they fought like life itself depended on the outcome and the people of the projects gathered around to watch.

Thin, having gotten the best of her after a while, was sitting straddle her waist with his fist drawn back. He was determined to punish her for the disrespect and humiliation that she had brought to him. When another female came running up and kicked him in the side. She kicked him so hard that he fell sideways off of Milkeila with a grunt and a sharp pain exploded between his ribs on the next breath.

"Fukkk nigga, gitjo fat, punk as offa her," she growled.

"BITCH! Yu betta …," he said as he turned to his attacker, only to lose his thoughts and words in mid-sentence. For an instant, fear replaced his anger when he saw Tieaa standing there with a mask of pure hatred on her face and her hands balled into fist at her side. It wasn't until he saw the murderous look in Juice's eyes as he walked up behind her that he really got shocked. "She betta whut muthafukkka?" Juice asked, moving around Tieaa and closer to him. All that he saw at the moment was spilling Thin's blood all over the courtyard. "I owe this son-of -a-bitch for what he did to my baby, and he's gonna damn sure get it now," Juice thought. "Fury is taking too long to kill this motherfucker. If there weren't so many people out here. I'd blow his motherfucking brains out right now."

"Yu're a real big fukkkin man when it comes ta smackin round females, ain'tja fukkk ass nigga?" Juice taunted. "Ya wanna try a nigga dat'll beat'cho punk ass real good fa once?"

Juice took off his wife beater and jewelry, muscles jumping in his arms and chest, fiending for some action. Thin having seen the handle of the big pistol tucked in his waist, almost pissed in his pants. He was sure that Juice was about to merk him where he was. Instead, Juice pulled the chrome 357 automatic out of his waist and handed it with his shirt and jewelry to his girl.

"C'mon pussy boi," he said taunting Thin further. "I've alwayz been told dat a nigga dat'll beat on a woman, ain't gon fight no man. So let's see whutja workin wit. Dis is yo chance ta prove datja ain't tha bitch ass nigga I thank ya really are. And I ain't gon wait all day fa ya ta gitja soft ass up offa tha ground."

Instantly, Thin's thoughts went back to the day at Milkeila's when Po Boy had mentioned the change in Juice. He could see it now. There was an indescribable evil in his eyes that wasn't there before and it shook him up even more. He knew that Juice was going to take him all the way out of the game, here and now if he slipped. Despite being scared shitless, he got up to try and save face.

"Let's do dis den lil nigga," he said, tearing off what was left of his already ripped and bloody shirt. "I been wontin ta spank yo young, slick rappin ass fa a long minute anyway. Vik nor dat fukkk nigga Fury, ain't here ta save yo ass dis time around."

No sooner than Juice moved in on Thin, Breeze, Dirty Red, Trey and Zee pushed their way through the crowd and stopped the fight before it could jump off. They too had the same murderous look in their eyes but they knew that now wasn't the time to handle that business.

"Leave dat lone fam," said Dirty Red, pushing him and Tieaa back the way they had come.

"Now ain't tha time, and dere's too many witnesses out here fa us ta fukkk his world up."

CHAPTER: 25

Tuesday night around ten o'clock, the entire family was at the Blue Goose in St. Augustine. Big Duke's clout in the game was so strong that we had no problem getting into the club without being searched. Once inside, the family spread out as we had always done to be able to cover one another's back from anywhere in the place if something jumped off.

Cee Lo, Vik and I were sitting at a table close to the bar, waiting for one of Dante's boys to come and escort me to the back for the meeting.

"Vik, do you and Lo always come here to handle this business?" I asked.

"No. We meet at a different location with every shipment," she replied. "To avoid becoming predictable for the jackboys or getting bagged by the alphabet boys. Why do you ask?"

"Because I don't feel comfortable in these surroundings. Don't misunderstand me, I respect and trust Big Duke and his decisions. I even understand the logic of not meeting in the same place twice in a row, but look around. It's too wide open and other than our own people, we don't know anyone here. How easily could we get into a conflict by being on someone else's turf."

"I understand you being uneasy on your first major buy. I was the same way in the beginning myself, but you will settle in the more you meet to conduct the business."

"Believe me when I tell you, even though Big Duke is behind the wall, he still has some heavy hitters on his payroll for if things get too hectic for us to handle, and I'm sure that there are two or three of them in here right now. As we speak."

"Trust me Fury, if anything goes wrong with this transaction while we're still in St. Johns county, you can bet your last dollar that Dante will answer for it in blood because he is the one that designates the meeting places."

It didn't take long before one of Dante's men came to our table. I nodded at Mesha and Zee who were sitting at the bar with two backpacks full of money at their feet as I got up from the table. They fell in behind me, as I followed Dante's man to the VIP.

He knocked twice on the door, and a slim, naked, blonde chick strapped with a mac 10 uzi opened the door and stepped to the side to let us in.

Inside, Dante was sitting on a plush red velvet sofa with two naked females, one on each side of him, sipping champagne.

"Come in and have a seat my friend," he said in broken Colombian accented English.

As we entered, Mesha and Zee stopped at the door with the money as I'd instructed them to do prior to the meeting, and I went forward as Dante stood to greet me.

"I am Dante," he said, embracing me in Colombian familia style just as we met beside the matching love seat to the sofa he had been sitting on. "And you are?"

"Fury."

"So Fury, you are a man of very few words I see," he said, pointing towards the love seat for me to take a seat, "that could be good and bad."

"Meaning what exactly?"

"Nothing my friend, nothing," he replied, sitting back down between his two companions.

"Everything means something Dante but we will get into that some other time. Did we meet here for business or social hour?"

"Maybe a little of both."

"Nah my man, my time is valuable. We can get together some other time and chop it up, but right now I'm here for business. Besides, I got people waiting on this shipment as we speak. Time is money."

"What if Dante decides not to sell it to you, being that you don't have time to be sociable with him?"

"That's your choice." I replied, getting up to leave. "I can take my money someplace else, and let you tongue wrestle with Big Duke over what happened to prevent this transaction from taking place. I'm sure that he's going to want some answers."

"Este chico sencillo está tratando de hacer negocios con hombres adultos," Dante said, *this simple boy is trying to do grown man business,* to the lady seated to his right. She looked at Fury, and smiled.

"Hold on a moment Fury, not so fast my friend. Please sit back down and have some champagne. I was only joking," he said, trying to smooth things over because he really didn't need to cause any complications between himself and Duke. He then snapped his fingers.

His henchman that escorted us in walked over with a briefcase and sat it on the table between the two sofas. He turned it to face Dante and opened it who then turned it to face me. Inside was three kilos of cocaine.

I reached in my pocket and pulled out a knife and a purity-narcoCheck kit.

"What are you doing?" Dante asked, indignantly.

"I'm gonna test the quality of the product," I replied. "What does it look like?"

"Don't insult me, Fury. Cee Lo nor Vik has ever tested my product whenever we've met and they bought for Duke. Why would I fuck up business by selling you some bad product?"

"No soy Vik ni Cee Lo. Si quieres hacer negocios, lo pruebo," I said. *I"m not Vik or Cee Lo. If you want to do business, I test it,* "Si dices que no, camino. Es tan simple como eso, para un niño que intenta hacer negocios con hombres adultos." *If you say no, I walk. It's as simple as that, for a boy trying to do grown man business.*

Dante was stunned at how fluently the Spanish had rolled off of his tongue, and embarrassed at the same time. Now that he knew that his snide remark had been understood, yet his kingpin status would not let him apologize.

"Do your thing," He said instead. "It's straight off the boat from my home country. You won't find anything on the east coast better than Dante's product."

After I'd done my test, I nodded my head in satisfaction. He snapped his fingers again, and his man brought over another, larger briefcase with the remaining forty-seven kilos inside. I, too, signaled Mesha and Zee, who brought the two backpacks of money over and dumped it on the table.

"I tested your product, would you like to count the money?" I asked. "Ten per for anything over ten, am I right?"

He did not respond. He just sat there and watched Mesha's every move, as she took the cocaine out of the two briefcases and transferred twenty-five kilos to each of the backpacks. Then handed them to Zee, before standing beside me.

"You don't trust so easily, do you, my friend?" He asked, after a long minute.

"What makes you say that?" I responded, with a question of my own.

"Because you could've simply closed the two briefcases and taken them with you like everyone else does."

"I just made a half million dollars off of you alone. The briefcases mean nothing."

"I'm not everyone else, Dante. You will come to understand that as well as we continue to do business. Just as you will come to understand that I have my own method of doing things."

CHAPTER:26

Nookie was on his way to his girl's crib in the Sugar Hill projects when his phone rang. "It's ya boi," he answered on the third ring. "Who dis?"

"Whut up cuzo, it's time," Thin replied.

"Hold on a sec fam," he said as he pulled over into the parking lot of Little Harry's liquor store on the corner of 19th and Madison Street and parked. "A'ight nigga, gimme tha rundown."

"Tha jits in tha Courts catch alla tha late night and afta shift action which ends about eleven thirty. And bein dat tha trap is always jumpin, nobody eva really pay attention ta tha whips dat come and go," he began. "If y'all time thangs right, say bout eleven forty-five. Y'all can catch'em dead ta tha right at Unique's crib countin up tha day's trap."

"Which crib is tha chick Unique's?"

"Tha green cinda block or tha fourth one afta yu turn right back on Jesse, comin outta tha projects."

"How many of'em usually be up in dere?"

"If all of'em are workin dat night, which more den likely dey will be. It'll be six of'em".

"A'ight cuzo, we'll be up dat way and handle dis business tonight. I'll hitja on tha hip as soon as it's done. So we can meet up and yu gitja cut befo we head back dis way."

* * * * *

The traffic going in and out of the Courts hadn't slowed down at all. Mainly because this was the time of the night that the undercover addicts and junkies from the suburbs would come to cop their drug of choice. Therefore, the two slow rolling Chrysler didn't look suspicious to Breeze at all who was sitting in the park on the bench facing Unique's, talking to one of the girls out of the projects name Stacii.

The two cars took the left off of Jesse onto Franklin following the other traffic going into the projects, and came back out to take a left, then a right to get back on Jesse. All the while, casing the green cinder block house. Four houses past their target, and out from under the streetlight, the drivers turn off the lights before pulling into the yard of an abandoned house. Two guys got out of each car dressed in blue camouflage and ski masks, and ran towards the back of the house to blend into the night. Moving quickly and quietly, the four sprinted through the backyards to come up in the back of Unique's house. There, they spit into two groups to come up on each side of the house and meet at the front. At the precise time that they had gotten into position to run up in the house, the front door opened.

"We had a really good week dis week fam," Trey said, being the first to walk out of the house.

"No doubt about that," I replied. "We've been at it so hard all week that I'm going to get at Vik about taking tomorrow off."
"I think we'll go to the Jaguars' game if y'all are down. I want to get Travis Etienne and Trevor

Lawerence to autograph my jersey."

No sooner than Zee, who was bringing up the rear, pulled the door closed behind him and stepped off the porch, our masked up guys materialized out of nowhere.

"Hold it right muthafukkkin dere," one of them said. "Y'all niggaz know whut muthafukkin time it is. Nobody move, nobody lose, nobody gits hurt. And keep ya handz where i can see'em. If nobody tries ta be a hero. Nobody has ta die ta'night."

Turning around slowly to face the jackboys put Zee in front and in the direct line of fire.

"Hold on my nigga. Y'all fools bout ta make a graveyard visitin mistake," he said. "Dis is Big

Duke's paypa, and dere are deadly serious repercussions behind takin it."

"Fukkk a Big Duke, muthafukkka. Dat's Panda and Trigga muthafukkkin bread y'all niggaz holdin. So drop dem bags right dere on tha ground and back tha fukkk up."

"How far do you really think y'all are going to get with this money, if you take it?" I asked.

"You're on our turf, and like my brother said, this is Big Duke's money."

"You take it, it becomes blood money. Your blood."

"Shut tha fukkk up nigga and drop tha muthafukkkin money, befo i murda yo ass. Big Duke or whuteva tha fukkk niggaz name is, can git tha same thang datjo ass is bout ta git if yu don't cut tha lip service and unass dat damn bread."

"Now, drop tha muthafukkkin bags on tha ground or die right here on tha muthafukkkin strength. Cuz I'ma git dat money eitha way it comes."

Breeze had seen Unique's front door open and close back, and more than the allotted time had passed without him seeing the family. Or anyone giving him the signal to fall back, caused him to instinctively think that they were in trouble. He got on his walkie talkie and Alerted Cee Lo and Dirty Red then got up off of the bench.

"Go home right now Stacii." He said, flipping the switch to automatic on the AK47. "I'll holla atja tomorrow." Then took off at a sprint towards Unique's.

Just as he got to Jessie Street, bright car lights came on as the driver stomped on the gas pedal, burning rubber, as the car took off in his direction. He turns in the direction of the oncoming car and squeezes off five quick rounds of rapid fire. Three in the grill of the car, bursting the engine block and two into the driver's side of the windshield. The car then veers to the right and slams into the big Oak tree in Unique's neighbor's yard.

The sudden burst of gunfire out in the street caused one of the jackboys to panic and he squeezed off two shots. Both shots hit Zee. One in the forehead and the other in the throat, killing him before his brain could register that he had been shot.

Instantaneously, guns seemed to materialize out of nowhere after that, and gunplay erupted right there in Unique's front yard. No sooner than the shit hits the fan, Dirty Red's Avalanche comes sliding around the corner off of McKay Street onto Jesse. Before the truck had come to a complete stop in front of the house next door, Cee Lo was already out of the truck sprinting with his gun in hand towards Breeze who was exchanging gunfire with the driver of the second car. Cee Lo raised his Glock forty-five and squeezed off two rounds, causing the window on the driver's side to explode and the gunman to duck behind the open door for cover.

At that moment, Breeze jumped up from behind the parked car at the curb that he was using for cover and sprinted to the wrecked car and put three rounds into the already slumped over driver.

Dirty Red was only seconds behind Cee Lo coming up out of his truck, with his nickel plated Calico nine in hand, sprinting towards

Unique's to help his family that were in her yard. By the time he intervened, two of the four were already down but by the sound of the rapid fire that was still being exchanged, he couldn't be sure how many were left. It didn't take long after Cee Lo and Dirty Red had entered the shootout that it was over.

Someone had called the police because sirens could be heard coming in the distance.

"Let's move," Cee Lo said. "Five-o is on the way."

"Whut about Zee fam?" Trey asked.

"Get his gun, vest and necklace," he said reluctantly, not wanting to leave him. "He's dead, and we need to get from over here now if we're going to stay out of jail tonight.
"This place is going to be on lockdown here shortly."

We all jumped in Dirty Red's truck when he pulled up, leaving our own cars in the projects. The last time that I had felt this numb was when I saw White Boy hanging from the tree in his front yard.
No more than a quarter mile after we had gotten off of Jesse Street, five of Duval County Sheriff cars passed us with the sirens blaring, speeding towards the projects.
"Damn!" Trey said, as it sunk in on him that his cousin was gone. "Cuzo didn't even have a chance."

"I know right," Breeze replied, in a soft voice filled with emotion, "but he didn't suffa and we put alla dem muthafukkkaz ass in tha dirt right beside him."
"Yeah, I know, but it ain't gon be tha same wit'out dat nigga round and it's gon kill Mesha." Trey leaned his head against the window and just stared blankly out at the passing scenery.

"Fury, call Juice and tell him to meet us at Vik's," Cee Lo said, "All of them. I'll call Vik and let her know that we're all on the way."

I took out my cell and dialed Juice's number. He answered on the first ring.

"Fam, are you still with the girls?" I asked.

"Yeah, we're at my crib countin tha trap. Whutz good?"

"Some niggas just tried to jack us coming out of Unique's, and Zee was killed."

"WHUT! I'm on tha way."

All three of the girls looked up simultaneously, when Juice's voice raised.

"No need, we've already left, but y'all need to
meet us at the house." "Say no mo, we leavin
now.

At the same time, Cee Lo was on the phone with Vik. He was informing her that the entire family would be coming to her house shortly.
"Is there something wrong, Lo?" She asked, in a sleepy voice. "It's after one in the morning."

"Yeah!" He replied. "Something is wrong. You will get the whole of it when we get there."

When we got to the house, Juice and the girls were already there waiting. Everyone, including Vik stood with questions in their eyes, when we walked in. Evidently, Juice hadn't told the girls or her about the shootout. Nor about Zee having been killed because they were all rather calm for the moment despite the fact that there was a crisis.

"Where's Zee, fam?" Mesha asked, being the first to notice that he wasn't with us.

"Sit down, Mesha. I need to address the family." I said, instead of answering her question.

Tears welled up and fell silently from her eyes when the reality of the meeting had something to do with the love of her life not being there. Instead of allowing her to sit, I grabbed her by the hand and pulled her to me. I wrapped my arms around her to be able to share the pain of what I was about to drop on her and those who didn't already know.

"Vik, fam, some jackboys tried to hit us up tonight coming out of Unique's with the week's trap. Zee was shot and killed before we ever had a chance to make a move."

"Do you have any idea who they were?" Vik asked, her eyes showing the heat that wasn't in her voice.

"No, they all were masked up and five-o had been called before we had the chance to unmask any of them."

"Somebody had ta set dat shit up doe," Juice said, not disguising the way he was feeling. "Big Duke been countin and stashin tha trap ova at Unique's fa years, and ain't nobody eva been stupid enough ta try and run upin dere befo ta'night."

"One of'em did call out tha names Trigga and Panda," said Trey. "If dat means anythang."

"Do you think that this might be some of Thin's doing?" Vik asked.

"I don't know, but anything is possible. He did say that we were going to feel him," I replied.

"We will know atleast who they were and where they are from soon." Cee Lo said, speaking for the first time. "Seven people were killed tonight, it's definitely going to be on the news."

*   *   *   *   *

Thin was still awake when the five thirty morning news came on. He stared at the television absentmindedly because he basically already knew what the headline story was about, and so did everyone else in the Gunby Courts projects. They had heard the massive shootout as if it had taken place in the middle of the projects' courtyard.

"Damn! I really fukkk'd up dis time," he said, talking to himself as thoughts of J.R and Po Boy crossed his mind. "I dun got my cuzo and my niggaz merked. I shoulda jus played my position like Vik said, and nuna dis shit woulda went down like dis. And when Vik figga out who Nookie is, I'ma fukkkin dead man fa sho. Big Duke will orda a hit on me his muthafukkkin self, when it git inside ta'em. Fukkk! I'ma walkin dead man."

His mind was so consumed that he got out of bed and started pacing the floor. He knew that he had stepped too far out of bounds. Especially with Zee having gotten killed, he knew without a shadow of a doubt that the blood draws blood street law was now in full effect, and he was soon to be on the top of Dirty Money's list.

"I need ta git tha fukkk away from here befo Vik put tha pieces togetha." He said, thinking out loud. "If I skip town right now, the only way I can protect Keila is ta take her with me." Stopping in front of the window, and looking down on the courtyard, he began to have a panic attack because he felt like he was running out of time and options. "I gotta figga out sumthin," he said as he started pacing back and forth. "How can I protect my people and stay alive in tha process? Maybe if I turn myself in and confess ta tha rape of Juice's bitch and tha setup of tha robbery dat went badacross tha street. Everythang'll be a'ight fa a long minute and my people'll be safe." He stopped beside the bed and looked down at Milkeila as he pondered actually turning himself in.

"Nah, dat ain't gon work," he said as he started to pace again. "I can't be caged up like an animal again. Besides, Big Duke still call shot out here on tha bricks from tha inside. So I know dat he could easily have me touched if I'm behind tha wall. Damn! I gotta find a way ta cripple dem or do sumthin dat'll buy me enuff time ta move my people outta harm's way".

Barney Fife ran across his mind out of desperation. "Dat's it," he said. He had formulated a plan from that single thought. He got his cell off the night table on his side of the bed, and went into the bathroom. Closing the door behind him. He sat on the toilet and searched his contact list for the number.

"Yeah," answered a male voice on the third ring.

"Dis is Thin," he said in a hushed voice.

"I recognize the number nigger. What do you want, calling me this time of the morning?"

"Yu need ta meet wit me. I got sum info fa ya."

"I thought you called yourself a thug. Since when did you become a fucking rat?" He asked, not being able to pass up an opportunity to hit him below the belt. "Tell me something to wet my appetite, and let me decide where it goes from there."

"Fair enuff," Thin replied. "Whut if I toldja dat I know who merked my niggaz J.R and Po Boy. And dem people ova on Jesse Street last night?"

"That sounds worth hearing. Tell me who did it and I'll meet with you to get your statement in writing."

"It wuz dem niggaz dat work fa Big Duke and Vik."

"Aren't you a part of that posse? What the name, Dirty Money, that's getting money out of the projects on Franklin Street?"

"Nah, not no mo. Dey kicked me and my niggaz ta tha curb fa dat young nigga Fury," Thin lied.

"I'm sorry homeboy," he said, mockingly. "What do you want me to do about it? I work narcotics, not homicide. And when Vik finds out that your fat, punk ass is putting the jake on. You will be another dead nigger like the others." He hung up.

"Damn Thin! Dat wuz a junkie move," he said to himself. "Yu know dat dat cracka is on Big Duke's payrol, and he's gon tell Vik datja called'em sho as shit stank."

He takes a couple of deep breaths to calm himself down as much as possible. He was all the way in now and he knew it. So he made another call.

"Duval County Sheriff's Office, this is officer Nadine Shaw. How can I help you?"

"Narcotics division," he said

Within seconds, the phone was ringing again.

"Narcotics. Detective Stacey McNeal speaking. What can I do for you?"

"My name is Kendrick Butler. I got sum valuable info fa ya, dat involves an ass of illegal drugs, and a dirty cop."

"Go ahead Mr. Butler," McNeal said. "I'm listening."

"Not ova tha fukkkin phone fool," Thin replied. "Meet me ta'night in Hooters down at tha Landing."

"Okay, but how will I be able to identify you?"

"Yu won't. Sit on tha last stool at tha bar, next ta tha jukebox. I'll come ta yu. Eight o'clock sharp, and not a minute afta. By yo'self or I'll walk."

"I'll be there." He hung up.

CHAPTER: 27

All of us were still in the living room the following morning when the six o'clock news came on. Everyone was gathered around the television, giving it their undivided attention.

"Good morning ladies and gentlemen," said the news anchor. "Last night on the east side was one of Duval County's deadliest bloodbaths in quite some time. Reporter Sharonda Miller is on the location."

"What appeared to be a robbery attempt gone badly, is what lead to mayhem in the yard and in front of 260 Jesse Street," said Miller. "As you can see here," pointing at the ground that had been spray painted in several places to indicate the numerous bullet casings then at the house. "The bullet hole riddled home of Miss. Unique Williams is only a small portion of the aftermath of a massive shootout that left seven young blacks dead.

"The Gunby Courts public housing apartments which are adjacent to Miss Williams," she continued, pointing as the cameraman moves into position for the projects to be seen, "were once known to be the major drug trade area of the east side. Run at the time by a well known drug kingpin, DeMarcus Daniels, who is known all around the city by the name Big Duke. He is currently serving a fifteen year sentence at Coleman Federal Correctional Institution for drug trafficking, money laundering and income tax fraud as a result of his chosen profession."

"Residents say that Zachariah (Zee) Williams, 21, of the Sherwood projects was shot and killed during the robbery attempt. He was the cousin of Miss Unique Williams. It is believed that he was mistaken for one of the local dealers that still hangout in the park and projects, when he went to visit her."

"No one knows exactly how many were involved in the shootout, but from the looks of things, and there being six dead wearing ski masks, it is evident that there were definitely more people than the assailants and unarmed Zee Williams in the yard last night, when the robbery attempt went bad."

"Witnesses say it sounded like being in a war zone."

"I've never heard anything like it in my life," said Georgie Merchant, "and I've lived in this house for over thirty years. There was so much shooting and glass breaking. I got so scared that I hid in my closet on the floor."

"Amongst the six that were killed in their failed robbery attempt are Parnell Pope 23, Tre'Maine Cohens 21, Bryson Anderson 20 and Naurice Butler 20. These four young men were killed in the same yard as Zee Williams," Miller said. "The other two assailants were found either in or near the two getaway cars that had been stolen from a used car dealership in Orange Park early yesterday evening. They were identified as LaFrenchie Hamilton 18 and Sequoquah Campbell 19. All six of the assailants were from Palatka, which is about an hour drive South of here in Putnam County."

Vik closed her eyes and repeated the six names she had heard over and over. As if searching the depths of her memory for some sort of a clue or connection, that would lead her to the setup man. When she finally opened her eyes. She looked at Cee Lo first, then at Dirty Red.

"I knew it," she said in the quietest voice that I'd ever heard come from her.

The rest of us could only look from her to Cee Lo and Dirty Red, and wait for her to reveal what she knew.

"Thin," Cee Lo said, putting it together at the same moment, and she nodded her head in concurrence.

I, on the other hand, could only assume that she knew that Thin was the one that had set the whole robbery thing up. Once the reporter mentioned that the six were from Palatka, and we all knew that Palatka was Thin's hometown. Or could it have been the fact that no one had ever even attempted to run up in any of Big Duke's spots before last night, a few weeks after him and his boys had been exiled. So I asked her as much.

"Not exactly, Fury, even though they were some good clues," she replied. "Niggas from Green Cove, Orange Park, Palatka and even St. Augustine comes up this way and tries to put in work, all the time."

"It was one of the names that gave him away. I had heard one of them before, even met the person. I just had to remember who and where.

"Naurice Butler. Thin called him Nookie when he brought him to meet Big Duke a couple of years before he got bagged. Naurice Butler is Thin's first cousin."

"I rememba dat," Dirty Red said, "now datju've mentioned it. Big Duke said dat he looked to sneaky fa him and he didn't thank dat he could trust'em. So he didn't take'em on."

Vik's cell rang, interrupting the meeting. When she looked at her phone and saw whose number it was, she got even more indignant but answered anyway.

"Hey giri, it's me." A male voice said.

"I know who the fuck you are!" She replied, letting the anger she was feeling be heard in her voice. "What do you want? I've got enough on my plate right now."

"Calm down. You are about to have more than you can digest if you don't listen."

"How much is it going to cost me?"

"Nothing, this affects me, just as much as it does you and your crew. Besides, we already have a nice little arrangement and I would like to keep it that way."

"If that's the case, give me what you got."

He told her everything from the time that Thin had called him to the end of the conversation. When he hung the phone up in his face. Leaving out only that he had called Thin a nigger because he knew that she was going to tell Cee Lo what he had told her. And like his father, he despised cops and white people. He knew the n-word having come out of his mouth would have been just enough to make Cee Lo pay him a visit.

"I don't know if he is going to go any further with this than me. But I've given you the heads-up on what's what. If you get knocked, it's because you have slept on this warning."

"Thank you," she replied. "I'll handle it from here."

"I hope so." He said, and hanged up.

When she got off the phone, everyone in the room was watching her and waiting to see what was next. "That was Barney Fife. Thin called him early this morning and tried to eat the cheese." She then told them everything that she had been told. "It's time to eliminate this problem before it gets any bigger. There's too much at stake to wait any longer.

"Cee Lo, tonight you take three and go down to Palatka.

"Fury, you take the other three and go to Milkeila's.

"I want that motherfucker dead. If y'all catch him before you reach your destinations, put his ass in a body bag then and there. Otherwise, kill everybody in both apartments, except his mother."

* * * * *

Eleven thirty that night found me and the girls in the elevator of building 6 of the Gunby Courts, heading for the 5th floor.

"Put on your gloves," I told them. "The masks aren't necessary until we're on our way out."

The elevator stopped on the 5th floor and the doors opened. The hallway was deserted. Quickly but quietly, we moved out with our guns ready for whatever, not breaking stride until we were outside of Milkeila's apartment door.

"Shhh!" I said putting my index finger to my lips after jimmying the lock and silently opening the door.

Quiet as a cat, we crept inside and I eased the door closed behind us. Creeping down the short hallway, the living room was the first room that we entered. There sitting on the sofa, is a naked jit with his head tilted back and his eyes closed, rocking his head from side to side as if enjoying some mello music that only he could hear.

238

Once we crept closer, we saw that it was not a jit at all, and why the person was in such an elated mood. Milkeila, who was also naked, was down on the floor on her knees between the legs of the bulldyke Octavia with her eyes closed, noisily and greedily eating her pussy. They were so caught up in their sexcapade that they never knew that we were in the room with them.

I signaled like I was opening a knife, then crossed my neck as if slitting my throat and pointed at Octavia. Mesha, having caught what I was insinuating, nodded her head. She and Yoyo tucked their guns in their backs and she pulled the straight razor from her back pocket. I grabbed the thickest pillow off of the love seat as I crept up behind Milkeila. Once I was in place, I nodded my head. Yoyo grabbed Octavia's forehead to hold her head back and in position. Her eyes popped open at the touch of Yoyo's hands but Mesha slit her throat from jugular to jugular, cutting off any words before she could make a sound.

Simultaneously to Yoyo grabbing Octavia's head, I pushed the pillow and the 9 mm glock that had been taken out of Thin's caddy to the back of Milkeila's head and pulled the trigger. Blowing her brains into Octavia's lap. Then dropped the gun on the floor behind her.

While Yoyo, Khandi and I searched the rest of the apartment to see if we had missed anyone. Mesha took a can of red spray paint out of her fatigue's cargo pocket and painted; STREET LAW: THE BLOOD OF ONE IS THE BLOOD OF ALL; NOOKIE, on the wall.

* * * *

At the exact same time that the order was being executed in the Gunby Courts, Cee Lo and his crew were down in Palatka on Eagle Street, in the courtyard of the White Projects, behind apartment 8.

"Don't forget Vik's orders," Cee Lo said in a hushed tone. "Everybody except Mrs. Butler. She'll be the oldest female in the apartment."

They gloved and masked up before dividing into twos and getting in position to run up in the place. As Cee Lo kicked in the front door, Juice kicked in the back. The four men rushed in and held the entire household hostage. Tre and Breeze quickly duct taped Mrs. Butler to one of the dinner table chairs, before positioning her so that she could see whatever was about to happen next.

"Dis is personal. Yo son Kendrick is tha cause of alla dis. He raped my gurl, den caused tha death of one of my people," Juice whispered in her ear, as he pulled a suppressor out of his pocket and screws it into the barrel of the Mini 14 submachine gun. "Tha only reason dat I ain't gon send ya home ta ya maka ta'night is b'cuz I need'em ta see tha pain he caused, in yo eyes."

Juice executed everyone else right there before her eyes without the least amount of remorse for their lives, killing a younger woman, two men, a child of about three and an arm baby. Before STREET LAW; PAYBACK IS A BITCH, is spray painted on the wall.

CHAPTER: 28

Thin had been sitting at a table near the bar for about ten minutes. When Detective McNeal took the last seat at the bar near the jukebox and ordered a beer. He sat where he was for a couple of extra minutes, to make sure that McNeal was alone. Once he was satisfied, he got up from the table and went over to the bar. He sat next to McNeal and ordered a crown and coke.

"That seat is reserved," McNeal said, showing his badge.

"I know my man, take it easy." Thin replied. "I'm Kendrick Butler. I've been here fa a little minute observin. Ta make sho dat thangs wu kosha."

"I can respect that," McNeal replied. "How do you want to do this? Do you want to go someplace private?"

"Nah! I feel safe in here. Dat's why I toldja ta meet me here."

"That's fine. You can start whenever you are ready."

"Yu ain't gon record dis?"

"No, it's unofficial at the moment. But I am going to take some notes as we go. Maybe ask a few questions if I get lost. Otherwise, I am going to listen. Once you give me enough to go on. I can take it to my superiors and get the authorization to investigate. Then we can get it in writing and make it official."

Thin nods his head in understanding after a few minutes of pondering, then began with a question.

"Have you eva heard of Big Duke from tha east side?"

"Yes, who hasn't?" McNeal replied. "He was one of the major players in the city in the distribution and sales of illegal narcotics."

"His government name is DeMarcus Daniels.

"It took us and the feds about ten years to take him down, but we got him."

"Whutja mean by wuz a maja playa?"

"He's in federal prison doing a stretch," he replied. "I was in the courtroom the day that Judge

Maxwell sentenced him and he was taken into custody."

"Whut if I toldja dat he's still got tha east side on lock from behind tha wall. And sat he's got a

Barney Fife from tha PD on his payroll."

"Hold on a minute, Kendrick. You're putting the cart before the horse. Daniel's is serving a fifteen year sentence at Coleman Federal Correctional Institution on tax fraud and drug charges. So you're gonna have to come better than that. How about you start from the beginning and give me the whole story."

"A'ght, a'ight," Thin said. "Big Duke gotta elite squad on tha east side dat's clockin some serious paypa slangin boy, girl and crack cocaine. Dem niggaz don't know no recession. Dat's jus how much money dey're makin."

"How much would you say that they are making on a weekly basis?" McNeal asked.

"I can't say fa sho or give ya a figga on tha amount all ta'getha but I know dat me and my boyz wuz makin fifteen bandz uh week as foot souljaz. If I had ta guess, I'd say dat dey're snatchin down anywhere from uh quarta ta a million dollaz uh week wit ease."

"Dey're trappin outta tha Gunby Courts projects, I know fa sho. Ova on tha Franklin Street side, across from tha park. But it's hard ta catch'em dirty out dere, b'cuz of tha Barney Fife from tha PD. He let'em know in advance when tha Duke boyz gon be ridin, and whut they drivin. He gives'em tha headz up on when tha narcs will be sent out dere, whut kinda whip and tha color dey'll be pushin, even how much dey'll be tryna spend."

"Even when dey do manage ta git in, dey always come up short cuz ain't nobody gon serve'em."

Thin sat there for a long minute, deep in thought, wondering what the outcome of this was going to be. Then thoughts of what had happened to Paypa Boy's people when he testified against Big Duke and Flex.

"In fact, everybody in tha projects are very close-mouthed when it comes ta answa'n questions bout dat crew or whutz goin on out dere. Especially when it's five-o askin tha questions," Thin said, breaking away from his thoughts. "Ah nigga ratha be in tha pen den hafta deal wit dat crew."

"Do you know the name of this dirty cop? Or Barney Fife?"

Thin ignited his question and continued to talk. "Dis crew ain't nuttin ta be fukkk'd up wit. Dey ain't got no problem putin a muthafukkka ta sleep permanently. I honestly thank dat dey're tha ones responsible fa alla dose bodies ova on Jesse Street tha otha....."

"You didn't answer my question about the dirty cop," McNeal said, cutting him off.

"I know," Thin replied, turning to face him. "If Big Duke's crew play fa keeps. Whut tha fukkk yu thank a fukkkin dirty pig'll do, and I ain't ready fa no dirt nap yet. I've given yu enuff ta wet'cha appetite. Yu go hafta take my word on whut I've toldja fa now. When yu can guarantee me dat my gurl and my family will be safe. Den I'll give ya names."

"I can't guarantee you anything because you haven't given me anything but speculation. How do I know whether or not any of what you have said is true or up to date?"

"Daniels has been off the scene for over five years. No judge is going to believe that he is still running a million dollar drug ring from the inside without mob ties. And we both know that the mob is leery about dealing with your kind."

"My kind? Whut tha fukkk is dat pose ta mean cracka? Evidently yo racist, punk ass ain't been listenin," Thin shot back at McNeal's statement. "I wuz a part of dat damn crew befo dey exiled me and my boyz a coupla months ago.

"Didn't I tell yo stupid ass dat me and my boyz wuz makin fifteen bandz uh week as foot souljaz?"

McNeal looked down at the notes that he had been taking. "Yes, yes you did," he said, "and that definitely makes a difference.

"Let me get with my boss and have him pull some strings. We will meet back here in two days. I should have everything in order by then for your family and your lady to be moved to one of our safe houses. But you will have to stay with us until we have made our case," he said, getting up from the stool. "Here in two days Kendrick. Two days."

Thin was still sitting at the bar after McNeal had left, when he had a premonition of something detrimental happening to someone that he loved. He tried to shake off the uneasy feeling by downing a shot of Jose Cuervo but it didn't go away. "Damn!" He said to himself, as he stared into the empty shot glass. "I can't stand ta lose nobody else."

Not being able to shake the uneasy feeling that continued to eat at him. He took out his cell and called home. When the answering machine didn't pick up on the third ring, instead of leaving a message, he hanged up, paid for his drinks and left.

In the car on the way home, all that he could think about was all of the bed decisions that he had made. All of the lives that had been lost due to his dislike of a situation that he had no control over. Then he wondered if he had done the right thing by going against the code and going to the man. Rather than dealing with the situation in accordance with the street laws because there was doubt in his mind that Barney Fife had already informed Vik about his calling and as soon as he got within earshot of knowing about his meeting with McNeal, he was going to inform her about that as well.

Her warning about having him erased before she would let Big Duke's operation fall because of him rang out loud and clear in his mind, and a cold chill ran down his spine.

"Fukkk it!" He said, thinking out loud once again and trying to shake off the chills. "Whutz dun is dun, ain't no goin back now. All I got left is my family and my gurl, and I'ma do whuteva I gotta do ta make sho dat dey're safe."

As he turned off of Franklin Street into the entrance of the his heart damn near jumped out of his chest . He put on brakes in the middle of the street and just stared ahead, directly in front of building 6. The parking lot was lit up and swarming with police cars and rescue units. The same uneasy feeling that he had felt back at Hooters came over him again. Only much stronger this time. The thought of something having happened to Milkeila caused him to jump out of the car and leave it in the middle of the street.

When he attempted to walk into the building without permission, a policewoman that was standing guard at the entrance tried to stop him. He pushed her to the side and ran up the stairs, taking them two at a time all the way up to the fifth floor. Opening the stairwell door on the fifth floor, he instantly panicked at the sight of so many police officers on the floor. His heart filled with dread, when he realized that it was Milkeila's apartment that they were going in and out of. He rushed the remaining few feet to the apartment.

The police officer that was posted at the door to keep the spectators out, extended his arm in an attempt to stop Thin from going inside the apartment.

"You can't go in there sir," the officer said.

"And who tha fukkk is gon stop me?" Thin replied, with a question of his own before pushing him to one side like he was a little child, and walking inside. "Dis is my bitch's crib."

The first thing he saw when he walked in was the street law that wass spray painted on the wall and Nookie's name to let him know that it was known that he had setup the robbery. His heart started to beat out of control as fear started to take over him. He knew that Milkeila had died in his place, but he needed to see how she had died. Whether it was quick or had she suffered a slow painful death for his sins.

Entering the living room where photographs of the crime scene were being taken. Everything seemed to go into slow motion. The bodies had not been removed from the premises yet.

Milkeila and Octavia were still naked in the same position, on and kneeling in front of the sofa. When he saw the love of his life on her knees, with her head between Octavia's legs, he howled in pain like a wounded animal. He didn't know how he knew but he knew that it was his fault that she had been turned out.

"Dey knew dat she wuz my whole world," he mumbled to himself as he stared at her lifeless body. "So dey gave her a sickness dat would cause her ta do anythang ta support it. Knowin it would hurt me more den it would her when I found out. Dey turned her into a junkie and trick bitch, jus like dat lil nigga Pimp had said when I caught'em trickin behind tha stairs." He had never felt hurt that deeply in his life as a pain like never before gripped his heart like a vise. He lost it right there.

Thin had to be physically restrained to be removed from the apartment then escorted out of the building. Once he was out in the night air, he was able to calm himself down a little. Sitting on the hood of his car, tears rolled down his face as he died inside all over again.

"Whut in tha fukkk have I done," he said, shaking his head in remorse. "I've lost everyone but my..." he stopped mid-sentence. In a near panic, he took his cell out of his pocket and dialed his mother's home number. The phone is answered on the second ring by a Putnam County Sheriff deputy.

"Dis is Kendrick Butler," said Thin who was in complete panic mode now. "Why yu answa'n my ol' gurl's phone?"

"Mr. Butler, there has been a massacre here at your mother's apartment," replied the deputy. "Everyone here is dead except for your mother. She was found duct taped to a chair, and by the way it was positioned, she was forced to watch the executions. You need to get here as soon as you possibly can."

The sixty-two mile drive to Palatka was done in less than forty-five minutes. When Thin pulled up into the White Projects, the spectators were still crowded outside of the crime scene tape trying to see more. He was stopped by a deputy, as he walked up to the apartment door. Too numb to say anything, he just pushed him out of the way and walked in on.

The first thing to hit him when he stepped inside was the stench of burnt gunpowder and the smell of fresh blood then he saw the street law spray painted on the wall. The bodies had already been removed, but the evidence and the eerie feeling of what had taken place was everywhere. "Damn!" He said, thinking out loud as the smell of death makes his stomach queasy and he almost throws up.

A cold chill ran all over him as he made his way towards the voices that were coming from the kitchen. The deputies stopped talking when they noticed that he had entered the room and the senior officer walked over to him.

"You can't be in here son," he said. "This is a crime scene."

"I'm Kendrick Butler," Thin replied. "Dis is my ol' gurl's crib."

"Oh okay, I talked to you on the phone a little over half an hour ago."

"Dat's right."

"Come with me," he said, leading Thin out the back door and over to his squad car.

"How is my ol' gurl? Whut have y'all done wit her?"

"She wasn't hurt physically, as far as we could tell. But she was psychologically fucked... I mean her mind had snapped," he corrected.

"She was taken to Putnam Memorial."

When Thin turned to walk away, the deputy put his hand on his shoulder.

"Hold on son," he said "Do you mind if I ask you a few questions before you leave for the hospital?"

"I don't know nuttin bout nuttin officer," he responded, shrugging his hand off of him. "I jus wanna go see bout my momma."

Back in his car, Thin just sat there for a few minutes with tears rolling down his cheeks. He finally realized that he had made the biggest mistakes of his life when he crossed Dirty Money and it had cost him dearly.

"How much mo can dey take from me otha den my life?" He said, as his thoughts escape him orally and he turned the key in the ignition.

CHAPTER: 29

At Putnam Memorial, Thin stopped at the reception desk to find out what room his mother was, before heading that way. Twenty feet or so from her soon, he slowed his pace as his heart began to pound in his chest. A sudden fear of what he might find when he entered her room tied his stomach in knots. He couldn't even begin to imagine what she must have suffered from seeing the ones she loved more than life itself executed before her eyes. Stopping outside of her room door, he took several deep breaths to compose himself, before knocking and going inside.

His mother was sitting in a chair, in front of the window staring straight ahead. Her mouth was moving as she rocked back and forth but there were no words coming out.

"Momma," he called out, before walking towards her to avoid traumatizing her any more than she already was. Yet, she still jumped in her seat at the sound of his voice before turning to look at him. It hurt him to the depths of his soul to see the fear and pain in her eyes as she stared at him. The fear and pain that he had brought into her life due to his own selfish deeds.

Milkeila had gotten off easy compared to his mother.

She put her hand over her mouth and closed her eyes as tears streamed down her cheeks. She jumped and quivered with fright as the scene of the executions of her husband, daughter, son, son in law and grandbabies flashed before her mind's eye.

"Mesha is coming Kendrick," she said, as she tried to break away from the brutal nightmare that won't release its grip on her. "They all are."

Silent tears streamed down his face as he looked into his mother's eyes because he knew that he had lost the one person who loved him most forever. He knew that she would never recover from that night, and it was all on him.

"Dis whole thang started wit dat lil nigga, Fury," he said, thinking out loud and trying to find somewhere to place the blame for his own fuckups. "I'ma take his ass down first. Him and his crew is vital ta Big Duke's operation. Wit him outta tha way, it'll buy me enuff time ta git at tha rest of'em."

He stepped over to his mother and kissed her on the cheek then walked out of the room without looking back. Momentarily stopping outside her room door and leaning against it, he closed his eyes to try and block out the guilt that was eating at his soul.

"Damn!" He said, pulling his cell out of his pocket as he started off down the hall towards the exit. He gave less than a fuck now, everyone he loved was dead one way or another anyway. His only desire now was revenge. He dialed a number.

CHAPTER: 30

McNeal was sitting on the same stool when Thin walked in Hooters. He went straight to the bar, sat on the stool next to him and ordered himself a drink.

"Dey've merked damn near everybody dat I love, while I wuz here witju earlier," he said.

"What are you talking about Kendrick?" McNeal asked.

Thin told him what he had found when he went home as well as about what had happened at his mother's apartment in Palatka.

"What have you done to these people? Why would they do this to you, if it's them?"

"I ain't dun nuttin ta my knowledge," he lied. "Dey're tha ones dat cut us off.

"But I'm sho dat it wuz dem."

"You can't swear to that in a court of law because you were here with me. And without a witness, your word is speculation. But if we can get this crew off the streets long enough to give homicide enough time to link this crew to the murders, they will be off the streets for good.

"So talk to me, give me some information that I can use to put things in motion with."

"A'ight," Thin replied, taking a deep breath. "Big Duke's unda'boss is dat lil nigga dat took my spot, Fury. He do alla tha coppin and distibutin of tha work. He has his own cfew of foot souljaz dat he roll wit, but I don't know where exactly dey're from."

"Dey're tha ones dat's got tha Gunby Courts on lock, and don't pay no games. Dey're real wit it and loyal ta dat nigga."

"How can I identify this Fury guy when I see him?"

"I doubt dat yu'll catch'em dirty or out on tha tracks. But he push uh triple black Infiniti QX56, wit TRU2IT on tha tag, or uh tricked out orange bubble Chevy Caprice, wit CBrown on it's tag,"

"Can you get in contact with this Fury?"

"I don't know if he's gon answa. He don't fukkk wit me," he replied. "He's tha one dat cut me and my boyz off. But I got his numba," Thin said, pulling his cell out of his pocket. "Ya wont me ta try and hit'em up?"

"Yes, but star sixty-seven your call to avoid your number showing up on his screen."

"He ain't gon answa no private call."

"It doesn't matter really. We just need to know that it's still an active line. So we can tap it."

Thin nodded in agreement before dialing star sixty-nine and the number then put it on speaker for McNeal to hear.

"We're sorry, you have reached a number that has been disconnected or is no longer in service. Please check the number and dial again, or stay on the line and the operator will assist," was instantly heard when the automated system picked up on the first ring.

McNeal looked at him as if he was full of shit but didn't comment on the disconnected number.

"Someone had to be incharge after Daniel's was taken off the scene and before Fury got there?" McNeal asked, after the failed phone call and a moment of thought. "Who was it?'

"It wuz Cee Lo and Vik, Big Duke's daughta and son." He replied, after a long minute of contemplation. "Dey ran thangz til dat young nigga came along and proved hisself. Den dey fell all tha way back and let him run it."

"Once he took ova, tha otha two disassociated themselves wit tha game alta'getha," he lied. "I'ma guess b'cuz Big Duke didn't need'em no mo."

"I checked Daniels' record on the NCIC computer and his visitation list at Coleman. According to the information in his files, he doesn't have any children and there aren't any names on his kiosk or visitation lists that comes close to a Cee Lo or a Vik. Does Alaisha Armstrong, Tavon Porter or Khalil Williams sound familiar to you?"

Thin could only shake his head no.

"So then, what are the government names of Vik and Cee Lo so I can have them checked out?"

"I don't know. Alls I've eva known'em by is Vik and Cee Lo," he lied again then wondered why he had done it because he knew that they were more a part of what had happened to his people than Fury. They were the ones that gave the orders.

"Hold on Kendrick, something is not adding up here. How can you work for someone and not know their fucking name?"

Thin sat there for a moment and contemplated the question. Knowing that he had slipped and McNeal had caught the lie. He knew that he had to keep telling half truths to avoid contaminating his credibility if he was going to make this work.

"I'd only been down wit tha family bout three months befo Big Duke got knocked. Me and my boyz spent dat time in trainin wit Big Duke's partna, at tha time, Flex who's in tha federal joint up in Bennettsville, South Carolina. Once Cee Lo and Vik took ova, dat young nigga wuz brought right in, and tha whole script wuz flipped."

"I neva got tha chance ta git close enuff ta find out much of nuttin beyond tha tracks. Neitha of dem did any bidness on tha street level. Dey left dat bidness ta him, befo he took ova completely. Tha only time I seen'em out and about wuz when me and my boyz graduated from trainin. Dat wuz at tha soiree dat's throwed fa dat occasion."

"I've heard you mention the name Flex more than once. Who is he, and how does he fit into the scheme of things?"

"I see yo ass ain't been listenin ta a damn thang I've said again. Didn't I jus tell ya dat Flex wuz Big Duke's partna. Dem two wuz tha ones dat tamed tha Gunby Courts and brought orda ta'em. Dey are tha ones dat turnt dem projects inta tha million dolla trap it is."

"You said that he's at FCI, Bennettsville. Am I right?"

"Yeah."

"What is his government name? So I can check his visitation list for Cee Lo and Vik."

"I doubt datja will, cuz him and Big Duke fell out befo eitha of'em got bagged. But, it's Malik Roberts."

"Why did Fury cut you and your boys off?"

"Me and him neva really vibed from day one. We wuz alwayz bumpin headz b'cuz he thought I wuz tryna unda'mind his authority wheneva I'd disagree wit tha way he wuz handlin' bidness." He lied. "So he started bitchin bout small shit, like tha trap money bein late or it wuz short of whut he said it should be. We bumped headz one night and it ended in a scuffle. He gave me tha boot afta dat and my boyz loyalty cause'em ta roll wit me."

McNeal scribbled something on his pad of notes, paused for a second to think then scribbled something else. He looked up at Thin, then back down at his note to scribble some more.

"Who is this Barney Fife that you said is on Daniels' payroll?" He asked.

"Alexanda Woods."

To hear the name of the alledged crooked cop almost knocked McNeal off of his stool. He looked up from his pad to stare at Thin because Alexander Woods was not from the PD. He was the head of the narcotics division for the Duval County Sheriff's Department. He was McNeal's boss.

"Alexander Woods," McNeal said, repeating the name. "Are you sure?"

"Yeah, I'm sho. Why tha fukkk would I wanna make up a fukkkin name fa a dirty redneck pig? I've been in tha car wit Flex when he met wit'em ta pay'em off." He lied, knowing that he had never witnessed anything. He only knew about the payoffs because they had them on video, and they were of Big Duke making the drop, not Flex. "Yu wont me ta give u his numba."

"No, I was only trying to make sure that I had heard you correctly, that's all."

If Thin would have been paying attention to McNeal's reaction to the name he would have realized that he had said too much, but he didn't. He was too intent on accomplishing his objective.

"Yeah, yu heard whut I said. I said dat Alxeanda Woods is tha name of tha Barney Fife dat's on Big Duke's payroll and dat I've been dere when he wuz gittin paid."

"Look man, I'm sho dat dat lil nigga is gon put uh hit out on me. So yu need ta git'em offa tha streetz befo word gits back ta'em bout dis meetin between us. Cuz i'm so dat when Woods hears bout it, he's damn sho gon put me out dere and goin inta protective custody ain't gon happen."

McNeal just looked at him because he was a dead man if what he had said about Woods being a dirty cop was true. Because he was in Woods' office talking to him about the case when Thin called, McNeal thought.

CHAPTER: 31

Thursday afternoon at about twelve thirty, I was heading for the door. When Vik stopped me.

"Little Daddy, what are you about to do?" She asked.

"I've got to make a few rounds before I meet up with Breeze and Trey over in the Courts," I replied. "Why, what's up?"

"Do you mind if I roll with you today?"

I looked at her like, that was the dumbest question she could have asked me. I work for you don't, before I answered her.

"Nah, boss lady, I don't mind. You know that you can roll with me anytime you want."

We took San Jose Boulevard to the 295 Beltway going East to get on Interstate 95 South. She and I both were wrapped up in our own little world as we rode listening to NeYo's 'In My Own Words' album.

About a mile down I-95, we passed a dark blue Dodge Charger sitting on the side of the road. I knew that it was an unmarked detective's car by the limo tint on the windows and the factory rims. It immediately pulled out behind us but I didn't pay it much attention because I wasn't speeding and no one knew that I'm making rounds today but me and Luke Dirty who didn't know what time I was coming through. Vik only knew because she was in the car with me.

I got off on the Golfair Boulevard exit to see if he was following me. When I stopped at the light at the bottom of the ramp. The car was right behind me. I could see the officer using his computer to run my plates through the rearview mirror.

"Vik, don't make any sudden moves to look back," I said, as the light changed to green,"but there is an undercover right behind us and he's running my plates."

"Are you sure, Fury?" She asked.

'I don't play games when it comes to Johnnie law Vik. Call one of the girls or Juice and tell them to pick you up from the Chevron on Golfair."

"What are you about to do?"

I didn't answer, I was going over every possible scenario in my head of why the police would be behind me, then it hit me. Thin had called Barney Fife and tried to snitch on us. When he couldn't get no justice there, he must have gone to someone else and they must have bought his story in order for him to be sitting on the side of the road, waiting for me to come by.

I have made this particular run at least three times a week, for only God himself knows how long and an undercover has never gotten behind me prior to today. I had never even had a black and white or a sheriff's car for that matter. He had to be looking for his particular car because I had made it a habit of never driving the same vehicle twice in a month whenever I was making rounds. So five-o had no reason to be tailing me, unless my thinking was correct.

"Do you have some work with you?" Vik asked, breaking the silence.

"Yes, a half for Luke Dirty. It's in the center console with my twins. That is why I'm going to put you off at the flea market. There is no need for both of us to get hit, and he is too close for me to throw it all out without him seeing it."

At the light, I made a right onto Golfair Boulevard, then another right into the Chevron Gas Station parking lot and pulled up parallel to the side walk. To let Vik out. The undercover followed me into the gas station parking lot, cruising past me just fast enough for it to look as if we just happened to be going to the same place and circled around the building.

"Fury, give me the dope and your guns," Vik said, just before opening the car door. "I can put them in my purse before I get out."

"Nah Vik, your purse is too small to put the work and guns in, and I'm pretty sure he's looking to see who's getting out of the vehicle. So he can stop and question them, if he gets the opportunity.

"If I can lose him, I'll see you back at the house. If not, have Tieaa to call to the county and see if I have a bond. Now get out before he sees you. He's circling the building."

Vik got the quarter bird out of the center console and stuffed it in her purse anyway. Then got out of the truck as if she was catching a ride and walked into the gas station.

Looking in the rearview mirror, I saw the front of the Charger coming around the building. I pulled away from the curb just as he turned to get behind me. No longer trying to look inconspicuous about following me, he sped up and got right behind me. So instead of taking a left and trying to get back on the interstate, I took a right onto Golfair West and stomped the accelerator to the floor. The powerful 6 speed 5.6 liter V8 engine in the Q didn't hesitate in response to the instant acceleration, which gave me a quarter of a block jump before the undercover could even pull out of the parking lot entrance.

I made the first left going South on Chase Avenue and stomped on the accelerator again. As I was crossing W 31st Street, I looked up into the rearview mirror. The Charger was a block back, just turning onto Chase, with the lights flashing and the siren blaring. I let down my window, just before taking the next right heading West again, I grabbed one of my twins out of the center console and threw it in the hedges of the house on the corner of West 25th and Barnett Street.

A car backing out of the yard in the middle of the block caused me to slam on brakes to avoid a possible fatal crash. I managed to get around the car without having to come to a complete stop, but not in time enough to stop the undercover from making up a lot of the ground in those few seconds. Pressing the accelerator to the floor once again, and the Q responded, reclaiming about half of the distance I'd lost. I knew that if I could get into the 20th Street Expressway traffic, I could survive going to jail until another day. Three half blocks to go, as I made the next left off of W 25th onto Fairfax Street, tires squealing as the Q slides around the corner, only to slam on brakes. The Fairfax and 24th Street intersection was barricaded with two patrol cars. As soon as I put the Q in reverse to back up, two city units along with the unmarked police car blocked me from the rear. Police officers were all over the place in a matter of seconds with their weapons drawn.

"JaMarius Brown," One of the officers said, on the loudspeaker of the patrol car, "turn off the engine and throw the keys out the window."

I looked around to see if there was anywhere that I could go. There wasn't, unless I wanted to die today. I was caught.

"JaMarius Brown, turn off the engine and throw the keys out the window."

I turned off the engine and threw the key out into the street. Before the sound of the key striking the pavement had stopped ringing in my ears, I was already snatched out of the truck and slammed to the pavement.

"JaMarius Brown, you are under arrest for reckless driving, fleeing and attempting to elude, failure to stop for a blue light and conspiracy to sell and distribute illegal narcotics."

By Sputnic

SNEAK PEAK

I was sitting in the interrogation room, handcuffed to the table when a white detective entered the room along with a black woman in a navy-blue business suit.

"I'm narcotics agent Stacey McNeal, and this is federal agent Qaasimah Nickerson," he said.

I didn't say a word or even look in their general direction, because I was tired of their little charade. So I just sat there as if I were still in the room alone.

"You know that you're in a lot of trouble to be so young, don't you?" Nickerson asked in a soft voice. "Conspiracy to sell and distribute one hundred or more kilos of cocaine, heroin and molly, could put you in prison for the rest of your life. And that's after the state is finished with you."

"But if you want to help yourself and work with us. I'll do all that I can to help you."

I looked up at her as if I'd just noticed that they were in the room and smiled. "You've got jokes lady, don't you?" I replied, with a question of my own. "You've got me on a few traffic violations and nothing more. All of that you're in a lot of trouble smoke that you're trying to blow up my ass. You can keep it."

"If all of that conspiracy to selling and distribution bullshit was solid, y'all wouldn't still be hounding me about it. Nor holding me hostage without bail on the petty shit y'all got me on, hoping that I'll break."

"Well, I'm going to tell you and this clown," I said, pointing at McNeal. "The same thing that I've been telling all the other toy ass cops here that have been harassing me over the past six months. I don't know shit about no goddamn drugs."

"Listen you little mouthed punk," McNeal said, pounding his fist on the table and getting in my face. "My man didn't lie to me. You know who DeMarcus Daniels is, just like you know who Vik, Cee Lo and Alexander Woods are too, don't you?"

"How else could a sixteen-year-old black boy," putting emphasis on black boy, "afford a brand new Infiniti truck? Not to mention the '91 Chevy Caprice that you've got with all of that dope money tied up in. You know something."

"What part do you play in the Dirty Money Mafia? What's your rank, boy?" Emphasizing boy once again.

"What? I got your boy hanging and swanging saltine, but you could always ask Phyllis what rank I am. She will definitely know."

McNeal's face reddened with anger when his better half's name was mentioned because he didn't even know that this JaMarius Brown existed before his street name was dropped in his lap. And here he sat with a cocky smile on his face after having called a name that some of his colleagues didn't even know now.

"Don't get mad, white bread. Y'all ain't never been better than us at nothing but incest, pedophilia, and spreading hatred. Besides, lil Meaghan has only called me daddy once."

"HOW THE FUCK DO YOU KNOW MY WIFE AND DAUGHTER NIG..?" He growled, biting off the racial slur before it could come all the way out of his mouth.

"I'm your nigger now, huh?" I asked, still smiling at him. "You would be surprised at what I know about that freak. Like where her hotspot is or that she prefers the African salami over the European Vienna sausage."

McNeal knew that he had already crossed the line when he used the partial racial slur in front of the black federal agent but he was beyond controlling his emotions by this time. He was so livid that he started sweating and trembling physically. Not only because this "nigger" had disrespected him by talking about his family or because he prided himself on being the very best in the department when it came to interrogation. Especially when it came to blacks because to his twisted way of thinking all niggers were beneath him, were too envious of each other to stick together or too jealous hearted of one another not to roll over when a little pressure was applied. Now, after fifteen years on the force, a sixteen year old boy was about to take a shit on his reputation and make him the laughingstock of his division when it was evident to everyone that he knew more than he was willing to say. But the main source of his ire was that he had to admit to himself that this boy was cut from a different cloth and that he was way out of his league. He had gotten to hardcore criminals in a couple of hours, yet here he had been bested by a child.

"I don't know why all of you black boys try to play hard, knowing damn well that you will drop a dime on your mother to avoid leaving that whore that your whole crew is banging but I have something for your smart-mouthed ass," he said, taking a sheet of paper out of a file. "Here's a warrant for possession of a firearm by a minor, for that loaded forty-five automatic that was found in your vehicle." He slammed it down on the table. "I hope the judge throws the book at your punk ass."

I smiled at him the same way that I had at Nickerson because the good-cop, bad-cop game that they were trying to play had me tripping before I let my face turn serious.

"Look cracker, there's only three kinds of boys where I come from; that's a white boy, a cowboy, and a pussy boy. I'm too damn dark to be a white boy. If it ain't on a plate cooked well done, I don't fuck with cows and I can throw hands with the best when it comes to knuckling up. So ain't no way in the hell I can be your boy."

"On some real shit, if you're trying to intimidate me, you've done a piss poor job of it. I've had females put down a more intimidating boo game on me trying to get the meat."

"And if you know so fucking much about me and who I'm supposed to be affiliated with, why the hell are you still here talking me to death? It's evident that you already know more about me than I know about myself."

"Ja'Marius, this is your last opportunity to help yourself," said Nickerson. "McNeal made a good point about your choice of vehicles, although you have not been caught with any illegal drugs. No matter what you say, you're sixteen years old with no job, and you drive a luxury vehicle. It has 'drug dealing' written all over it."

"You're going before the judge tomorrow, and Easton hates drug dealers or anyone who has any dealings with drugs. You see, his daughter died from an overdose of fentanyl and his son shot and paralyzed him after he wouldn't give him money to support his meth addiction. If the prosecutor can link you to Daniels in any way or to any other drug dealer, the judge is going to try to put you away for a very long time. But if you help us, I'll talk to the judge and prosecutor for you before court starts tomorrow morning and see if I can work something out in your favor."

"So, tell us something."

266

I sat there for a long minute as if I was contemplating what she had said, or if I was about to tell them something. Knowing that snitching was not in my DNA, they both stood there waiting impatiently, thinking that they had finally gotten to me.

"Look you two," I finally said, looking up at them. "I will see you in court in the morning."

* * * * *

The next morning, my attorney met me at the courthouse. When we walked into courtroom number three, the entire family was sitting in the third row on the right-hand side. I nodded at them as I passed and each nodded in return.

"I talked with Cordell and LeVickia when I first got here this morning," my attorney whispered to me after we were seated behind the defense table. "He says to tell you not to worry about anything. Your truck has been released and put up with the other. He also said that if you get some time, you will be well taken care of while you're down."

Within three minutes after I'd entered the courtroom the court was called to order and I was called up to stand before the judge.

"Ja'Marius Brown, your charge of conspiracy to sell and distribution of illegal narcotics has been dropped due to the lack of evidence, or proof that you have had any ties to the drug kingpin DeMarcus Daniels or any knowledge of any illegal drug activities," Judge Easton said. "The trust fund that was left to you by the late Jamaal Brown has justified your means to be able to afford what you have in spite of you being so young."

I smiled within, because despite the fact of me not being able to remember Jesi and Jule's father. Nor having any knowledge of a trust fund. He had reached out from beyond the grave and covered my tracks.

"However, I believe that you know a lot more than you have chosen to speak," he continued. "Evidence of that is present in the courtroom with you. Knowing is one thing, but proving it is something else."

"I commend you for knowing how to keep your mouth shut though because if the prosecution could have found one shred of solid evidence that linked you to Daniels or any other drug dealer, I would have waived you over to an adult and sent you to the Florida Department of Corrections for no less than thirty years before the feds even got a shot at you. I don't give a damn what kind of a deal the prosecution would have offered you but being that I can't for your charges of reckless driving, fleeing and attempting to elude, failure to stop for a blue light, and possession of a firearm by a minor, I remand you to the custody of the Department of Juvenile Justice where you will be sent to the Authur G. Dozier Reformatory School until you are twenty-one years of age," he said, striking his gavel on the bench.

Instantly, my attorney asked the court for sentencing reconsideration because he knew that the judge was prejudiced against drug dealers and that five years was outrageous for a first-time offender. Easton cut his eye at Jenkins as if he had interrupted his court without permission. Then looked back at me, as if I was the one who sold his daughter the drugs that killed her.

"Denied," he sneered. "His ass is going to jail. What do you have to say to me? I don't know shit about no goddamned drugs? Get your high-priced drug attorney to cover that up."

I looked to my left towards the prosecution's table and saw Detective McNeal sitting behind the partition with a smile on his face. I smiled to myself before looking back at the judge.

"Fuck you, you cripple redneck son of a bitch," I replied. "If I would have known anything about Daniels, you motherfuckers would never have gotten it out of me. But he's not the one you should be worried about. It's that crooked motherfucker sitting behind the D.A., Stacey McNeal."

The whole courtroom was in an uproar and McNeal's face reddened with baffled surprise at being exposed. He had never had any dealings with Ja'Marius Brown before this case, which caused him to wonder just how well-connected the young man really was.

"And by the way, that junkie bitch of a daughter you had, the skeezer gave the best brains in Duval County. Me and my boys pulled an all-night amtrak on the nasty ass-licking bitch for three dollars a piece before she killed herself."

"GET HIM OUT OF MY COURTROOM!" Easton yelled, banging his gavel furiously on the bench. "GET THAT BLACK SON OF A BITCH OUT OF HERE NOW!"

* * * * *

Thin was sitting across the street from the courthouse when the Dirty Money family came out without Fury. He knew that none of them were strapped and that he had caught them with their pants down. He looked over at the 454 Casull laying on the passenger seat.

"I could easily erase alla dem muthafukkkaz right nie and takeova tha Courtz fa my own." He said, thinking out loud.

When he looked back across the street, he noticed that the entire family was standing on the curb looking in his direction like they knew that he was there and it unnerved him. Then unexpectedly, the passenger side door was snatched open. In a panic, he momentarily forgot about the big pistol laying on the seat.

"Whut tha fukkk!" He exclaimed as his head whipped around to see who was about to jump in the car with him. To look down the barrel of a 9mm Ruger, in the hands of a beautiful, caramel-skinned, petite sister.

"You won't be needing this," she said reaching down and picking up his pistol off of the seat, "and I think that it would be best if you rode your fat ass up out of the Ville and never come back. Because if I ever see your pussy ass again, I'ma remember that you are the nigga that got my baby sister killed."

Thin grimaced as he looked in the broad's face, and Milkeila's materialized right before his eyes. Guilt and pain stabbed at his heart greater than it had been the night that she had been murdered.

'I know that them motherfuckers put it out there that I had been the reason that Keila was murdered, for Maisha to get it' he thought. They knew that Maisha and Milkeila were close and that she would want to get some get back for her sister.

He turned his head to look back across the street. The Dirty Money family was gone. When he looked back at Maisha, the look in her eyes said that a murder was only a few seconds away, right there across the street from the courthouse if he did anything stupid or made a false move. He put both of his hands on the steering wheel to show her that he was not a threat before he spoke.

"Yu win babygurl. Gimme a coupla feet and I'ma git on through," he said. "Yu won't hafta worry bout seein me round no mo."

Without saying a word, she backed away from the car holding both guns on him then kicked the door closed to allot him the distance needed to get light.

Less than ten minutes after he had left Maisha standing across the street from the courthouse, he was on the interstate heading South with the music pumping and no thought of where his final destination would be. When his phone vibrated, he turned down the music to take the call. It was short and straight to the point.

"One down", he said, thinking out loud when the calling party hung up. A satisfied smirk crossed his lips. His nemesis was out of the way for a little minute and he knew that he had time to regroup and come back for the other. Despite the major price that he had paid for his sins, he could breathe a little easier now.

Printed in Great Britain
by Amazon

40102376R00155